LIES
of my
MONSTER

RINA KENT

To every girl who's proud of loving villains

AUTHOR NOTE

Hello reader friend,

If you haven't read my books before, you might not know this, but I write darker stories that can be upsetting and disturbing. My books and main characters aren't for the faint of heart.

Lies of My Monster is book two of a trilogy and is NOT a standalone.

Monster Trilogy:
#1 *Blood of My Monster*
#2 *Lies of My Monster*
#3 *Heart of My Monster*

For more things Rina Kent, visit www.rinakent.com

ABOUT THIS BOOK

In our brutal world, there's no such thing as the truth.

Lies overflow until they become a reality.

But I'm determined to uncover what happened to my family.

One problem, though.

My monster, Kirill.

We are not the same anymore.

It's become hard to trust one another.

But it's downright impossible to stay away from each other.

It's mad, chaotic, and wrong, but it's us.

And we might have to pay for it with blood.

PLAYLIST

Saints—Echoes
Blur—MO & Foster The People
The Raging Sea—Broadside
Shoot and Run—Josef Salvat
Cursive—VOILA & Kellin Quinn
How Villains Are Made—Madalen Duke
Bleeding Out—Molly Hunt
Pyrokinesis—7Charlot
Stay—Thirty Seconds to Mars
A Beautiful Lie—Thirty Seconds to Mars
Victim—Halflives
Cosmic Lover—Florence + The Machine
Still Worth Fighting For—My Darkest Days

You can find the complete playlist on Spotify.

LIES
of my
MONSTER

PROLOGUE

Kirill

Age Thirteen

IF YOU LOSE, IT'S YOUR FAULT.

If you win, it's natural.

Those are the words my father has engraved in my mind ever since I learned how to talk. I've come to the realization that I'm nothing more than a commodity to him. He invested in me, and he expects returns in any form he deems necessary.

Roman Morozov isn't my father. He's my keeper.

One day, I'll get out of this fucking house and take Konstantin and Karina with me. Better yet, I'll kick him and Yulia out and live in the mansion with my siblings.

Why should we leave when they're the abnormal ones?

I step through the school's gate and wait for the driver to pick me up. The gloomy sky casts a shadow of sadness over the school grounds, but a certain cheerful atmosphere fills the air since it's the last day before the Christmas holidays.

Everyone attending this private school is either rich, influential, or both. It goes without saying that my father would enroll me in this fucking circus where everyone's first question is, "What does your father do?" I can't exactly answer with, "He kills people," because that would be frowned upon due to their fragile morality. I settle for ignoring them instead.

Usually, Viktor would be glued to my side like a magnet, and his stonelike presence is enough to ward off unwanted attention. However, he was forbidden from attending today due to some guard event.

Whenever Roman feels Viktor has gotten too close, he doesn't miss the chance to remind him and the rest of my personal security that they're only guards—servants—he can get rid of whenever he pleases.

Or, more like, he does it to remind me that if he chooses to, he can isolate me from everyone. My father insists on grooming me to believe that my only role in life is being his heir. Not anyone's friend, sibling, or son.

I'm just a fucking commodity.

A few students whisper as they pass by. I don't have to hear them to know what they're saying about me.

"I heard his father is in the Russian mafia."

"He'll become a gangster one day."

"Don't look at him, or he might get you killed."

"Have you seen the way he glares?"

If Viktor were here, he'd terrorize these kids until they pissed themselves. Me? I couldn't care less. Let them gossip all they like. After all, that's the only thing weak people can do.

Adrian trudges in my direction then stops beside me. He's a few years older than me, but since I was an early bloomer, I'm not that much shorter than him. While I ignore all the other kids, I have an excellent relationship with the teachers and make it my mission to charm them for good grades. Adrian, however, only talks to his closest guard, Kolya, who's currently standing on the corner.

Adrian has made himself an outcast on purpose. His expression is closed off and his hands are shoved in the pockets of his khaki pants. I was a bit taken aback when he approached me since students usually avoid me like the plague.

He definitely has no reason to stay away from me, considering his father and mine are two of the New York Bratva kings.

He has no reason to initiate contact, either. We're not friends.

In fact, the concept of friends doesn't exist in our world. There are two categories—allies and enemies. He falls under neither.

"Waiting for your ride as well?" I ask, tilting my head to the side.

He says nothing and continues staring ahead with his depressing gray eyes that could be mistaken for a wayward cloud.

Adrian's mother was a mistress who somehow snatched the wife position after a lot of drama. He's never appeared to feel comfortable at any of the events we've been pushed into together. And he rarely talks, no matter how much the other children and I try to bring him out of his shell.

He acts like such a drama queen, as if he's had it worse than the rest of us or something.

"You know." I jut my chin in his direction. "You'll never get anywhere in this world with that attitude of yours."

He meets my gaze and then motions at my neck. "Worry about yourself and those bruises you're doing a shitty job of hiding."

I grin despite the tingling that starts in my neck and slithers down my spine. "Battle scars shouldn't be hidden."

"That's called abuse, Kirill."

"Oh yeah? Are you an expert?"

"I know it when I see it." He faces me fully and steps closer so we're toe to toe. "That is *not* okay."

"Fuck off."

"You being defensive is also a result of abuse."

"Hey, don't push your luck, and stay out of my business."

"Closing oneself off is a symptom, as is defending one's abuser."

"If you don't shut the fuck up right now, I'm going to punch you."

"That's another form—"

Before he's finished his words, I've already driven my fist into his face. He stumbles back a step, but then he swings his arm and punches me in the cheek.

I reel back but catch myself before I trip.

We exchange a few more blows until our noses are bleeding, our lips are busted, and we need to lean on the stone wall for balance. A few onlookers gather around, but Adrian's guard, who's around his age, scares them to death while kicking them away. He did try to stop us at one point, but a single look from Adrian was enough to derail him.

We're both panting as we glare at each other while hunching over to catch our breaths.

"You need to stop it, or it'll go on forever," he says.

"I swear to fuck, Adrian, if you don't shut up..."

"What are you gonna do? Punch me like a girl?"

"I'm going to kill you." I lunge at him again, and he's waiting for me, his eyes blazing. Seems that this motherfucker woke up today and chose violence. How could I not make his wish come true?

He doesn't lift his hands to protect himself and, instead, strains from between clenched teeth, "You can stop it."

"And how do I do that, genius?" I stand before him and let my fist fall to my side. "Unless I get stronger, I won't be able to stop anything."

"Then do it faster. For starters, stop punching like a girl."

"You wouldn't be saying that if you saw how *prettily* I decorated your face, motherfucker."

He harrumphs and turns toward his guard. "We're walking home, Kolya. A certain presence has soured my mood."

"I should be the one saying that!" I shout at his back. "I wish you a shitty Christmas."

He flips me off without turning around, and I want to run at full speed and knock him to the ground. I don't, because even I realize that I already gave in to violence more than I should've allowed myself.

I'm trying to have better control of that part of myself, and to do that, I need to be more levelheaded. I touch the corner of my lip and wince. One of these days, that fucker Adrian will have his throat slit in his sleep.

A black van pulls up in front of me, but before it's fully stopped, the side door opens, and a shrill, excited voice yells, "Kirya!!!"

My brother jumps from the car and slams into me, knocking me off balance. I pat the top of his light hair. Despite being only two years younger than me, he's way shorter. I'm having a growth spurt he can't keep up with.

"Hi there, little Kosta."

"I'm not little." He still nuzzles his nose in my chest like when he was a toddler. My ribs ache from when Adrian punched me, but I wrap my arm around his back.

"Kirill!! Kirill!" Another much smaller figure crashes into my side.

My five-year-old sister, Karina, reaches her hands up to me even though I've told her she's too heavy to carry. Does she understand that logic? No way in hell.

She looks pretty today in a pink dress with white ribbons. Her blonde hair falls in styled curls to the middle of her back.

"Kara." Despite my sore body, I still lift her high and she sits snugly on my shoulders.

She taps the top of my head and then gasps. "Blood, blood. Are you hurt?"

That's when Konstantin pushes back to actually stare at me, and his eyes widen. "Why...what happened?"

"Just a meaningless fight. Nothing to worry about."

He pouts, and Karina starts to cry, so I have to console them both and assure them that I'm really okay. If I'd known they were coming to pick me up, I wouldn't have risen to Adrian's provocations or talked to the slimy fucker.

I might not be strong enough to put an end to my father's tests and training, but I will be. If for no other reason than to protect my siblings.

In the car, there are two of my father's guards and the driver. No matter which angle I view the situation from, it's weird that my father sent Konstantin and Karina to pick me up from school. It's even more strange that Yulia allowed Konstantin out of her sight when she's usually overprotective of him.

"Why did you guys come along?" I ask.

"Because we miss you! Miss you!" Karina shouts, then breaks into a fit of giggles. She has a habit of repeating her words because our dear mother always tells her to speak clearly and not like an idiot.

"Papa said we're going on a Christmas holiday." Konstantin grins, his face brimming with excitement. "As a family."

I narrow my eyes. We have never, and I mean *ever*, done anything as a family, so the fact that we're starting now makes me suspicious.

In fact, I'm fucking paranoid about this change of events.

Christmas is usually me decorating a tree for my siblings and giving them presents because Roman doesn't do it, and Yulia only has Christmas presents for Konstantin. I've come to expect that from her, but it still makes Karina cry every year. So Konstantin divides his dozen presents between him, me and Karina behind Yulia's back. I don't take them, but that act soothes our baby sister's hurt feelings. She's the one with an eternal love for glitter, bright colors, and everything pretty.

Does Yulia care? Absolutely not. It's like Karina and I are invisible to her. I wish she was our stepmother. That way, this whole disdain would make sense.

How the woman who actually gave birth to us could treat us this way is the part that I can't find an explanation for.

"Is that what the guards said?" I ask my brother.

He nods. "We're finally going on a trip together!"

I cast a glance at my surroundings. All the other students have left, so it's only us. My gut twists as I put Karina down and let her grab my hand, and then I clutch Konstantin's with my free one. "We should leave this place. *Now.*"

"But why?" He tries to resist me. "Kara and I want to go on the holiday."

"We want to go, go." Karina pulls on my hand, too, but she has little to no effect.

Because I'm already dragging them down the street.

"Sir, come back here." The guards' heavy footsteps sound behind me as they soon catch up to us. "We have clear instructions to drive you."

"We're walking. Go back on your own," I say without turning around.

The heavy footsteps disappear, but they're replaced by others. Lighter but more of them. I lift Karina up so that she's glued to my side and scream, "Run, Kosta!"

There's a small pause before he nods and complies. He doesn't even ask me why or where we're going. Konstantin has always trusted me with everything. Including thoughts about how he hates Yulia sometimes because she treats me and Karina like shit.

He tells me how one day, it'll be just the three of us because my baby brother decided that my dream is also his dream.

We don't look behind us as we run down the streets, breezing past the Christmas-decorated shops. But we're not fast enough. Karina is slowing me down, and Konstantin keeps lagging behind. Suddenly too overwhelmed by the pace, he trips and falls, calling my name.

I curse and start to go back to help him, but the moment I

do, it's too late. Men dressed in black combat clothes and balaclavas have already gotten hold of him.

He thrashes and kicks, but it's impossible when he's surrounded by six of them. Karina screams at the sight, and I put her down, then hide her in a small alley. I hunch to her level and say in a soothing voice, "Stay here, Kara. I'll get Kosta and come back, okay?"

"Okay, okay." She keeps her hand on my arm as if not wanting to let me go, so I gently wrench it free.

I rush back to my brother to find him thrashing and cursing. Upon seeing me, hope blossoms in his eyes, "Kirya!"

I fetch a rock and throw it at one of the men. It hits him, but two others lunge at me at supersonic speed. Just when I'm devising the best plan of action, Karina shrieks.

"Kirill!" both she and Kosta call.

My mind turns into a mess, and I don't know where to look first. But before I can decide, I'm whacked in the side of my head, and my knees hit the ground before my body follows.

Through my blood-soaked vision, I see the men carrying a screaming Konstantin and Karina away.

I try to reach out to them but realize I'm also being dragged away, but in the opposite direction.

Just like that, my world turns black.

ONE

Kirill

I BELIEVE IN INSTINCT.

Not only has it saved my life numerous times, but it's also helped me in solving many mysteries.

It was in my early teenage years that I began to predict what type of torture my father had in store for me. He started using Konstantin and Karina to get to me, so I gradually kept my distance so as not to get them involved.

That time when I was kidnapped in front of their eyes when I was thirteen terrorized them to the point that they couldn't sleep for days. The guards dropped them off at home, but I was in for my special torture endurance 'training.' A little Christmas gift from dear old Papa.

And while my father only meant to scare them, it went above and beyond and actually traumatized them.

I went back home a few days later with bruises all over my torso and cutting scars on my abdomen. Like a damn psychopath, Roman had made sure none of the torture was visible on my face.

As Konstantin and Karina hugged me, I had to bite my lip to endure the pain. They cried their hearts out and crowded my bed that night. Not even Yulia could take Konstantin away. It was the first time they slept after nights of terror.

But I couldn't sleep. The pain didn't allow me the comfort of shutting my brain and relaxing. In fact, it was soon after that incident that I found it hard to sleep. My mind was on high alert, thinking about solutions in case I was ambushed again.

That's when I realized that if I didn't create distance from my siblings, they'd be collateral damage in my father's grand plans for me.

Since then, I've learned to trust my gut when it tells me something.

Like now.

I knew something was amiss the moment Sasha asked for three days off. One, she barely utilizes her vacation days, and when she does, it's to spend time with Karina or with fucking Maksim.

Two, her going to Russia for this particular vacation told me everything I needed to know.

She was returning to the slimy motherfucker she was talking to on the phone seven months ago.

The one she told she missed and would come back to soon. Not only that, but she also shot the device so I wouldn't be able to find his details, then proceeded to threaten to kill me if I hurt her beloved snowflake.

The reason I know he's Russian? She spoke the language when she said those affectionate things I didn't think she was capable of.

I never brought up the subject of her lover again, because I knew that if I did, her walls would be up in no time. That doesn't mean I forgot about him, though.

In fact, he's been in the back of my mind every second of every day. Whenever I fuck her, I go harder and faster at the thought that she has feelings for someone else.

I see her face each morning and wonder if today is the day she'll decide to leave me and go back to his side. The only thing that's offered a small form of solace is knowing she followed me to New York for a reason, and until she gets what she wants, Sasha will simply not give up.

That's just not part of her personality.

And while I don't know her reason, I haven't actively searched for it either since I've had her by my side, and that's what's mattered the most.

But then she asked for those three days off so she could go see her lover in Russia.

In the beginning, I contemplated locking her the fuck up in the dungeons so she'd never consider leaving my side again. However, I thought better of it.

This is my chance to not only meet her lover, but also eliminate him once and for all. That way, she'll have no one to be with but me.

When I dropped her off at the airport, though, I wanted to abandon the whole plan, and I was ready to if she'd just stayed.

I all but fucking *begged* her to stay, but she left anyway.

She chose him over me.

Did that drive me to nearly lose my shit during the flight? Absolutely.

Even Viktor was eyeing me like I was an alien, despite my numerous attempts to remain still.

I initially planned to come here alone, but Viktor, who likes to think he was born as my shadow, vehemently refused to stay behind.

He did keep his questions to himself when I told him we were going to Russia. But that's only because I threatened to throw him out of the plane if he said anything.

My mood went from bad to colossally terrible when we landed

in Russia and I found out that Sasha had left her phone in an airport locker.

She knew I'd send someone after her and abandoned the method that's susceptible to being tracked.

The joke's on her, though, because that's not the only tracker I have on her. Since I anticipated this, I placed one tracker in her bag and another in the lining of her jacket.

I check my phone, and both of them are working.

She's moving, and judging by her location and the speed, she's in a vehicle on the highway.

Russia's fucking winter slaps me in the face and nearly freezes me during the walk from the private jet to the car I arranged to have waiting for us. We're definitely not dressed for Mother Russia today, and it shows. Even Viktor's jaw tightens at the stabs of cold.

The heavy snow turns my jacket white in seconds and by the time we're inside, it's soaking wet. I remove it and send the live location to the GPS in front of Viktor. "Follow that dot, and don't lose it."

He stares at me through the rearview mirror. "Can you tell me why we're in Russia and following fuck knows who?"

"No. Do as you're told or get out so I can do it myself."

"Kirill—"

"It's personal, and that's all you need to know. I swear to fuck, Viktor, we lose that dot, and I leave you to freeze on the side of the road."

He narrows his eyes as if he wants to take this already tense situation further, but he chooses to be smart and starts driving.

In the meantime, to keep myself from self-combusting, I continue checking the location on my smartwatch.

Sasha stops at one point and begins moving at a slower pace, probably on foot, then a few minutes later, she increases her speed again

Interesting.

She's using different means of transport. Again, to avoid being followed.

The fact that she's going to such lengths to protect her fucker of a lover fills my vision with red.

Of course, she could also be here to meet a family member, but according to her army records, she's an orphan. She's just mentioned her family once, that day in the sauna, and she never uses personal names.

The only other possibility is her fucking lover.

I push my glasses up my nose and lean my chin against my fist.

It should feel blasphemous for me to have these emotions toward anyone, let alone a girl I know practically nothing about.

She's just a fuck buddy. Someone who submits to my dominance and gets off on it.

And yet...she isn't.

I have no clue why Sasha is special to me, but I know she is. She. Fucking. Is.

And I'll be damned if I let her reunite with her lover before I get to the bottom of these turbulent emotions.

We keep following her for over two hours, until she stops, then appears to be running toward what looks to be a giant field on the map. If my guess is correct, she's used at least four means of transportation at this point.

By the time we arrive, she's about half an hour in. I can't follow her on foot, because I'll probably miss her. Or, more accurately, I'll allow her to reunite with the fucker without my being there.

"Get me a snowmobile," I tell Viktor.

"It might take me a while."

"I don't give a fuck. Make it happen."

He steps out of the car, but juts his head back in.

"What?" I snap.

"If you were a woman, I'd say you're PMS'ing, but you're not. So I'm not sure how to categorize this behavior."

"Then don't, and do as you're told."

He stares at me for a beat, as if making sure I'm the same person he's known his whole life, shakes his head, and finally goes to make himself useful.

It takes him fifteen minutes I don't have to bring me a snowmobile, but Sasha still appears to be running, so I can make it.

Viktor throws me a thick white coat and thermal pants. I hastily change into them, pull on the snow binoculars, and hop on the snowmobile.

My guard clutches the handlebars. "I'll drive."

"No, you'll stay here until I get back."

"I'm not letting you go in the middle of nowhere alone."

"You don't have a say in it. Don't follow me."

"But—"

"That's an order, Viktor. Wait here."

He goes rigid, seeming taller and even more like a mountain than at any other time. He's never liked being separated from me for any reason. Viktor really thinks his role in life is to ensure my safety and that if he fails that lifetime mission, he has no purpose.

"It's not a dangerous situation," I offer in a half-assed attempt to lessen the blow, but I don't wait for his reply as I cut off the GPS transmission to the car. If I don't, he'll follow the signal until he finds me and insist we fly back to New York immediately.

After making sure I'm the only one with the tracking signal, I grab the snowmobile's handlebars and go off like a bullet in the snow.

It takes me about fifteen minutes to reach her, but Sasha stopped moving five minutes after I started.

Her location is inert in the middle of the vast field she was running through earlier, and the area looks to be deserted. I had thought she was headed toward a village nearby, but that doesn't appear to be the case.

I pick up speed to climb a hill that separates me from the field. After I reach the top, I catch a glimpse of a warehouse. The structure is creepily similar to the one where my men died in our last mission for the military.

I'm someone who's always followed his instincts. That, coupled with quick reflexes, has saved me from death countless times.

And now, my instinct is screaming at me to turn around and speed in the opposite direction.

I don't.

Because that would mean leaving Sasha with her lover, and that option is simply not on the table or even beneath it.

However, the view that materializes in front of me does make me question my reasons for being here.

Not far from the warehouse stand men dressed in black, their faces hidden with balaclavas like in some terrorist snuff movie.

All of them have rifles slung across their chests, except for one who's holding a gun.

Although her coat looks different and her face is hidden, I know it's Sasha. I gave her that gun soon after we got to New York, and she scratched an 'S' on the handle because it looks too similar to Maksim's gun, and she wanted to avoid a mix-up.

Red alerts go off in my head. Most of them start and end with 'run.'

A lot of questions sling through my head. First, who the fuck are these people? How is Sasha related to them? But most importantly, why the fuck does this smell like a trap?

Because it is, you fucking idiot.

I start to turn the snowmobile, but it's too late. The man beside Sasha opens fire.

Pain explodes in my chest, and I lose my grip on the handlebars. The snowmobile and I tumble down the hill, flipping twice.

Motherfucking fuck.

I try to control the fall, but it's impossible on such a steep hill. Pain flares from my wound, but I don't think it's near any vital organs—

"No!" Her raw shout echoes in the air as another bullet hits me in the chest. Again.

This time, I can't attempt to control anything.

I fall and roll, and my vision turns misty red. Not due to the wound or the fact that I'm probably dying.

It's the reality of knowing that Sasha led me here so that whoever these men are would kill me.

She betrayed me.

Fuck.

Sasha *betrayed* me.

All the fight leaves my limbs as my world turns black.

TWO

Sasha

THE SCENE STARTS IN SLOW MOTION, BUT THEN IT'S TOO fast. Too raw.

Too...surreal.

It's strange how some events overlap in a completely different rhythm while they happen in real time.

For a moment, I think I'm dreaming. Maybe this is another one of my cruel nightmares where I keep losing the people I care about the most.

That's a plausible explanation...right?

The person who's rolling in the snow after being shot for the second time can*not* be Kirill.

He just *can't*.

When his huge body comes to a halt at the bottom of the hill, my heart nearly does the same. Then, within a fraction of a second, it roars back to life and almost explodes out of its confinements.

This is not a nightmare or a cruel play of my imagination. This situation is happening.

Right now.

Right in front of me.

Uncle Albert raises his rifle, but before he can take the lethal shot, I jump in front of him.

My limbs tremble and the only thing that plays in a loop through my mind is: what makes you think the first or the second shots weren't the lethal ones?

Kirill is probably dead—

No. I kick that thought out of my head as I remove my face covering and throw it down, my upper lip unconsciously lifting in a snarl.

"Get out of the way, Sasha," my uncle orders in a foreign voice. Papa was the one who spoke in this authoritarian tone—not to us, but to the people who worked for him. Uncle Albert would never.

It feels like I'm seeing him through new eyes. As if maybe he's not the same uncle I've known for my twenty-one years of life.

He starts to push me aside, but I push back as hard as I can and actually manage to make him stumble in the snow.

"Stop it!" I scream, my raw voice echoing in the emptiness surrounding us.

"What do you mean by stop it?" Uncle Albert steps forward. "He's the man behind our family's death, Sasha."

I shake my head more times than needed. "I don't believe that."

"Why the hell wouldn't you?"

"I just don't!" I jut a finger at his chest. "I'm going to get him medical help, and if you try to stop me, I don't know how I will react. I'm warning you. Unless you want one of us to die today, do *not* stop me, Uncle."

I don't wait for his reply as I run through the snow. My boots get stuck and I fall to my knees, but I lift myself up and rush to Kirill. I expect Uncle Albert to try to clutch my hand or forbid me from getting on with my mission, but neither happens.

I run the fastest I ever have and that includes training, military missions, and high-speed exercising. A foreign energy grips hold of me until all I can focus on is reaching Kirill.

It takes me more time than I have to finally get within touching distance. His large body is sprawled out on the snow facedown. Splashes of blood surround him and leave trails of red in the snow. Nausea rises in my throat and my heart shreds to pieces.

This feeling is no different than when I realized my cousins were dead on top of me four years ago. For a moment, I'm frozen in place, unable to move. My nostrils fill with the metallic tang of blood, and my heart all but spills out and crawls up beside Kirill's inert body.

Falling to my knees beside him, I grasp his shoulder, then turn him over. A small gasp leaves my lips when I see the huge hole in the middle of his chest and his white coat that's soaked with red. The stubble covering his cheeks looks too black and harsh against his paling skin. My trembling fingers gently touch the blood that's gushed out of his mouth.

Did he…vomit blood?

Oh, God. Oh, no.

Please *no*.

I reach my shaky hand beneath his nose and my breath catches as I wait for a sign of life from him.

In the grand scheme of things, the amount of time I wait is insignificant, but it feels like years. The longer I don't feel any breaths, the harder my heart beats.

I taste salt, and it's then I realize I'm bawling my eyes out. My hand is a trembling mess, and the sight of blood makes me want to throw my guts up. It's not because I'm squeamish, but it's the fact that it's Kirill's blood.

He's lost so much blood.

Faintly, almost as if it's not there, I feel a fraction of a breath. It's not much, but it's all I need. I rip a piece of my shirt and put pressure on the wound in a hopeless attempt to stop the bleeding.

Then I contemplate lifting him and carrying him to the snowmobile that's stuck on the middle of the hill, but I'm scared about aggravating his injuries.

So I sit him up and crouch behind him so that his back is against mine. Then I hook my arms through his and start to lift up.

I fall right back down.

It's impossible.

Not only is he way bigger than me, but he's also unconscious, so he feels much heavier.

If I do it this way, I'll never be able to get him help in time.

I abandon the idea of lifting him and lay him on his back. Then I grab his feet and start to drag him across the snow. This way, I won't aggravate his injuries. It's still hard, though. Not only is he literally made of muscles, but the hill is so steep, my legs burn and shake, nearly giving out from beneath me.

But I don't stop or pause—except to ensure that I'm not hitting his head on any bumps. The moment I reach the snowmobile, I release him and gently lay his feet on the snow. Then I use whatever inhuman strength I have to flip the vehicle and drag it to where he is.

My heart squeezes and shatters at the sight of the huge wound on his chest, but I don't allow myself to get stuck in that loop.

I'm the only one who can get him help.

I *have* to save him.

Those thoughts fill me with renewed energy that allows me to pull him onto the snowmobile.

I try to keep him upright as I sit down in front of him, draping his body around mine for more security, and then strap him to me with my jacket tied around our middles. I'm going to go as fast as possible, and I can't have him falling in the middle of the trip.

Once I make sure he's secured, I search the GPS for the closest hospital, then drive the snowmobile at supersonic speed. I ignore the sound of other snowmobiles following me. Probably Uncle Albert and the mysterious men he brought with him.

I don't give a fuck, because I meant it. If he so much as tries to stop me from getting Kirill help, this situation will get really ugly really fast.

It takes me thirty minutes to reach the hospital, and that's only because I actually drove at the snowmobile's highest speed, while leaning forward so that Kirill had good support and wouldn't fall.

I'm ready to drive the thing through the hospital door, but a few nurses come out of the building with their equipment. I try to help them lift Kirill onto the stretcher, but I step back when they push me away since they know how to do it properly.

A doctor straps an oxygen mask to his face, and then all of us are running down the depressing white hall.

"He has two gunshot wounds to the chest," I tell them in a clear voice I don't recognize. "He also fell down a hill and lost a lot of blood."

The doctor shouts some instructions at the nurses, then jumps onto the stretcher, straddling him, and cuts Kirill's coat open.

My throat closes at the view of the two bullet holes gushing with blood. One is higher than the other. One has more blood around it than the other and causes red to stain his abs and tattoos.

Oh, God.

Is that…where his heart is?

I try to go with them all the way, but the nurses forbid it and ask me to wait outside. The moment the emergency room door closes, I slide to the floor, tears and blood dripping onto the white tiles.

I lift my red hands and stare at their harsh contrast against the fluorescent lights. They look blurry through my tears, and this state—the fact that I'm losing my grip on reality—feels so final, it's crippling.

While staring at my bloodied hands, I see the last time I talked to Kirill. In the car. When he dropped me off at the airport.

I can still taste his lips on mine when he kissed me like he never had before. When he set my world ablaze and nearly had me confessing every twisted feeling I have for him.

If I could go back in time, to that moment when he asked me not to go, I'd stay.

I'd do things differently.

But I can't, and the damning fact remains...Kirill is fighting death because of me. He has a hole in his heart because I stupidly thought I was here for Babushka and that I could actually avoid being tracked by him.

I'm the reason he's in there, and that breaks the heart that, before him, I thought was long dead.

A heart that was overlooked in my conquest for revenge, ignored and considered irrelevant in my current life. Kirill is the one who brought it back to life and nurtured it to its current state.

And the fact that I indirectly put two bullets in his chest as repayment makes me want to claw my skin off and scream until my lungs give out.

"Care to explain what you think you're doing, Sasha?"

My uncle's clipped question wrenches me out of my gloomy state. I wipe my tears with the back of my hand, stand up, then whirl around to face him.

He's still in his combat clothes, but there's no weapon—none that's visible, at least—and he removed the balaclava. "Why don't you explain what *you* were doing, Uncle? How could you use me to get Kirill here?"

"Would you have come if I'd told you the plan?"

"No!"

"That's your reason, then. You're getting close to Morozov, and while that's good, not protecting your own feelings isn't. Anyone who goes undercover should be extra careful not to allow the subject they're spying on to affect them. Needless to say, you failed, Sasha."

"I don't give a fuck!" This is the first time I've cursed in front of my uncle, but I don't give a flying fuck about that either. "How could you… How did you know he'd follow me?"

"I didn't for certain. Until he boarded his private plane right after yours took off. It's not a coincidence, and a man like Kirill doesn't do things arbitrarily."

"You…have spies in New York?"

"I have spies everywhere."

"Just…what do you do, Uncle? Who were all those men from earlier? What's going on?"

"I told you what's going on. We're taking revenge on the people who annihilated our family. Or we were in the middle of doing that before you took him to the hospital and threatened that one of us would die if I intervened."

"That's because you're not making any sense!" My arms and legs are taut with tension as I get in his face. "How could Kirill be responsible for the massacre? It was his father who came to our house!"

"And it was Kirill who devised the plan to wipe us out."

My feet falter, and I shake my head slowly. "That's not true. Kirill…was in the army at the time of the attack."

"Our family's demise was his last mission before enlisting."

"Do you have proof?"

"Not yet, but I don't need it. In the beginning, I thought Roman had come up with the entire plan, but things didn't add up. He wasn't that cunning. Besides, weren't you the one who told me that Kirill was the mastermind behind his father's success before he left for the army? That's when I started to dig deeper and found out that he was indeed behind every successful operation Roman conducted in the last ten years, whether in Russia or the States."

I continue shaking my head, my heart beating fast and so damn loud, I can hear the roaring in my ears. "You're projecting, Uncle. You're just trying to find someone to blame, and Kirill happened to be in your path."

"And you're in denial, Sasha. You know, deep in your heart, that he is the one."

"I said no!"

"Sasha…"

"He's not. I'll wait for him to wake up and ask him myself."

"And reveal your identity?"

"I don't care!" Uncle doesn't know that Kirill already found out about my gender, and I'm keeping it that way.

"Your grandmother won't like this," he says with an aggravated tone. "She's waiting to hear about his death, and if she knows you stopped it, she will…"

"What? Punish me? She can do whatever she wants, and it'll mean nothing to me anymore. I went through hell for this family, but you and Babushka chose to *use* me. I'm going to bet she's not sick at all and all of this was a setup."

"Sashenka—" He reaches a hand for me, but I step away.

"I'm not your Sashenka when you fucking used me, Uncle. You forced me to indirectly put two bullets in the chest of the man who saved me when I was on the brink of death. You weren't there when I nearly died on that mission, but he was, Uncle! He carried me and got me medical care. He *saved* me."

"After he killed your entire family."

"I told you I don't believe that!"

"You're being unreasonable right now, but that's fine. We'll talk about it. Come back to see Mother and Mike with me."

"Not now." I stare at the emergency room door. "I'm not leaving until I know Kirill is all right."

"What is this fixation you have on Kirill?" He narrows his eyes. "Is there something I need to know?"

"No." I point at the exit. "Now, go, Uncle. I don't want you here."

He purses his lips, probably irritated at how I spoke to him, but that's the last thing on my mind.

After he leaves, I stand in place, staring at the door, unmoving.

Three whole hours pass before the doctor finally emerges, his face worn out and his posture defeated.

My legs barely carry me, and my eyes blur with tears as I ask in a voice so low, I think he doesn't hear me, "How…"

The doctor speaks in a rural accent, "We were able to remove the bullets, but some fragments hit the heart and caused damage to the fine arteries. He also lost a lot of blood. We did our best, but the rest is up to him now. We're moving him to the ICU. The next twenty-four hours will determine whether or not he survives or slips into a coma."

He talks about the cause of the incident and how he's obliged by law to call the authorities, but I'm not listening. Once he's out of sight, I fall against the wall and sob so loud that my heart feels like it's bleeding along with Kirill's.

What have I done?

THREE

Sasha

I'M A MESS.

After I cried my eyes out upon hearing about Kirill's slim chances of survival, I haven't been able to fully gather myself together.

The only reason I don't crumble is because I can't leave Kirill alone. If I do, he might be in more danger. Yes, Uncle Albert left, but that doesn't mean he or his men won't come back.

I've been standing guard in front of the ICU the whole time, then when I get tired, I sit down. I haven't left to change my clothes or wash my hands, not even when the nurses asked me to. So they brought me some disinfectant wipes to at least get the blood off my hands.

It's been five hours since I heard the news, and only now has the doctor come back to check on him.

I wait on pins and needles, but when he returns, there's no change in his expression.

"He's still unconscious, but that's not out of the ordinary," he says before I can ask anything.

"Can I see him?"

"Not unless you're a family member."

"I'm…" I can't even lie and say I'm his girlfriend since I look like a damn man. "His cousin."

He eyes me suspiciously probably because Kirill and I look nothing alike. However, the doctor nods and points down the hall. "Take a left, and the nurse will direct you."

"Thank you."

I'm about to head there, but the doctor blocks my path. "As I mentioned earlier, we have to report gunshot wounds to the authorities. The police will be here shortly and will have questions for you."

I nod, not really thinking about the police right now. I'll manage to mislead them when it's time.

Before I'm allowed to see Kirill, I clean up and change into fresh clothes from my backpack. After I'm done, I follow the nurse with heavy steps.

She leaves once we reach the window, through which I can see him. A large ball clings to the back of my throat, and I suppress a sob at the view in front of me.

Everything is white—the lights, the bed, the bandages covering his naked chest. Even his skin is pasty, making the dark tattoos contrast harshly against it.

His face is too colorless, too lifeless, as if he's given up and is already crossing to the other side.

My hands touch the glass slowly, carefully, as if I'm actually stroking his cheek. "I'm sorry, Kirill. I'm so sorry…if I'd known…I wouldn't have come, I would've listened to you and stayed, I would've…"

I curl my fingers on the glass, knowing full well that any excuse I offer or what-ifs I think of are futile. It all happened, and

Kirill is fighting for his life because of me. That's the truth that I can't change no matter what I do.

That knowledge doesn't erase my sense of culpability and frustration, though.

I taste salt, and I realize I'm crying again. What's wrong with me today? Since when did I become a crybaby?

My body is just not able to contain all the emotional turmoil inside me. The regrets, the adrenaline, and especially the feeling of being torn between my family and my strong sense of loyalty to Kirill.

I don't know if this type of loyalty started in the army or after he saved my life or even after I went to New York and became close to him on more than one level, but the loyalty is there.

Which is ironic since I brought him to this state.

"Please come back, Kirill. I beg you."

I don't want to think of the possibility of him being gone. That's simply not allowed. I've known him for about a year, and while that might not seem like a long time, it feels like forever.

I just can't imagine my life without him in it.

Worse, I'm starting to forget how I lived before he came along.

And if he's gone, I have no idea how I will be able to cope or survive.

"You have all these plans to rise to the top, right?" I murmur as if he can hear me. "You'll go so high, people will break their necks looking up at you. You'll build and smash as many houses of cards as possible, just because you can. You have too many plans and things to do, so you can't just give up on them now... Also, Karina will lose whatever progress she's made if something happens to you. She really loves you but doesn't have the confidence to express it, because she's scared you might leave again. I think Konstantin loves you, too, but he's just badly misguided by your mother... And Viktor...what will happen to your shadow if you're gone? He can't be anyone else's shadow after he's invested so many years in you. And Anna...she'll be devastated. Yuri, Maksim, and the rest of the men, too. They respect you because they see you as a role model. Not because they're scared of you... All these people depend on you, so you can't leave..."

I'm blabbering and bawling again until I can only see him through blurred vision.

"Sir..."

As I raise my head at the nurse's voice, I use the sleeve of my jacket to wipe my eyes. I imagine they're probably bloodshot and red since she double-checks me before continuing, "You have visitors outside."

Probably the police.

After taking one last look at Kirill, I stroke the glass as if I'm caressing his face, then leave the ICU area.

The moment I step outside, my cheek flies to the side due to a ruthless slap. I freeze in place as none other than Babushka comes into view, accompanied by my uncle, who's changed into a casual shirt, pants, and a heavy coat.

My grandmother is a short woman with a square face and gray hair that's gathered in a stiff bun. Her wrinkles form a map of the decades she's lived on this earth. She's dressed in a conservative gray knee-length dress with a thick golden brooch on her chest. A matching necklace, bracelet, and the family ring complete the look. Oh, and the cane that she's tapping on the floor.

I always knew my grandmother didn't prefer me over my cousins or brother, but this is the first time she's looked at me with pure contempt.

"Mother..." My uncle tries to pull her back, but she pushes him away and hits her cane on the floor again.

"How dare you stop our revenge on that rotten family?" she asks with an extremely upper-class Russian accent—the way I used to speak before I joined the army and had to lose it.

My shoulders hunch like every time I'm scolded by her. I've always worked for Babushka's approval but have never gotten it, which makes me lack confidence whenever I'm in front of her.

The cane with a golden strip and a crow's head in her wrinkly hand has been the bane of my existence. I, more often than not, got hit by that when I was growing up.

Sometimes, even hearing it tapping on the ground is enough to start a ticking sound at the back of my head.

I swallow twice before I'm able to speak. "Kirill has nothing to do with our revenge."

The cane swishes in the air before it crashes against my side, and I wince, but I don't move out of the way. "So you are switching sides now?"

"No. But I won't allow anyone to kill him."

"You're defending him with everything in you. I wonder how he'll react if he finds out you're an Ivanov." She lifts her nose in the air. "He and his father did everything in their power to eliminate us. Do you think he'll take the knowledge of survivors lightly?"

"He's not like that." And I mean it. Kirill might be ruthless, but he cares about Karina and Anna. He wouldn't hurt children, no matter what the agenda is.

"Sasha," my uncle starts. "You are in denial, and that won't only be a threat to your life but to ours as well. I need to kill Kirill while he's alone and defenseless. We'll never have a chance like this one again."

"No." The word comes out too raw and guttural, and definitely not in the way I'd usually speak to the two most revered members of my family.

"What did you just say?" Babushka asks in an incredulous tone.

"I said no. You have no proof. Besides, Uncle, didn't you say the one who ordered the hit was a higher-up in the military? Didn't I enlist to find him?"

"The one who executed the hit was in the military," Uncle says. "I didn't know his name at the time, but I found out from trusted sources after Roman's death that he was General Abram Kuzmin. But here's the thing. Before I could get to him, he was found mysteriously murdered in the streets of Moscow not long after Kirill became the head of the Morozov family. Do you think it's a coincidence that the lone witness to Roman's deeds was killed after he died? The only one who could've ordered that hit is Kirill. Roman has no reason to hide information after his death. His son, however, is going to great lengths to cover up his tracks."

My mind is about to explode from the onslaught of information, but I still shake my head. "He has nothing to gain from eliminating a witness to a murder when he thinks the entire family was killed, which means your source is unreliable. You don't know Kirill, but I do. He's not the type who does anything unless there's some sort of gain."

"How dare you defend him in front of my face, you preposterous child!"

"I'm sorry, but I won't allow you to hurt him, Babushka."

"Go do your thing, Albert." She hits me with the cane on my other side and pushes. "Move out of the way."

I seize hold of her cane for the first time in my life. My hand trembles, but I lift my chin and continue to stand tall. "I said no."

"Sasha, don't make this harder than it needs to be," Uncle says.

"If you want to kill Kirill, you'll have to kill me first."

"Sasha!"

"Aleksandra!" Babushka screeches, pulling her cane from my fingers and stomping it on the ground. "I should've known a girl would be good for nothing. You've fallen for the monster, haven't you?"

"N-no." I clear my throat. "He's my savior, and I refuse to betray him."

"If you don't move out of the way," she warns. "Mark my words, Aleksandra Ivanova, I will *disown* you."

I pause, my fingers shaking and my heart thumping so loudly, I can hear it in my ears.

Sweat breaks out on my temples and upper lip as I stare at my grandmother.

The thought of being a stranger to my family rips my chest open, but no more than the mere thought of losing Kirill.

So I stand there, unmoving.

"Sasha," Uncle pleads, but I shake my head.

"You are dead to me," Babushka says with another stomp of her cane. "I will think that you were killed that day with everyone else."

Then she turns around and leaves, hitting her cane on the ground all the way. Tears fill my eyes, but I don't let them loose.

"It's not too late to fix it, Sashenka," Uncle says gently, pleadingly almost. "Do the right thing."

"Killing my savior is not the right thing. Far from it."

"This is not over even if I walk away right now. I will come back for Kirill's life. It's my duty toward this family. If you decide to stop me, be ready to kill me." His eyes soften, and he releases a long sigh. "I wish I'd never sent you to the army."

Then he follows Babushka out.

As I watch their retreating backs, a part of me rips through my chest, spills out in front of me, and dies a slow death.

The worst part is that I can't do anything about it.

I've always thought I'd be with them for the rest of my life, but now, it feels like everything was for nothing.

I don't pause to wallow in misery for too long, though. I need to get Kirill out of this hospital. *Now.*

If Uncle said he'll come back, he means it. And this time, one of us really has to die.

I run to the hospital's public phone and dial the number I learned by heart.

"Who is this?" Viktor's gruff, tension-filled voice sounds from the other end.

"It's me. Sasha."

"Lipovsky, you fucking fucker! What happened to Boss? I knew he was following you after your impromptu visit to Russia. I went searching for him, and although it took me hours, I only found traces of blood. That blood better not be his, or I swear to fuck—"

"It's his. He was shot, and he's in the ICU at the local hospital."

"What the fuck—"

"Listen to me, Viktor," I cut him off and lean closer to the phone. "His life is in immediate danger. You need to make the arrangements to fly him out of here now. I'll remain on guard until you have everything sorted. Hurry. His life depends on it."

"Are you the reason he was shot?" he asks with frightening calm.

I bite my lower lip and then quickly release it. "That's not important right now—"

"Are you?"

"No." *Lie.* I was completely the reason behind it, though indirectly. But if I tell Viktor that, he'll separate me from Kirill, and I can't have that.

He inhales sharply. "Now, *you* listen to me, motherfucker. You will guard him with your life until I get there. Once I do, you better not show your face, or I will punch you on sight."

I tighten my hand on the phone, but I don't say anything.

It doesn't matter if Viktor, Kirill, and everyone else hate me as long as I can get him to safety.

FOUR

Sasha

VIKTOR MIGHT BE THE MOST STOIC PERSON I KNOW, whose personality can only be compared to walls and steel, but he's also the most efficient.

In just a few hours, he managed to find not only transportation to the airfield, but also a few bodyguards, a doctor, and a nurse who will accompany Kirill on his flight back to New York.

I haven't been able to stop studying my surroundings for the past hour, even with all the security that Viktor specifically hired to ensure Kirill's safety.

There's no telling what my uncle and his men will do. Hell, Babushka might have given him the green light to get rid of me as well if I dare to get in the way of their revenge.

I tap my chest, fruitlessly trying to eliminate the knot that's growing there.

No, it's not *their* revenge. It's mine, too.

I lost as much as they did. And I don't only mean my parents and the rest of my family, but also my identity and my femininity. I'm nothing more than an entity of violence now who can never go back to the way things were.

That doesn't mean I'm giving up on retribution, but right now, as Kirill battles against death, I can't think about that lifelong mission.

My main concern is getting him out of here alive. I might not have been able to save him on that hill, but I'll put my life on the line to ensure his safety now.

"Lipovsky."

I turn around at the sound of Viktor's voice, and my face flies sideways from his brutal punch. My cheek stings and red drips on the hospital tiles from my lip. I can feel my mouth swelling within a fraction of a second.

That *hurts*.

What's with people slapping, hitting, and punching me today? And that's not counting the metaphorical stab I felt when my own uncle shot Kirill.

Why can't this day fucking end already?

Despite the pain, I stand erect and face my assailant. Viktor's expression has never been welcoming, but as he stares at me right now, I have the urgent need to run before he squashes me between his fingers.

"I told you I'd punch you. In fact, I'm in the mood to shoot you, but I need you to answer my questions first."

"If you shoot me, we'll have less security for Kirill. You and I both know we need all the help we can get under these extraordinary circumstances, so why don't we call a truce?"

"Fuck that. How could you let this happen? In fact, care to explain why he was shot right in front of you?"

I purse my lips. If Viktor finds out the truth, a punch will be the least of my problems. He'll kill me without thinking twice.

And I can't just die before making sure Kirill is home safe and sound.

Sure, he might be the one to kill me once he wakes up, but I'm ready to face his wrath and everything he has to dish out as long as he's alive.

I wipe the corner of my lip with the back of my hand. "That's not important right now. If we don't get him out of here soon, he'll be in mortal danger."

"Haven't you heard what the doctor said? We can't move him out of the ICU before he wakes up."

I know that, I do. But the threat of an attack from my uncle is imminent at this point. I can't hurt the only father figure I have or indirectly cause harm to Mike and even Babushka.

She might have disowned me, but the three of them are all I have left.

But at the same time, allowing anyone to hurt Kirill is out of the question.

"What happened, Lipovsky?" Viktor insists.

"He'll tell you when he wakes up."

"Bullshit." He grabs me by the arm and shakes me until he nearly dislodges all my cells. "What's the deal with you, little fucker? You're always roaming around him and sticking close, despite your subpar skills. Are you perhaps threatening him with something? Why would he put trackers on you and follow you all alone to the middle of fucking nowhere?"

He...put trackers on me? *Plural?*

Now, it makes sense that he could follow me so closely. I honestly thought the only tracker he could put on me was the one on my phone, but, of course, he's always one step ahead. He must've slipped one in my jacket when he kissed me or something.

God, to think that I could've prevented this whole nightmare by checking my belongings makes me want to scream.

"Answer me." Viktor shakes me again.

I twist my arm free from his brutal hold and raise my chin. "I told you to ask him when he wakes up. Our priority is to get him out of here before we're attacked again."

"Listen to me, Lipovsky—"

"No, you listen to me, Viktor! I know you're suspicious and want to find out what happened, but I'm telling you that now is not the time. You need to channel your energy into flying him out of here, and only when he's safe can we talk about this."

He reaches an open-palmed hand to me, but before he can bash my head against the nearest surface, a nurse peeks from around the corner.

The smile on her face falters upon seeing the tension between us, but she still says, "The patient just woke up."

My stomach dips, and an urgent need to cry hits me again, but I manage to rein in those emotions as I kill the distance between us and ask in a word vomit, "Is he fully conscious? Were there any side effects? Did he speak? Can he breathe without the machines? Did the doctor mention anything about his ability to fly? Will there be any complications due to cabin pressure?"

She offers me a kind smile. "You can ask the doctor all of those questions."

Viktor and I basically jog to the room Kirill is being treated in. The bodyguards, probably mercenaries, judging by their aloof stance, are stationed by the door.

Through the glass, I catch a glimpse of the doctor and another nurse injecting something into Kirill's IV drip.

His eyes are open, but they're unfocused and look almost dead. Their intense blue color is dull and washed out, like the endless snow in Russian winter—lifeless and without purpose.

Heartless and...cruel.

My heart shreds to pieces as I continue to stare at him, but at the same time, I can't control the euphoria I feel at the knowledge that he's alive. I don't care what happens as long as he continues to breathe.

Maybe he senses a presence or sees a shadow, but Kirill's eyes slowly move in our direction.

I stop breathing as they clash with mine.

For a moment, it feels like we're no longer in the hospital. Instead, we're both standing in that field he followed me to. We're surrounded by the bloody snow as he looks at me with the most terrifying expression I've ever seen.

One that says he's my enemy now.

Without realizing it, I shake my head slowly.

I didn't know, I say in my mind. *I swear I didn't. I would never do this to you.*

But that changes nothing in his unwelcoming gaze or the small muscle that tightens in his jaw.

It hits me then; he doesn't like me being here.

As fast as his eyes opened, they close again, and I think my heart falls to my knees due to the impact.

Soon after, the doctor emerges from the room, and I rush in his direction until I nearly collide with him. "What's going on? Why did he lose consciousness again?"

"He didn't lose consciousness, he fell asleep." The doctor is apathetic and collected, and it reminds me of Kirill's manner of speech.

There's something seriously wrong with me. I'm even seeing him in other people now.

"Will he be okay?" Viktor asks.

"Yes. His vitals are almost back to normal, and he's not suffering from an infection."

It takes everything in me not to sag against the wall from gratitude. Instead, I keep my head in the game. "We need to fly him home. Now."

"I don't recommend that," the doctor says. "It might put a strain on his injury. It's better to wait at least forty-eight hours—"

"We don't have one hour," I cut him off with a nonnegotiable tone. "We have a medical crew who will take care of him during the flight, so I'm sure he'll be okay. Viktor, have you gotten everything ready?"

The mountain of a man narrows his eyes on me. "If this is another one of your games, I swear to fuck—"

"This is about ensuring the boss's safety. You and I might not get along, but we have that in common." I face him, chin up. "I'm asking you to put our differences aside and focus on him. After we get to New York, you can do whatever you want."

He still stares at me with apparent suspicion. Viktor has never trusted me, and he hasn't shied away from voicing it to Kirill, but I really hope he sees that we're on the same page here.

If we clash, we have no way of fixing this situation.

After almost a full minute of silent contemplation, he faces the men he brought and orders them in curt Russian to get the plane ready.

I still don't breathe in relief, though. I can't until Kirill is safely out of Russia and my uncle's reach.

Even if temporarily.

⁓

I'm on edge.

The claustrophobic sensation I've had since the hill hasn't disappeared. Not when we left Russian soil, not when we landed at the airport, and not even during the trip to the house, throughout which we were accompanied by most of Kirill's bodyguards—Yuri and Maksim included.

I only manage to release a breath when Kirill is settled in the house clinic, and the doctor says that he only needs rest to make a full recovery.

Anna wails upon seeing him. Karina runs the length of the garden, trips and falls, but she stands up again and bawls her eyes out when she gets to his bedside.

Yulia watches from the doorway with her emotionless expression, then turns and leaves. As if the man fighting for his life isn't her flesh and blood or her eldest child.

It's like she couldn't care less what happens to him. Hell, she might even wish for his demise.

Konstantin, however, comes over and holds his sister as she sobs and calls Kirill's name.

The scene digs the black hole in my chest deeper until it's hard to breathe or remain in the same place as all of them.

Despite not wanting Kirill out of my sight, he has many people who care about him by his side.

And I need to get out. *Now.*

I slip out of the clinic's back entrance and stride through the side garden without purpose or destination.

When I'm far away from all the chaos, I lean against a tree and close my eyes.

The cold breeze slips through the barrier of my clothes and clashes against my bones. I inhale deeply, but I'm still unable to breathe properly.

I tap my chest as I stare at the cloudy sky through the tree's leaves. But the longer I tap, the harder it is to breathe.

Something is trapped inside, and it's impossible to let it out.

What am I supposed to do now?

I clearly chose Kirill over my family, and if I ever want to see them again—under peaceful circumstances, at least—I need to prove that he had nothing to do with the massacre.

But since this incident happened, I doubt he'll ever trust me again. Hell, he might kill me.

What do I do then? Beg? Abandon ship and look for a new career?

Maybe I need to dedicate my life to looking for my brother, Anton. It's been years since I last saw him, but I still like to think he's alive somewhere. That he's searching for me like I'm searching for him.

Once upon a time, he used to be the only one who told me the truth bluntly. Papa loved me too much to ever scold me. One smile, a kiss, or even an innocent blinking of my eyes is enough to have him completely forgive any mischievous things I've done.

Mama gave me lectures, but she also spoiled me rotten, and was part of the reason why I was excruciatingly sheltered.

Anton, however, was the one who told me, "You need to grow the fuck up, Malyshka. Our parents won't last forever."

I hated how abrasive he was at the time, but I came back to his words after the safe haven my parents built for me splintered and turned into a pool of blood before my eyes. I had to grow up in no time and I had only myself to rely on.

But now I'm tired. I wish I had Anton. I wish I could find him and tell him I'm sorry for being a spoiled brat.

But that means I'd have to leave.

The thought of losing everything I've had with Kirill so far makes my heart bleed. But so does the thought of losing my family.

My purpose.

The reason why I'm pretending to be a different gender.

How does one deal with being torn apart? How do I put myself back together again after forty-eight hours of pure hell?

"Sash."

I dab at the corner of my eye and turn around to face Maksim, who's accompanied by Yuri.

The sight of them makes me emotional again. I just want to hug them and cry, but that would just be weird.

Maksim squeezes my shoulder. "You okay?"

I nod. "Boss was the one hurt, not me."

"We don't mean physically, Sasha." Yuri crosses his arms and leans against the tree beside me. "Anyone can see this incident has impacted you both mentally and emotionally."

A ball constricts my throat, and I have to swallow a few times before I'm able to speak. "I'm okay."

"Liar, liar." Maksim slaps me teasingly on the arm. "You don't have to act so strong."

"Am I that obvious?" I ask in a small voice.

Maksim winces. "It's written all over your face. Everyone knows how close you are to Boss, so of course you'd be this affected."

"What happened?" Yuri asks in a soothing tone.

I shake my head. "Let him tell you."

"Why can't you tell us?" Maksim's brows draw together.

Because you'd hate me and might kill me before Kirill has the chance to.

"Viktor mentioned that Boss was injured because of you," Yuri continues when I don't speak. "We know there's more to it."

"Yeah! No way would you hurt Boss." Maksim pulls me to his side by the shoulder. "Everyone knows Viktor is an asshole. Don't mind him."

But Viktor is right this time.

Everything happened because of me, and now, I'm in that uncertain phase where I have no clue what will happen next.

Kirill might kill me for all I know.

But I still won't leave until I find the answers to my family's death.

And hopefully, to Kirill's forgiveness. No matter how impossible that seems.

FIVE

Kirill

DESPITE MY BEST EFFORTS, I KEEP SLIPPING IN AND OUT of consciousness.

The more I hold on to the sliver of light, the deeper I fall into the pit of darkness.

This situation is no different than playing a game against my body and obviously losing.

It doesn't matter how strong the brain is. If the body can't keep up, then it's a wasted effort.

At times, I contemplate just closing my eyes and never opening them again, but then I remember that I have so much to do, too many places to go, and unfinished business to attend to.

I remember the promise I made to the weaker, younger version of me.

We'll never be weak again. We'll be so strong that no one can reach us.

And I'm under the binding obligation to keep that promise and never fall into the pit of hopelessness again.

If you're low, you'll be stomped upon and ordered around, but if you're high…no one will dare look you in the eye.

And I will never, *ever* stoop so low again.

I don't know how long it's taken me, but I manage to open my eyes and not feel the need to fall back into slumber almost immediately.

My surroundings slowly come into blurred focus. The white walls, the smell of antiseptic, and the familiar scent of…lavender?

"Kirill!" My sister's brittle voice sounds like it's been plunged underwater.

My ears ring as if I'm stuck in the aftermath of a brutal bombing, but I fight the urge to give up and make myself squint. Karina's small face comes into view, all messy with tears, a runny nose, and puffed-out lips, probably from all the nibbling she does whenever she's anxious.

"Can you hear me? Are you okay? Viktor! Call the doctor. He's woken up again!"

The word *again* confirms that I was, in fact, slipping in and out of consciousness.How much time did I lose in this extremely inconvenient situation? Worse, how much time will I continue to lose in order to become fully functional again?

Soft hands grip mine as Karina strokes them and stains them with her tears."I was so worried. I couldn't sleep and watched you every night and…and…I even…even came all the way here. If you'd died, I would've killed you!"

I smile, but the small motion triggers a throbbing pain in my chest. I cough, and that nearly makes me throw my guts up.

Fuck.

I was really hit in the heart, wasn't I?

"Oh, Kirochka." Anna takes my other hand, her eyes molten, face sunken as she brushes my hair back with her soft palm."Do you need anything?"

I do need something, but she's not the one who can bring it to me, so I shake my head.

She continues stroking my hair and pats my face with tears rimming her eyelids. If anyone was watching this scene, they'd think Anna was my mother. It doesn't matter that we have a different skin color or that she didn't actually give birth to me. This woman has given me more affection than my actual mother—who's probably doing some satanic rituals to pray for my death as we speak.

The doctor comes to check on me and helps me to sit up. He does a few tests and some speech, memory, and mobility exercises. During all the time, Anna, Karina, Viktor, and almost every single one of my guards stack up at the entrance of the room to watch.

The idiots are leaving their positions to be spectators of an utterly boring show.

After the doctor finishes his checkup, he discloses the good news. There's no permanent damage from the fragments that hit my heart, and I've also been recovering during the five days I've spent slipping in and out of consciousness.

I shouldn't strain myself for the upcoming two weeks. I need constant checkups, and no surprise here, the bullet wounds will scar.

My men basically fight over who gets to buy the medication when the doctor writes a prescription until Viktor glares at them and pushes the piece of paper into Yuri's hand.

As in, the only mature one who didn't take part in the watching or the fighting. Maksim, who was the first to quarrel, insists on joining Yuri.

They're both here, but their closest friend isn't.

I know because I scanned the crowd earlier, and there was no sign of her fucking presence.

Not that I expected her to come back after what she's done.

The doctor insists that I need rest, so Viktor kicks everyone out—Karina and Anna included, though he does use more diplomatic methods with them.

Once it's only the two of us, he clicks the door shut and stands by my side like some fallen angel.

"Didn't you hear the doctor?" I speak like I've gained a few decades of age. "I need rest. Pretty sure that means you should leave, too."

He glares down at me. "What happened after we separated? Who did this to you?"

Interesting.

When I woke up to find myself in New York, I was sure that Viktor had followed me, saved me, and brought me back here. But according to his words just now, that wasn't the case.

Was that dream where a soft voice was calling my name and crying not a dream, after all?

"How much do you know?" I ask instead of answering him.

"Nothing except that the fucker Lipovsky somehow got you to the hospital and called me from there."

My eyes narrow.

What does that mean? She had no reason to take me to the hospital after she led those men to ambush me.

The thoughts that plagued me when I was getting shot weren't losing my life, my ambition, or leaving everyone I cared about here unprotected. It was the very fact that she'd *betrayed* me.

And for one foolish moment, I actually lost all fight and surrendered to the implications of that knowledge.

But that moment has ended. That foolish, sentimental, absolutely illogical part of me was killed by those two bullets.

"Is he behind this?" Viktor insists. "Give me an order. Anything."

"I want you to turn Russia inside out. Find him."

His brow creases as if he hasn't heard me right. "Why would I do that? He came back with us."

My lips fall open. "He's…here?"

Viktor nods slowly, still appearing bemused.

That doesn't make sense. Why would she accompany me back

to New York after that stunt? If she thinks she can fool me, I swear to fuck—

Pain throbs in my chest. Maybe the doctor needs to give me more painkillers so I can deal with this situation more efficiently.

"Is he not supposed to be here?" my guard asks in his usual suspicious tone.

"Where is he? He wasn't with the others just now."

"Probably training and punching things. He's been doing that a lot since we came back. And you didn't answer any of my questions. Did Lipovsky have a hand in what happened to you?"

The short answer is yes, but if I give it to Viktor, he'll torture and kill Lipovsky without giving it a second thought.

It's not that easy and *can't* be that easy.

I'm the only one who's allowed to deal with her.

No one but *me*.

So I shake my head.

"If it wasn't him, then who was it?" Viktor asks.

"Mercenaries." I tell him part of the truth. "They had masks on, but I recognized them from the way they handled their weapons. They could have been my father's enemies or my own from the army."

"I will look into this."

I nod in agreement. "Make it discreet. I don't want anyone else to dig into this incident."

"Could it be your mother?"

"She's not the type who sullies her hands."

"Konstantin, maybe?"

"Maybe."

Viktor clears his throat. "He...has been here every day since we landed in New York. It looked like he was consoling Miss Karina, but he visited even when she wasn't here."

I close my eyes and lean my head back. Viktor's words barely register. It's not my newfound life, my siblings, or my men who are occupying my thoughts.

It's that bitter taste of betrayal that's been clogging my throat since the moment I was shot.

That fucking taste is the worst medicine I've ever swallowed, and it nearly made me lose all my power.

But it didn't.

I'm here now, even as I continue to swallow that god-awful taste with each passing second.

"I'll leave you to rest," Viktor announces. "If you need anything, I have three of our best men guarding your room. Just click the intercom button, and they will be here. If you need me personally, call me."

I nod, still closing my eyes and seeing blood red. In the middle of the snow. The stark contrast makes my head dizzy.

"Boss."

"Hmm?"

"Lipovsky's here. He must've heard about you waking up."

My eyes open slowly but pointedly. I stare at Viktor, who's at the door, waiting for a reply.

Behind that door stands the woman because of whom I'm experiencing this irrational burning pain. And I'm not talking about the physical discomfort from the wound. That doesn't compare to the constant squeezing in my injured heart.

"Don't let him in," I order. "From now on, Lipovsky is not allowed in my vicinity. Assign him to clean and maintain weapons."

Viktor raises a brow. "Is there a reason for this?"

"Do as you're told. I don't want to see his face."

"We can fire him."

Of course Viktor would suggest a permanent solution to get rid of him. But I won't release her for good until I get to the bottom of this.

I will find out the why and how and who. Especially the fucking *who*, and only when I'm satisfied will I put an end to this.

Until then, I'll make her lose her mind with boredom.

"Just execute the order." I close my eyes again. "Don't let anyone in."

"Yes, Boss."

I was supposed to die on that snowy hill, but I didn't.

When I'm done with her, Aleksandra will wish that she'd finished me off instead of taking me to the hospital.

SIX

Sasha

KIRILL DOESN'T WANT TO SEE ME. When Viktor first told me I wasn't welcome in the boss's company anymore, I don't know why I thought he was joking.

Surely, it was some sort of a mistake. Yes, I'd anticipated that Kirill's reaction to what happened in Russia wouldn't be pretty, but I didn't think he'd go as far as...completely erasing me from his surroundings.

It's been a week now since he fully woke up and even started conducting business deals from home as if nothing had happened.

Karina and Anna always try to forbid him from that, but no one can change his mind if he sets it on something.

I know because I've tried countless times to visit him, talk to him, or just see him from afar, to no avail.

Viktor is always by his side like unbending steel. Whenever I ask him for a mere minute in Kirill's presence, he shuts me down so quickly and harshly that my pride is wounded.

Yes, it's true that Viktor doesn't like me—or anyone, for that matter—but this silent treatment wasn't his idea. It was Kirill who ordered him not to let me approach him.

I stare out of my new prison—the weapon vault—at the small, secluded garden, where no one comes near. Maksim and Yuri only show up because I'm here. Otherwise, they wouldn't step foot on these premises.

Before I was forced to this place, I vaguely knew it existed.

The only staff here are me and two older men who are no lon-ger in-field bodyguards. We're tasked with taking the weapons and ammunition up to the rest of the guards. However, Viktor clearly ordered me not to show my face upstairs and to let the two men handle the deliveries.

Even my stuff was moved from Kirill's suite to a small room in the basement of the weapon vault. So I can't get together with the guys. It's like I'm being caged without actual bars.

That, combined with the fact that this house is fucking huge, has ensured that I've only managed to see Kirill twice and only from a distance when I've snuck around at night. The first time, I saw him standing by the window of the clinic, his merciless eyes staring blankly into the distance.

I wanted to go inside so badly, but the sight of the other guards made me change my mind. They're under strict instructions to stop me from coming in contact with the boss, and if they don't do as they're told, Viktor might go as far as firing them. At least, that's what Yuri told me.

My friends asked why I was relegated to weapon vault duty, and I said it was because I defied a direct order and, as a result, put Kirill's life at risk, which is why he got shot.

Yuri thought it was odd the boss didn't fire me, and Maksim said, "If he's only punishing you, then it means he still wants you around, so hang in there."

That's the hope I held on to as I snuck around like a spy.

When I saw him at that clinic, I stayed there as long as possible, greedily memorizing every inch of his face—his eyes covered by the black-framed glasses, his stubborn nose, his square chin, and his mouth that was set in a line. I wanted to touch his knitted brows and relieve the tension lurking there. I wanted to lay my hand on his chest and make sure his heart was working properly and that the haunting faint sound I heard when I was taking him to the hospital had actually disappeared.

I wanted to do many things, but most of all, I wanted to look into his eyes and have them look back into mine. Even if it was in anger or contemplation or whatever his emotions are toward me. I didn't care as long as he actually looked at me.

This silent treatment and complete apathy are hitting me harder than any anger he could express. I was ready for his physical punishment, but I had no clue the mental effect would be ten times worse.

The second time I saw him was when Karina invited me to her room for lunch two days ago. It was around the time when Kirill leaves the clinic and goes back to his room in the mansion. I was on pins and needles hoping to see him. Although I paced the hallway with Karina for a whole ten minutes, not only did he not leave his room, but Viktor also showed up and kicked me out, then said, "The house and its premises are forbidden. You only have access to the weapon vault's immediate surroundings. Are we clear?"

It didn't matter how much Karina protested. The titan was on a mission and was only satisfied when I left. It was either that or cause Karina needless stress.

However, on my way out of the mansion, I caught a glimpse of Kirill at the top of the stairs. I swear I felt his eyes on me, but when I looked up, he turned and walked away.

My heart and soul have been bruised ever since he came up with this torture method. It's worse than if he'd hit me or let the others physically torture me.

LIES OF MY MONSTER | 53

I could handle that. His indifference, however, is proving to be my undoing.

Maksim keeps telling me that it's just a phase and he'll get over it.

But how can he get over it if he refuses to see my face, let alone talk to me?

How am I supposed to clear the air between us and make amends if he won't listen to what I have to say? Over the past two weeks, I've thought of many things that I want to tell him. Maybe it would be futile, but I need him to hear me out.

Just once.

So I wait until after my hours for the day are done. Usually, I go to my new room in the lonely basement that could be mistaken for solitary confinement. Then someone from the kitchen delivers my food since I'm not allowed in the other guards' quarters. After finishing dinner, I toss and turn all night or train until I'm physically exhausted and eventually pass out.

Usually, my nights are plagued with nightmares. Some of them are about Mike, but most of them are a replay of Kirill being shot and the gruesome images of his bleeding chest and unconscious face at the bottom of that hill. I wake up with tears in my eyes and a heart so heavy, it feels like it will burst.

Tonight is different, though.

During the last few days, I've spent time planning how to get around the security cameras and sensors installed all over my route to the mansion.

So now, it takes me minimal effort to avoid them. I have no doubt that Viktor has someone specifically watching my movements so he can stop me whenever I get too close.

Still, I spend about fifteen minutes getting to the mansion because I was basically put at the farthest point of the property while still being inside it.

I head to the back of the main building and use the bushes as camouflage. Once I reach my destination, I ensure my surroundings are clear and silently crawl to the huge tree closest to the house. Then, after one last look around me, I grab onto the trunk and climb.

I always told Kirill that this tree is a security hazard because any sniper could use it as base to attack the property, but he said it actually strengthens the security because it offers privacy.

At any rate, I'm glad he didn't listen to me.

Once I reach the level of his balcony, I realize that the distance to the ground is actually greater than I thought. I stare down and wince at the height—about three stories. If I fall, there won't be any happy endings.

I start to scoot across a branch that's less sturdy than I anticipated and suppress a yelp when it breaks. Two other branches catch my fall and once I get my balance, I leap toward the balcony. My left leg hits the railing, and I nearly stumble out, but I dig my fingers into the wall and glue myself to it before I jump onto the balcony as silently as a ninja. I don't stop to inspect my injured leg, but I do lift it off the ground to keep from putting weight on it.

The balcony door is closed, but voices speaking in Russian reach me from inside. The first is Viktor's—gruff and unwelcoming—but the second…my heart picks up speed, and I have to tap my chest to be able to breathe properly.

It's been so long since I listened to Kirill's steady deep voice, and although I don't hear the words clearly, I can't help leaning in. I'm no different than an addict who's finally getting a hit after nearly two weeks of deprivation.

If this plan doesn't work, then I at least got to hear his voice. He's alive. He's right here.

And nothing will change that.

Whenever I close my eyes, I only see his dying face. I can't erase it, no matter how much I try. But this…witnessing him speaking, might help keep him alive in my nightmares.

A few minutes later, Viktor's voice disappears. Then so does Kirill's.

But I know he didn't leave. I can feel his presence in the room and even sense a hint of his warmth through the walls.

Him being alone gives me the opening I've been waiting for, but now that it's here, I can't bring myself to move.

I remain in place for what seems like forever, forcing my limbs to step forward but unable to move. After a few moments, I finally clutch the handle of the balcony door, inhale deeply, then slide it open.

The sound is heightened in the silence, and I pause for the time it takes me to fit myself in the opening.

Then I slip inside soundlessly and freeze when a gun clicks at my temple.

Shit.

I underestimated Kirill. Since he was injured, I thought maybe his reflexes would be slower, but the weapon pointed at me proves that those thoughts are a far cry from reality.

"What the fuck are you doing here?"

Slowly, I start to turn to face the owner of the cold question, but he pushes the gun against the temple.

"You don't need to change your position to answer."

"Can't I at least look at you?" I hate how my voice sounds so emotional and weak.

Even if he's harsh and indifferent. Even if he's holding a gun to my head right now.

"No," comes his closed-off reply.

Still, I turn.

"I said. No."

"And I want to look at you." I lift my chin. "So if you're going to shoot, do it."

The more I continue turning, the faster my heart beats. I know he won't shoot me. If he wanted to kill me, he would've done that when he woke up. He wouldn't have chosen to torture me by depriving me of him.

Sure enough, the moment I fully face him, he's lowered the gun to his side.

I'm rooted to the spot as if struck by lightning due to being able to look at him closely. *All* of him.

Although he's wearing casual sweatpants and a black T-shirt, neither can conceal the masculine perfection of his physique. He's lost some weight due to the injury, but his build has retained its charismatic edge.

Tattoos in the form of skulls, roses, and a human heart swirl along the visible parts of his forearms and biceps, but they don't look hauntingly black now.

The color has returned to his face, and his lips are no longer pale and chapped. His hair that's usually styled currently falls over his forehead and brows. He's also grown a thicker stubble that complements his cut jawline.

But something else leaves me gasping for air.

It's his eyes.

They're…different.

While not as lifeless as when I last saw them when he woke up in the hospital in Russia, they're also not those intense eyes that caused my stomach to drop whenever they fixated on me.

My stomach is dropping now, but it's due to knots of dread and anxiety building up. Because these eyes? They're cold and apathetic. Almost like…a stranger's.

And that hurts worse than a gunshot wound. I realize now that while I've been missing him like crazy and going out of my mind worried about him, he probably hasn't even thought about me.

"What the fuck do you want?" he asks with that lethal voice again.

I motion my chin at him. "I wanted to see you."

"You saw me. Leave." He starts to walk to the bathroom, but I jump in front of him, arms open wide.

"That's all?"

His expression remains the same, except for a smidge of annoyance. "Should there be something else? A ceremony in your honor, perhaps?"

"Kirill...please."

"It's Boss or Sir. You have zero rights to call me by my first name."

My spine jerks upright, and I have trouble swallowing past the lump in my throat. "I know you must have a lot of questions about what happened in Russia, and while I can't answer all of them, I promise to answer as many as I can. You have my word, I would never—"

"I have no questions for you. I got my answers in the form of two bullets."

His calmly spoken words trigger the claustrophobic sensation I had when he was shot on that hill. My chest constricts, and it feels as if I'm falling down a spiral, unable to put on the brakes. That's when I realize I've been shaking my head. "That's not...I swear I didn't know. I wouldn't...have gone there if I'd known. I'm sorry that you were shot because of me. I have no clue what I can do to make you believe me, but I'm willing to do anything."

His eyes taper to a frightening blue—a color that I've never seen in them before. For a moment, I think he'll shoot me with the gun in his hand, after all.

Maybe he's figured out that keeping me alive has no meaning and it'd be better if he finishes me off.

But instead of doing that, he speaks with deceptive calm. "What's the name of the man who was beside you? I'm not interested in the mercenaries. I want the identity of the man who shot me."

My lips part, and I stand there unblinking. How did he figure out the men were mercenaries when everyone's face was covered? But then again, Uncle Albert was the only one who shot at him with the sole purpose of killing him. So he must know that he's the one with a vendetta against him.

Sometimes, Kirill's intuition really frightens the hell out of me. I often wonder just how much he knows and how much he doesn't.

He steps forward, filling my space with his addictive cedar scent. It's a welcome change after the stench of death that he picked up from the hospital. "You said you're willing to do anything."

"Disclosing his identity is the only thing I can't do," I whisper.

Uncle Albert is still my family, and even though I protected Kirill from him, I have to do the opposite as well, because I have no doubt that Kirill will kill him if he finds him.

One moment I'm standing there, then the next, Kirill wraps his fingers around my throat and slams me against the wall. Air is knocked out of my lungs as he towers over me, his breathing harsh and his eyes blazing. "Is this some sort of an elaborate plan between the two of you? Did he put you up to spying on me and then, when the time was right, ask you to lure me to his den?"

Shit, shit.

How does he know that? Did he already figure out my family ties?

Even though Uncle Albert was initially against me coming to New York, he was practically using me as a spy after I told him I was getting close to Kirill.

"So it is true," he says in a frighteningly low voice. "Let me ask you something, Aleksandra."

I hate my full name. I never did before, but now that Kirill only uses it when he's mad at me, I loathe it from the bottom of my heart.

He advances further into my space until his chest almost touches mine. "Was seduction part of the plan, or did it only happen because I was *convenient*?"

"No, no...that's not—"

My words are cut off when he squeezes his fingers, effectively cutting off my air supply.

"Shhh." His voice comes near my ear like a whip. "Shut the fuck up. I could and should kill you right now."

Oh, God.

Is this how I will die? Staring at these cruel eyes that I once dreamed would soften?

"I should choke the living fuck out of you and watch as your eyes turn blank, just as you stood there and watched while *he* shot me." His fingers sink into my skin as he tightens his grip. "But I won't. You know why?"

I shake my head, my eyes nearly bulging out.

"Because you'll eventually lead me to that motherfucker. Mark my words, I will kill him in front of your fucking eyes even if it's the last thing I do." He releases me with a shove, and I fall to my knees on the floor, coughing and splattering on my choked breaths.

When I stare up at him, it's like I'm looking at a raging monster.

I've always thought of him as one, but this is the first time I've actually been afraid of him and what he might do to reach his goal.

"You should've let me die while you had the chance." He leans down and squeezes my chin between his harsh fingers. "I'll make you regret playing with me when I turn your life into a living fucking hell."

SEVEN

Kirill

I'VE ALWAYS BEEN PROUD OF MY ABILITY TO REMAIN CALM. It took me some time for that side of me to grow, but as soon as I was out of my teenage phase, no one could get into my head.

Not my parents, not my siblings.

No fucking one.

I've always been self-sufficient and entirely self-reliant. As a result, it's impossible for anyone to provoke me.

That steel-like will is being tested to its limits right now. Or more like, since that fucking Russia episode.

Every night, when I'm all alone, I stare at the two ugly stitched holes in my chest and replay the scene on that hill. The images of the man who opened fire and of Aleksandra standing right beside him plague me.

The complex feelings I had at that moment refuse to be erased. It's been three and a half weeks since the incident. A week and a half since she snuck into my room, apologizing and promising to do anything so I would forgive her.

Anything but disclosing the identity of her fucking lover who was out to kill me.

And she helped him.

I flick my hand on the desk, sending the house of cards flying in all directions.

Viktor and Yuri, who are sitting opposite me relaying updates about the club and the cartel, freeze at my sudden burst of motion. Something they're definitely not used to.

"If it's about the cartels," Viktor starts. "Don't worry, Boss. Yuri and I will keep them occupied until you're in better shape to personally meet them."

"You don't even have to," Yuri supplies. "Juan doesn't come all the way from Mexico. He sends his underlings. It's neither disrespectful nor strange that Viktor and I take care of these shipments on your behalf. As for the club, Maksim and your late father's senior guards are doing a good job keeping everything in check."

I nod absentmindedly, just so they'll think this irrational fucking mood is indeed about the state of affairs.

After they're done with their daily reports, Yuri leaves, but Viktor lingers behind and locks the door.

He stands in front of the desk, legs shoulder-width apart and hands clasped. "I have gathered some information about the attack in Russia."

I pause picking up my cards, then continue. "And?"

"I used the trackers you had on Lipovsky to pinpoint the location's coordinates. The warehouse in that area as well as the surrounding landscape and my placement are almost identical to that of the warehouse where we had the last Special Forces mission."

So my gut was right. That place was linked to the cursed mission where I lost my men. I was so sure Roman was behind the whole scheme, but maybe there's more to it.

I neatly stack the bottom row of cards. "Have you figured out who owns that place?"

"According to our last mission, it's insurgents and illegal weapons dealers, and while that's true to an extent, I believe there may be hidden information about that particular mission." He pauses. "You know of the Belsky Organization scheme, right?"

"The organization that clashed against the government and stored weapons, only for them to be wiped out?"

"That's public and military general knowledge, but it's neither as simple nor as justifiable as the tales indicate."

I keep building my house despite the volatile nature of my dimming patience. "I don't see why the Belsky Organization has anything to do with those two warehouses."

"They were owned by the family."

My gaze meets Viktor's through the small triangles. "Didn't the military have them wiped out?"

"Not all. It's impossible to locate the entirety of their warehouses, considering they kept them hidden in places even the KGB doesn't tread near. They could also have allies in those areas to help maintain their anonymity."

"You're talking as if they're still alive."

"I suspect that a few members are, yes. Otherwise, those warehouses wouldn't have remained functional."

"Some other group could've gotten hold of them."

"They could, but it's highly unlikely. That organization operated like a cult and no one aside from their inner circle members are aware of their strategic weapon vaults."

"So you think the Belsky Organization members are the ones behind the last Spetsnaz mission failure and my getting shot?"

"It's a possibility, yes. I'm not saying the late Mr. Morozov didn't have a hand in it as well, but all the arrows point in their direction."

"Riddle me this, Viktor." I clasp my hands to form a steeple at my chin and lean my elbows on the table. "Why would they target me when I've never dealt with them?"

"Could be a mercenary mission or for a reason we're not aware of. Their guards certainly turned into rogue assassins who are only interested in money after the organization's famous cleansing."

I adjust my glasses with my middle finger. Where does Aleksandra, who's definitely not a Lipovsky, fit into the picture?

Is she in a relationship with the leader of the remaining Belskys?

Maybe she's a Belsky herself. It makes sense with all the spying and acting suspiciously. There's also the fact that she supposedly hid her gender because it's dangerous to be a woman.

Whatever the case, she clearly thinks of me as an enemy. It's no secret that Roman was involved with the Belsky Organization— one of his multiple foolish decisions. That one nearly got him in trouble with the Pakhan, so he said he'd take care of it.

If by 'take care of it,' he meant the annihilation of the organization, then I'm not surprised they would come after his heir— aka me.

I'm going to also take a wild guess that the people who kidnapped, tortured, and then sent Konstantin back in a duffel bag as a message belong to the same faction.

Was Aleksandra getting close to me to gain information?

No, she clearly passed that stage and moved on to the execution part, where she watched as her lover shot me down.

The red haze from that day blurs my vision and I have to close my eyes briefly to disperse the energy. When I open them again, my hawk-like focus returns. "I need all the information you can find about the Belsky Organization. Every file, every member, and every movement they've made before and after their alleged annihilation."

Viktor appears stunned for a second, but then recovers. "That's impossible, Boss. Even the government and its intelligence agency couldn't figure out much about them, which is why they called for outside help to eliminate and get rid of their influence."

"Dig deeper. Call your friends in the KGB, the Spetsnaz, and the military. I don't care what you have to do in order to get me information."

"I can try, but I'm afraid I can't promise any results this time."

"Just make it happen, Viktor. If we don't know who's after me, how can we stop it?"

"Got it."

"Don't get anyone else involved."

"Not even Yuri?"

"To an extent. Don't disclose all the information to him. Make it look like you're still digging into the setup from the final military mission."

He nods, then, after making sure I don't need anything, steps out of the room.

My mind is left bubbling with different possibilities. I wasn't in the military when the Belsky Organization was annihilated, but I'm apparently involved in some way. Otherwise, I wouldn't have been targeted.

It must be because of my genetic relationship with Roman. That old man was always up to no good. Not that I'm any better, but I at least know which battles to pick and which to steer the fuck clear from.

One thing's for certain, though. Aleksandra and her lover have something to do with that scheme.

A foul taste explodes in my mouth at that thought.

Lover.

I should fucking kill her for betraying me, but that's just too light a punishment. She has to wake up every day and fall asleep every night tasting the bitter pill I've been surviving on ever since I woke up in the hospital.

With another flick of my finger, I destroy the half-built house of cards and stand up.

My physical strength has been slowly coming back, but I still have to be careful or else I'll suffer a longer recovery period, and that's just not something I need.

I step out of the office and go down the stairs.

"Kirill!" Karina catches up to me halfway to the entrance and interlinks her arm with mine.

She's been joining me for my daily walks around the garden ever since I was able to start getting around.

Now, I only do them because she actually willingly leaves her room, usually dressed in some princess dress and boots, as if she's going to a fashion show.

I don't like the way some of my men look at her, which is why I had Viktor threaten to gouge their eyes out of their sockets if they ogle her again.

What? My sister is still too young.

She's the same age as Lipovsky and you've been fucking her regularly for almost a year.

I shut down that sinister voice as a muscle works in my jaw.

"Are you better today?" Karina asks in a super cheerful voice that's a reminder of her younger self. It's reminiscent of a time when she either rode on my shoulders or hung onto my and Konstantin's pants.

She used to ask him to carry her, too, but after she was yelled at by Yulia for being a spoiled brat, she's never done it again.

"I'm fine."

"You look so much better." She strokes the stubble on my cheek and grins. "I like this look."

"Should I keep it?"

"Yes! I'm going to get you the best suit that goes well with this look so when you get back out there, people will think you're a model, because, duh, you totally are—" Her humor disappears as Yulia comes inside the mansion, followed by her 'only' son.

Karina subtly cowers behind me, her hand gripping my bicep

hard. That woman not only failed as a mother, but she also made her own daughter scared and wary of her—for reasons unknown.

She lifts her head high like an arrogant monarch and doesn't speak to us as she passes us by. It's almost as if we don't exist.

"It was nice to see you by my bedside, *Mother*," I say out of pure spite.

She whirls around and narrows her eyes. "Oh, I was by your bedside, but only to make sure you finally died. I even prepared a funeral dress for the occasion. Unfortunately, you survived like the devil."

"Aww, were you worried about me? I'm so touched."

"*Worried* about you?" She laughs, the sound so venomous that even Konstantin cringes. "You are nothing to me, Kirill. *Nothing*."

"Glad we feel the same." I step closer to her, and Karina tightens her grip around me. "Since we mean nothing to each other, I'm happy to inform you that I have allies in your bank, dear Mama. Your own brothers and sisters prefer me in business matters. After all, I'm part of their family, too, no matter how much you try to convince yourself otherwise."

"You—" She lifts her hand, probably to slap me. Karina forces her eyes closed, but the hit doesn't come.

Konstantin grabs that hand and interlinks his arm with hers as he leads her to the stairs. "Don't waste your breath on the likes of him, Mother. I will talk to my aunts and uncles..."

He continues offering vague consolations and everything someone like Yulia wants to hear. Before they disappear up the stairs, he subtly casts a look in my direction.

It's brief, almost unnoticeable, but there's that soft edge of my little brother who always tried to shield me and Karina from his mother's toxic favoritism.

That side of Konstantin was supposed to be long dead, so why the fuck—

"Did you see that? Did you see that?" Karina asks with contagious excitement. "Kosta stopped her for us!"

"Don't be so sure. He's too far up his own ass to do anything for us."

She swats me on the shoulder. "Don't talk like that. He was really worried about you when you got shot and visited every day. Well, every day until you woke up, because he knew you'd be an asshole if you saw him."

"He was probably spying for Yulia."

"Stop it, Kirill. Just stop it. If you're suspicious of people all the time, how are you ever going to be happy?"

What the fuck is *happy*?

Maybe happiness is reaching the top. Being so far above people that they fall and splinter to pieces if they ever attempt to get near me.

I don't answer Karina, though, as we step out of the house. She's about to tell me about a book she's reading—which is usually what she talks about with this much enthusiasm—but stops herself when we're faced with a small commotion.

My jaw clenches, and my wound burns as I stare at none other than Lipovsky. She's standing by the main entrance wearing a dark gray suit and a blue button-down. Her hair is styled back, and her expression is solemn, cold, and, most of all, determined.

I want to grab her by the throat like I did over a week ago when she dared to demand to talk to me.

But this time, if I choke her, I can't guarantee that I won't accidentally kill her. Just the thought of her lover and her betrayal turns me into a raging volcano.

I don't let it show on my face, but the fire is splintering me on the inside.

"You can't be here, Sasha." I hear Yuri whisper to her in a kind voice. "If Boss finds out—"

"I will kill you," I finish for him.

Yuri and Lipovsky straighten. Her expression softens, but only for a moment, and then it's closed off as she steps forward. "I want my previous position back."

My eyes lock on her face. "That won't be happening."

"I'm not a weapon caretaker. I'm a sniper and a bodyguard. I demand my post back."

"You think you have the right to demand anything from me, Lipovsky?"

Her spine jerks, and her lips part before she swallows. "I… won't leave this place until I get my actual job."

"I'll take him back," Yuri tells me and starts to drag her.

"No. Let him be." I meet her darkened eyes that have been invaded with brown. "No one is allowed to feed him. When he's starving to death, he'll leave on his own."

"I. Will. Not." She has the fucking audacity to lift her chin and even glare at me.

I have to step away before I actually act on my depraved thoughts. All of them start and end with her beneath me confessing why the fuck she stood there when her lover shot me, then, apparently, took me to the hospital.

Viktor told me that, and he's not the type who'd offer Lipovsky any sort of credit if it wasn't true.

I can feel Lipovsky's gaze at the back of my head as Karina and I wander into the garden.

Once we're out of earshot, my sister blurts, "Why don't you just give him his job back? What did he do? Didn't he and Viktor save you? I just don't understand."

"Let it go, Kara."

"But… Oh! He can be my bodyguard if you don't want him!"

"No. He's not allowed near you."

"But why?" She glares up at me. "Just so you know, Kosta asked Sasha to be the head of his bodyguards."

I slide my attention to my sister. "Did he, now?"

"He *so* did! But Sasha said he's only your guard."

A guard who lured me to my near death.

But that doesn't matter, because the fact remains—her life is all mine now.

EIGHT

Sasha

AM I DOING THE RIGHT THING?

Honestly, I don't know. What I do know, however, is that I refuse to move from here unless Kirill stops this madness and at least hears me out.

And not talk at me, but actually talk *to* me.

I know it's an impossible thing to ask for since he thinks I betrayed him, but I also won't be exiled to the other end of the house indefinitely.

Maybe he'll never be satisfied, and I'll grow old and gray in that boring weapon vault.

It's better to put an end to it now. Whether I win or lose, at least I'll have proper closure.

Three days have passed since he told me to either return to my post or remain here and starve to death. I foolishly chose the latter because, as I mentioned earlier, I won't be forced back into exile.

Despite the determination that flooded me at the beginning

of this mission, I'm finding it hard to keep up with my body's deteriorating state. I'm sitting with my back against the pillar near the mansion's entrance, where everyone who goes in or out can see me.

I must look pathetic, begging for a chance from a boss who won't even listen to me.

The thought of facing Kirill draws goosebumps over my skin. But I would rather experience this surreal discomfort than know I'll probably never see him again.

As time passes, he'll completely erase me from his life and continue living as if I never existed.

The mere thought of that possibility makes me shiver with dread. I have this irrational fear that he'll never appreciate or respect me as much as I do him.

That, in the great scheme of things, I'm nothing but a convenient pit stop on his path that he was always meant to leave.

And that scares the shit out of me.

As per Kirill's order, no one has offered me food, except for Maksim and Yuri, who tried to slip me some protein bars. Karina brought me a feast, too, and told me to ignore her 'stupid' brother.

I shook my head and refused to eat anything. If I'm meant to starve for my cause, then I'll do it. I definitely won't cheat the system just because I can.

I hadn't had anything to drink until Viktor himself threw a large bottle of water next to me two days ago and again last night. "Don't even think about dying while we're still investigating what happened in Russia."

I wanted to refuse that, too, but there's only so much I can do without actually dying.

So I drank the water and kept the bottle beside me. If Kirill objected to that, he didn't show it or threaten to throw me off the property.

He comes out every morning for his walk with Karina and doesn't look in my direction. It's as if I'm invisible. His sister, however, comes to check on me, and asks me to end this already and return to the weapon vault until he calms down then attempts to persuade him to give me my post back. Not only does he not reply, but he also continues to ignore my existence.

No matter how much I try not to be affected by his cold behavior, knowing that he can erase me so easily hurts more than I'm willing to admit.

A shadow hovers over me, and when I look up, I find Anna standing there with a tray of food. She pushes it in my direction while still wearing the same stern expression she always has for me. "You need to eat before you pass out."

My spine straightens. "Did...Boss ask you to bring me this?"

"No. I just don't like seeing people starving to death."

Oh.

My shoulders hunch.

I thought that since Anna only follows Kirill's orders, the fact that she brought me food had to be because he told her to.

The small hope that blossomed in my chest turns to ashes in a fraction of a second.

I shake my head. "I'm not eating. Besides, didn't you hear what Boss ordered? No one is allowed to give me food."

"Listen, young man. I don't care what he says. No starvation will happen under my watch."

I vehemently shake my head again. If Kirill is stubborn, then I'm ten times worse.

"If you don't pick up the spoon and eat, so help me God, I will force you," she threatens. "You're too starved to stop me."

"I can still fight you, Anna." I sigh, finding it hard to even speak due to sheer lack of energy. "Seriously, I'm thankful for the effort, but I refuse to eat or move unless I can go back to my previous post."

Anna is about to say something, probably to scold me, but stops herself when Konstantin strolls out of the house. He approaches us, and Anna places the tray by my side, nods, and leaves.

Kirill's brother stares down at me with eyes way warmer

than his brother's, probably because they're not as hauntingly icy. Besides, ever since he was kidnapped and tortured, I've started to see him through new eyes.

He's actually more classically handsome than Kirill. Sharp jawline and cheekbones, sandy blond hair, and a more clean-cut aura. Where Kirill has a nefarious edge, Konstantin has a protector feel. Which is weird since when I first met him, I thought he was a cliché of an evil brother who only cared about power. It was only over the last few months that I learned he has a completely different personality when Kirill is around—antagonistic, foolish, and repellent. Almost as if he was doing it on purpose.

"This whole thing is beyond idiotic," he informs me matter-of-factly. "If you think he'll change his mind just because you're doing this, you don't know Kirill."

"I refuse to be buried in the weapon vault for the rest of my life, so if this is what I have to do to be able to escape that place, I don't mind."

He crouches and tilts his head to meet my gaze. "You could always become my senior guard. That would piss off Kirill more than this futile plan."

I thought about that the last time he asked me this, and he's right. Considering how mad Kirill was when I helped Konstantin all those months ago, this tactic might get his attention, but it could also backfire. Besides, I'm trying to prove that I'm loyal to him, and I can't do that if I go to the brother he considers an enemy.

"I can't do that. I'm Kirill's guard."

"You're awfully loyal to someone who doesn't give a fuck about you." Konstantin rises to his full height. "Take it from me, Sasha. That man only cares about himself. No one else matters."

I shake my head but don't say anything. I've gotten to a stage where I need to preserve my energy.

"My offer still stands," he says, then climbs into the car that's waiting for him. I'm guessing Yulia will join him and probably glare at me as if I'm a pest.

I wait for a few moments, but the car leaves without her.

It's rare for Konstantin to go to any meetings without his mother glued to his side. Could there be something more to this? Are they colluding against Kirill again?

Not that they've ever stopped, but they really couldn't do him any damage when his aunts and uncles—on Yulia's side of the family—actually prefer doing business with Kirill rather than Konstantin. Yulia has been fighting it tooth and nail, but it's safe to say that she's losing.

It may be weird that I'm thinking about Kirill's well-being when he's indirectly starving me, but I really meant it about being loyal to him.

Because that's the only way I'll get to be by his side. If I'm not here...where would I go?

I can't go back to my family. And I don't want to. Not when Kirill thinks I betrayed him and they might try to get me to kill him the next time I see him.

Besides, I need to prove that he had nothing to do with my family's massacre. He's just not that type of person.

Before he woke up, I got the chance to snoop in the office after they temporarily paused the security. I even managed to check the safe, but there were no files that Roman may have left about my family.

The only thing I found were a few contracts, valuables, and paperwork about some shady deals that he kept as evidence against the people involved—mostly politicians and celebrities.

The scent of food, soup, fish, and some type of salad fills my nostrils, and my stomach growls the loudest I've ever heard it. I grab the plate Anna brought me and it takes everything in me to push it away instead of bringing it closer.

A droplet falls on the top of my head, then another follows, and I'm soaked within a few seconds as rain pours down.

Usually, I'd try to take shelter, but that'd mean hiding and not proving how resilient I am about this.

It's been a long time since I've felt the rain. *So…long.*

I stand on wobbly feet, and a wave of dizziness nearly knocks me back down.

The world starts to blur, but I still stand with my feet shoulder-width apart with my hands on either side of me, then stare up at the angry rain.

I close my eyes and get lost in the moment, not caring that my clothes are sticking to my skin or that I can barely remain upright. I spent so much time the last few years running, living for duty, and trying to work on myself that I missed these small moments of feeling and enjoying the simple moments.

The last thing I was able to feel properly was that kiss in Kirill's car before everything went bust.

I've spent a long time wanting to return to that moment, but the bitter reality is that there's just no going back once things are done. All I have is the aftermath, his silent treatment, and the scary feeling that no matter what I do, I've already lost him.

My legs give out on me and I stumble, then fall. I'm ready for the impact, but instead of hitting the ground, I land on something warmer and safer. Through the slits in my eyes, I think I catch a glimpse of Kirill's masculine face. Even though he's glaring down at me, I can't help the smile that lifts my lips.

He came for me.

That's the last thought I have before darkness takes me under.

❧

Drip.

Drip.

Drip.

I slowly open my eyes due to the continuous sound near my head. For a moment, I think I'm in a nightmare, but then a very familiar room comes into focus.

The same room I was kicked out of not too long ago.

I stumble to get out of bed but pause when a tube pulls at my wrist. The reason for the dripping is an IV stuck in the back of my hand. I start to inspect it, but a deep, authoritative voice stops me in my tracks.

"Don't move until it's finished."

Slowly, almost as if I'm scared, I lift my eyes to where Kirill is.

Earlier, when he caught me in the rain, I thought maybe I was dreaming. Kirill wouldn't go that far for someone he considers untrustworthy. But I was right, after all. He was there and chose to help me.

He's sitting on the sofa opposite the bed, legs spread wide, one hand holding the back of the sofa and a tablet in his other. The intense color of his eyes isn't dimmed by the glasses. In fact, they appear more sinister now.

"I...uh...thank you," I stutter like an idiot.

He tilts the tablet to the side so that his complete attention is on me. "For what?"

"Saving me earlier."

"I didn't save you."

"But you prevented me from falling."

"Only so you didn't crack your head on my doorstep."

Ouch.

Okay.

My teeth sink into my lower lip, stopping me from blurting out something that will definitely not play in my favor. He's probably being mean on purpose, and if I rise to his provocations, that's no different from letting him into my head.

"Why did you bring me to your room then?"

"You needed to get nutrients in you."

"You could've had the doctor do that in the clinic or the annex. Why your room, Kirill?"

"Because it's closer. And it's Boss, not Kirill."

My hands fist on my lap as I try but fail to breathe properly.

Every inhale is filled with his scent—cedar, woods, and passionate animalistic memories from on this very bed.

That's the wrong thought to have. Wrong thought—

"What are you playing at now?" His question drags me back to the present.

"I'm not playing at anything. I told you I won't stop until you give me my old post back."

"Are you threatening me with your life, Lipovsky? Does it hold so little meaning for you?"

"It's not that it holds so little meaning, and it's not easy to do this, but I refuse to be pushed aside by you."

A silent moment falls between us before he abruptly stands and heads in my direction. I instinctively push back against the headboard before realizing I'm cowering away. What the hell?

Kirill stops by the side of the bed and stares at me with those cold eyes that could be mistaken for a weapon. "You should've left while you had the chance."

"I don't want to leave," I murmur. "But I also don't want to be allocated to other departments. I came here to be your bodyguard, and my place is by your side."

"After everything that's happened, you have the audacity to say your place is by my side?"

"It is. I know you don't trust me, but I'm ready to prove my loyalty. Just give me one last chance, Ki…Sir."

I bite my lower lip. I really hate calling him that. It's like I'm rebuilding the wall between us brick by brick.

"You lost my trust, and, therefore, I will only see you as a potential enemy."

My chin trembles, but I lift it. "I'll gain it back."

"Doubt it. So why don't you leave? Be my enemy for real, so we can fight properly."

"I'm not your enemy, and I refuse to leave. If you still insist on throwing me in the weapon vault, I'll stay outside again and starve to death. I'd hate to waste your time if you have to carry me and nurse me back to health every time…wait, did you carry me? How is your injury—" I start to reach a hand for him, but he slaps it away.

My heart squeezes. It wouldn't have hurt this bad if he'd punched me in the face.

"Don't even try to act worried."

But that's the thing. I wish I were acting, but I'm genuinely worried about him, so I'm rethinking the whole scene of him carrying me. Was he exerting himself while holding my dead weight? I really hope he got someone else to take me inside and change me into dry clothes…shit. My bandages are gone, so that means he did it himself.

Now, I'm mad at myself for not being awake during that time.

But then again, if I were, I probably wouldn't have woken up here.

He adjusts his glasses with his middle finger. "You want your job back?"

I nod frantically.

"You got it."

Before I can grin and do a celebratory dance in my head, Kirill grasps my chin with two harsh fingers. "But you're no longer my trusted person, Lipovsky. You're nothing more than a stranger that I'm keeping for information. You want to prove you're loyal to me? That won't be possible when I already consider you my fucking enemy."

NINE

Sasha

"WHAT THE FUCK IS THIS SUPPOSED TO MEAN, Kirill?" Damien lunges in our direction as soon as we're out of the Pakhan's house.

I step forward, my shoulders squaring for a fight or the possibility of one.

Before he manages to grab Kirill in a chokehold, I'm already standing between the two men. Viktor, Yuri, and even Damien's guards don't move an inch, despite the clear war that's about to take place.

"You, step the fuck away before I fuck up your pretty boy face." Damien speaks so close that I smell the nicotine on his breath.

Most days, Damien has casual and sometimes amusing moments, but today is definitely not one of them. His shoulders are taut with tension, and his eyes blaze in a mixture of light green and a raging gray.

Still, I can't let him attack Kirill. The rest of the guards might choose not to interfere in such instances due to orders from both men, but I already promised Kirill my loyalty, and I intend to prove it in action, not words.

It's been three months since I got back my bodyguard job. Or more like, kind of forced Kirill to offer me back my job. I thought that as long as I was where I was supposed to be, everything else would work out. That, sooner or later, he'd learn to trust me again.

I definitely thought wrong. I greatly underestimated Kirill's ability to completely erase me even while seeing each other every day.

And he has erased me for three months. Didn't speak to me directly for a whole month until I thought I was going insane.

The only reason he went back to speaking to me, and only in clipped direct orders, was because I nearly got myself shot during a shipment gone wrong. He pushed me to the ground—like that time when we were a captain and a soldier—clutched me by the nape to hold me in place, and told me, "Stay the fuck down."

They were harsh, cold words, but I wanted to cry. Beneath the callous edge of his order, I could hear the smidgen of care he has for me. Something I thought I'd lost for good.

After a whole month of starvation, it felt like a sweet reward.

It's not an exaggeration when I say it took all my willpower not to hug him or at least grab onto the hand he held me down with.

Since then, he's given me direct orders instead of using a middleman, usually Viktor, who—to be fair—was getting sick of being a messenger.

But the state of things hasn't changed. He doesn't like me in his presence for any extended time or if we're alone. I'm tasked with activities that are far enough from his vicinity that he doesn't have to see or hear me.

It's like he's allergic to me.

No. It's worse.

He's disgusted with me. He doesn't look me in the eye without a slight tic in his jaw and a subtle darkening of his gaze.

I'm still trying to convince him that he can trust me, and he still believes I'm an enemy of sorts.

Back to the present, we're the last ones to leave the Pakhan's house after the weekly meeting, and Damien is clearly pissed off that Kirill suggested stopping an ongoing war with another organization and got the majority of the others to agree.

Damien, who, unsurprisingly, led the on-ground war with his brigade, reacts badly to the prospect of taking away his favorite hobby.

So the fact that he came after us the moment we stepped outside was expected. Now, we have to deal with his bursts of anger and whatever unpredictable things he has in store for us.

I shake my head once, placing a palm on his chest. "Step back."

He seizes my wrist and starts to twist it with brute force, but I free myself before he breaks it. Then I use my hold on his hand and push him back as I move so that I'm standing fully in front of Kirill.

Damien pauses and narrows his eyes. So, yes. I'm no longer the weakling he could send flying during that first meeting. Kirill might have given up on me, but Maksim and especially Yuri haven't.

Yuri even has a special program for me that I've been following to hone my skills to a T, and I never skipped a day of strength training.

Unlike Viktor and Maksim, Yuri isn't as strong in combat and always withdraws or has a subpar performance in physical training. However, he's the best teacher alive. Unlike Kirill, he doesn't teach using force or terrorizing methods. He's more of a steady progress type, and it's been working perfectly for me.

He's patient and understanding, and most of all, I feel like I'm going out to see a friend whenever we have our daily sessions.

"I'm warning you, pretty boy." Damien balls his hand into a fist. The veins pop on the tattoos decorating the back of it. "If you don't move right this instant, I'm going to break your fucking neck and feed your fucked-up corpse to my dogs."

I don't change position. In fact, my shoulders snap backward, and I jut my chin forward, ready for the fight. Damien's upper lip lifts in a snarl as he steps forward. Before I can get into a defensive position, large hands fall on my shoulders from behind, pressing down, then effortlessly pushing me to the side.

Or maybe it's so easy for him because I'm too dumbfounded to think or react. Kirill steps in front of me so that he's toe to toe with Damien, and the only view I have is of the taut muscles of his back.

Ever since he recovered from his injuries, he's been spending all-nighters at the gym or doing hand-to-hand with Viktor. As a result, he has gained more muscle than before.

His shoulders have broadened, and his physique has sharpened to a level that looks more menacing than when we were in the army.

This noticeable change in his build certainly doesn't help when I'm trying to stop being affected by his presence, warmth, and intoxicating scent that I'm currently breathing into my starved lungs.

Kirill slips a hand in his pocket and tilts his head as he speaks to Damien in a bored tone. "As I told everyone inside, and you obviously weren't listening, this war is draining our resources and offering nothing in return but some form of entertainment for you. Therefore, it's tasteless, needless, and, most importantly, profitless. It's more logical to work on gaining allies than indulging in meaningless wars."

"Blah, blah, and fucking blah!" Damien gets in his face. "Those wars are my only source of entertainment and the one thing I do best. If you take them away, what the fuck am I supposed to do?"

"Take a rest and work on your anger issues?"

"Only if I get to kill you. Pretty sure my anger issues would be fucking resolved."

"I will refuse that offer, but here's another one for you. How about you explore endeavors other than fighting like a madman? Don't you get bored?"

"Fuck no."

"You need other sources to help you let go of all this toxic energy. How about you learn more effective ways to invest your fortune? I can help."

Damien raises an eyebrow. "Does that mean you finally agree to fight me?"

"How did you get that from my last sentence, I wonder?"

"The fact that you killed my fun and are under obligation to offer me something in return, or I will break your fucking neck while you sleep."

"That won't be possible, but here's the deal." Kirill clutches Damien by the shoulder, and I step to the side to get a better view of him.

His face is serene, calm, and since he's kept the light stubble after his injury, he looks like a different type of beast. He's scarier, more closed off, and…unreachable.

I can watch from afar, but it's impossible to touch him. It's even more impossible to know what he's thinking anymore. It's like he locked himself in a vault and threw away the key.

"Allow me to invest twenty percent of your assets. One condition, though. I get fifty percent of the gains."

"You fucking high? Fifty percent?" Damien, who everyone knows doesn't give a damn about finances and would've already gone bankrupt if he didn't have the right people by his side, thinks that amount is crazy. "My broker guy takes care of my investments. I don't need you."

"I'm telling you that, even with my fifty percent cut, I can give you more than what your broker currently does."

Damien narrows his eyes, seeming frustrated, then he lifts his hands in the air. "I don't give a fuck about money. So if this is the master plan you came up with to dissuade me from stopping that war…"

"I'll get you another war."

Damien pauses, and his eyes shine like a kid who's found countless presents under the Christmas tree. "How soon?"

Kirill adjusts his glasses with his middle and ring fingers. "Pretty soon."

"If you're fucking with me—"

"If I don't give you that war in the span of a few months, I'll fight you."

"Not *months*. Only one month, and even that is fucking pushing it. I don't know what the fuck I'll do during all that time. I might start killing people randomly, and no one wants that drama in their lives, now, do they?"

"You need to rein in the fucking craziness, Damien. It's your weakest point and the only thing that's holding you back from moving up."

"I don't want to move up. I want the fucking war that you'll give me in a month, and if you fail me, you'll fight me anytime I wish to." He pushes him with his shoulder. "If you fuck with me, I'll kill all your men. Starting with the pretty boy Sasha."

On his way out, Damien pats my shoulder. "No hard feelings. It's only business." He leans over to whisper in my ear, "Get in my way again, and I'll stab Kirill while he sleeps, got it?"

My spine jerks, and I remain frozen long after Damien and his men have gotten in their cars.

Kirill spins around and faces me with those emotionless eyes that I'm starting to dread seeing. "What did he tell you?"

"You…heard him."

"What did he whisper to you just now, Lipovsky?"

"That…uh…I shouldn't get in his way again." I omit the last part, and something tells me Kirill can feel I'm hiding something, because he narrows his eyes, a muscle clenching in his jaw, and he remains like that for what feels like an hour but is actually a few seconds.

Then, as if he didn't just turn my world upside down, he walks to the car.

Viktor follows after him, but Yuri stays behind and even approaches me as I catch my breath.

"You okay?" he asks in a soft tone.

I hate that he always has to check on me lately. Maksim doesn't. Yuri, however, is more attuned to people and changes, and he said that he feels like I'm not myself lately—despite all the effort I go through to appear normal.

Not myself is an understatement, though. I used to think that it was only a matter of time before I got Kirill back, but that hope dims with every passing day.

Now, I think I'm on the verge of mourning him. No, we weren't best friends or anything, but we were intimate, and he let me hold him sometimes—mostly after sex. He used to joke and lash out his sarcasm and made me feel so safe in his company that I actually considered never leaving.

Everything is different since fucking Russia.

"Sasha?" Yuri asks again when I don't answer. "Did Damien say something that bothered you?"

I shake my head. "It's not that. I'm just…not on my game, I guess."

"No, you're good." He squeezes my shoulder. "You were able to escape Damien's hold. Not just anyone can do that. I'm proud of how far you've come."

I grin. "It's all thanks to you."

"Don't be humble. None of this would've happened if you weren't disciplined." He releases me. "Come on. We should go before Viktor starts being a pain in the ass."

We're about to leave when I catch a glimpse of Rai—the Pakhan's niece—being guided by her guards into her car. She got married a week ago to someone chosen by her granduncle. Her new husband is dangerous and mysterious. Everyone is keeping an eye on him.

Their wedding day was complete madness, and everything that followed was weird.

Since then, she's changed, but I'm not sure if it's for the better. Rai has always been a careful businesswoman who's made of steel. She used the secret she held over Kirill's head to make him vote for her to become the executive director of V Corp—the organization's legitimate front. Since that time, she's been slowly but surely eliminating his and even Adrian's spies from the company. Something both men don't appreciate and have been secretly plotting to get back at her for. How, I don't know.

Under different circumstances, I wouldn't care, but I'm sure Rai is also planning something. For instance, she's glaring at Kirill as he gets into the car now. And I'm not sure how much longer he can piss her off in meetings before she decides to put his position and all the wins he brought to the organization in jeopardy.

All because of me.

Logically, Kirill has no reason to protect my identity. He could tell her that I'm a woman, and that might get me killed by the Pakhan, but Rai would have nothing to threaten him with anymore.

But he hasn't.

Why hasn't he?

"Move it." Viktor glares at us, forcing me to break eye contact with the situation.

I climb into the passenger seat. It's now my usual place since I'm forbidden from sitting with Kirill. Viktor, who took that position, would gloat if the man knew how to display normal human emotions.

I'm in the middle of checking my ammunition when my eyes clash with Kirill's through the rearview mirror, and he's glaring.

Or I think he is, because the contact only lasts for a fraction of a second before he focuses back on what Viktor is telling him about the club's numbers this month.

I swallow. What the hell was that for?

"Is there a reason why you're not putting Rai in her place?" Viktor asks after he's done discussing the club. "She has the audacity to subtly threaten you at the table with everyone there."

I go still, but I don't dare check the rearview mirror or look behind me and, instead, focus on the tall buildings blurring past us.

Even Viktor notices her not-so-subtle animosity. Which means everyone else does, too.

"She's all bark and no bite," comes Kirill's casual reply.

"She didn't sound like it. Besides, it's demeaning, Boss. Adrian, Igor, and Damien's men are asking me and Lipovsky if you're not able to remove Rai from your path. We don't know how to answer them."

"Then don't," Kirill says simply. "You don't owe them anything."

I've been telling them there's nothing to it, but, of course, they don't buy it. Especially Vladislav, Damien's senior guard, and Yan, Adrian's guard. Yan acts clownish like Maksim, but he's the best at getting information. And I'm sure he told Adrian that Rai must be threatening Kirill with something.

Shit.

"If Adrian knows…" I trail off when I realize I'm speaking out loud. Silence falls over the car, so I clear my throat and look at Kirill through the rearview mirror. "I'll try to find out from Yan. We've become close."

Or more like, we're constantly milking each other for information while pretending to be friends. Neither of us will admit to that fact, and we keep dancing around it in this weird limbo where we're aware of each other's intentions but still go with the act anyway.

"You'll do no such thing," Kirill orders in his frightening tone.

"But I can do something. If Adrian has any information, you can be in the know."

"What the fuck did I just say, Lipovsky? Are you defying direct orders?"

"No…sir." I want to bite my lower lip until it bleeds, but I ball my fists on my lap instead.

Tension grows in the car for a few seconds before Viktor says, "Lipovsky is actually close to Yan, Boss. Let him do his thing and be useful."

"I said—No. And that's fucking final."

This time, no one tries to persuade him. There's a shift in the air, and the tension swirling around Kirill could be cut with a knife.

The rest of the ride, Viktor talks more about the club, but that doesn't really kill the unwelcoming atmosphere. Once we arrive at the house, Kirill tells us he has work to do alone.

Pressure grows in my chest and I have to tap it a few times in order to breathe properly.

It's times like these when I start to question my choices and everything I've done since Russia.

I'm so close to giving up, but then he does something like saving me or paying attention to details about me and I go back to my stupid hopeism.

Only for the cycle to begin again.

It's downright toxic at this point, but I can't put an end to it.

Sometimes, when it gets to be too much, I try to call my uncle to make sure they're doing okay, but his phone has been disconnected.

At this point, I've been truly cut off from my family, and this place is the closest I've ever had to belonging. I've found dear friends in Yuri, Maks, Kara, and the others.

Even Viktor's mountain-like presence feels like an anchor.

Konstantin's, too. Sometimes, he joins me and Karina for breakfast, but only when Yulia isn't around.

Kirill always, without fail, glares at us whenever he sees us, and soon after, I get an order that we're leaving the house.

Still, I don't want to lose the relationships and the belonging I feel in this place. Kirill might not approve of me, but I can at least do my part to ward off unnecessary enemies.

I wait for Yuri to go back to the annex and make sure Viktor has headed to the gym to torture the others, then I follow Kirill to the office.

Once I'm in front of the door, I take a deep breath, but before I knock, it opens, and he appears at the threshold, tall, big, and downright frightening.

My fist hovers over his chest for a few seconds before I finally come to my senses and drop it.

He crosses his developed arms over his chest, making his shirt stretch over his biceps. "I know what you're here for and the answer is still no, and mark my words, Lipovsky, if you go behind my back on this, I'll fire you."

I purse my lips. "But—"

"No buts. If you're going to prove your loyalty, you will not disobey my orders."

"Let me ask you something," I whisper. "Why didn't you just expose my real gender and get rid of the threat Rai poses to you? She might have lacked power before, but she has influence now, and she can use it to strip you of all the accomplishments you've made."

"That's none of your business."

"Uh…I'm sort of in the middle of the problem, so I think it's my business."

"Do as you're told and stay put."

"I…can tell her myself."

"Are you in the mood to fucking die?"

"If it proves my loyalty."

"Don't be an idiot."

"I'm not an idiot."

"You acting suicidal is the definition of being a fucking idiot. How will you prove your loyalty when you're dead?"

"You'll finally know it then and stop treating me like I don't exist. I'm right here, Kirill. Always beside you, in front of you, and anywhere you want me to be, so why…" I choke on my words. "Why are you erasing me?"

"You know exactly why."

"Will you ever trust me again? Am I fighting a losing battle?"

"I might consider trusting you if you don't go trying to get yourself killed. Got it?"

My heart warms, and I think it'll explode from the sheer pressure his mere words have put on it.

He might trust me.

Well, consider to trust me, but it's a beginning all the same.

Kirill is a lot of things, but he's not the type who dishes out empty hope.

"And do us all a favor." He narrows his eyes. "Stop befriending people and being a busybody, Lipovsky."

"It's Sasha." The words get stuck at the back of my throat. "I hate it when you call me by my last name."

His face remains the same, short of the clenching of his jaw and the slow adjusting of his glasses.

"Stay. Fucking. Put." He enunciates every word, then, just like that, he closes the door in my face.

TEN

Kirill

I HAVE A BAD FEELING TODAY.

There's nothing out of the ordinary in my routine, but something isn't clicking. I'm not sure if it's people, food, or even my fucking men.

Everything is wrong in some way—a bit crooked, twisted, and completely...out of reach.

The last time I felt this way was when I was on the top of that hill in the middle of nowhere and saw the mercenaries behind Aleksandra.

I haven't started to deal with that, and now, we have this. Whatever *this* is.

"Is everything in order?" I ask Viktor on my way to the car.

"As usual."

That still doesn't erase the uncomfortable feeling.

I stop in front of the house and cast a glance at my

surroundings, which are shrouded in the night's darkness. Three vans, all full of my men, who I might as well be leading to their deaths.

Like I did to Rulan and the others.

"Maksim," I call.

He lifts his head from checking his weapon. My focus shifts briefly to Aleksandra who's standing next to him. At my appearance, she straightens until her shoulders nearly snap.

For over three months, I've been attempting to erase her from my reality and have only managed to fail miserably.

On one hand, I want to tie her up and torture her for answers, using unorthodox methods that are more sexual than physical. But that thought soon fades.

If I go down that road, I'll be the one with a problem that's been manifesting itself every day in the form of my cock's hate speech. He's been my enemy for months after failing to put him to use.

Last week, when she came up with that idiotic idea about spying on Adrian, it took all my self-control not to indulge in my cock's sadistic plans.

Do I have contempt for that woman? *Absolutely.* That doesn't stop me from seeing her as the subject of my fucked-up desire.

I should probably put more effort into actually searching for another woman to fuck. One problem, though. My cock is a dick—literally—because he's been excruciatingly not interested in any other pussy.

The only time he jumps to life is when she's in sight. He doesn't care that she's a deathtrap waiting to happen. Even right now, when she's looking more nervous than Karina when she's outside, my cock strains against my pants, demanding to be fed.

I'm supposed to be attending to something important, but I find myself watching her instead. Her posture is erect, translating the clear discipline she's been maintaining for years. While she'll never be as muscular as the other men, she has been following a strict routine that Yuri specifically made for her, and she's easily the best sniper we have.

Which could be bad news because she colluded with other people against me.

By other people, I mean her fucking lover that I still can't find. Viktor has come up empty regarding the whole Belsky Organization that could offer us some insight into the situation.

Apparently, his friend in the KGB has the same level of information we do. He did promise Viktor that if anything comes up in Russia on this matter, we'll be the first to know.

What the fuck are you hiding?

I know Aleksandra wants my approval. She's been working tirelessly for months, even when I gave her the cold shoulder and excluded her from important meetings to make her feel less important.

What? She got me shot, or her lover did and she's still helping him.

Call me Petty Fucking Betty because I won't stop acting this way until she finally confesses the bastard's name.

She tightens her fingers as if she's suppressing something and subtly lowers her head. It's then I realize I might have been staring at her longer than socially acceptable.

"Yes, Boss?" Maksim stands before me, oblivious to the tension he cut through.

"I'm going to need you and your team to stay back."

His brow furrows. "Why? We're always at these shipments."

"We have no use for too many men. Guard the mansion instead."

"Yes, Boss."

Aleksandra starts toward the main car, but I face her. "You stay back, too, Lipovsky."

"But I have my position as the lead sniper—"

"Someone else will take it."

"But—"

"That's an order. You'll stay behind with Maksim's team."

Her lips purse, and an unnatural shine covers her eyes, but she does everyone a favor and remains silent. She doesn't move, though, until Maksim grabs her by the shoulder and drags her to his side.

I narrow my eyes for the slightest bit before I catch myself and swiftly slide into the back of the car.

The feeling of doom I've had since this morning lessens, but it doesn't completely disappear.

As Yuri drives out, I catch a glimpse of Aleksandra balling her hands into fists. Her lips push forward in what looks like a pout.

I have no fucking clue why that draws a smile on my face.

When we arrive at the port, it's about eleven-thirty. This month's shipment will hit the dock around thirty minutes from now. The mayor is cooperating. The police won't stick their noses in our business, and some of the feds eat our money like pigs.

So they're out.

What else could disrupt this shipment aside from Juan's betrayal, which is highly unlikely. I offer him the best rate around, and he even suggested expanding our ventures at the last meeting we had.

I step out of the car and stare into the distance at the hidden part of the dock and the containers stacked everywhere, forming a maze. The chilly breeze freezes my face and I slide a hand into my pocket.

Viktor joins me after doing the rounds. "Everything's in order."

"Go with two of our best men to the other side of the marina. If you sense a hint of danger, drive a boat out and warn Juan's men."

"I can send the men, but why should I go? If there's danger, as you said, who will protect you?"

"I'm no dainty princess, Viktor. I can protect myself."

He narrows his eyes. "Like back in Russia, you mean."

Touché. "Those were different circumstances." *There's no Aleksandra to distract me now.* "Besides, Yuri and the others are here. Go."

He hesitates for a beat, then he barks at two men to follow him.

"Yuri." I tap on the window of the driver's side. "Keep the car running."

He nods, brings out his gun, and checks his bullets. I don't have to tell him that the situation is dire. He already understands.

I must say, though his accident was unfortunate, I prefer him post-accident than before it. He was a nice guy who kept to himself and had trouble keeping up with the others. Now, he's an important weapon in my arsenal.

Not a fighter, per se. I wouldn't send him on an on-ground mission like I would Viktor or Maksim. He's more of a strategist.

I walk to the other men who are positioned down the length of the dock and tell them to keep their cars running, too, and to take cover.

I'm about to get to the third group when there's movement behind me. I spin around fast, pulling my gun at the same time.

No one's there.

No. That's not it. There's no one there now, but there was definitely an intruder a few seconds ago.

I click the interphone in my ear. "Viktor, take that boat and intercept Juan's men."

"Yes, Boss."

I'm thinking it could be Juan or some of his rogue men who decided to cause trouble, but it seems that the shipment has been used as an excuse to get close to me.

The sound of screeching tires echoes in the distance, and my men go on high alert.

"Take cover!" I'm not even finished with shouting the words when a stream of bullets fire in our direction as if they're being shot from a machine gun.

Thankfully, my men hide behind the cars in time and start firing their own weapons. I jump behind a large red container to get a better read on the situation.

The intruders have vans like ours and are in ski masks to hide their identity.

But that's not the part that gets my attention.

It's the weapons.

I've seen those specific sniper rifles that can't be found in the US somewhere, but where?

One of my men gets hit in the arm, but before the masked man finishes him, I shoot him in the head. That easily gives away my location, so I use the cover of the container to run to another one before I shoot two more men.

But I also miss a few times, mainly because my men come into view, and I'd hit them if I took the shot.

Ten minutes later, I'm low on ammunition. As in, I only have two shots left. I can only use one and leave the other until I get to Yuri. The problem is, due to the constant running between the containers, I lost him, so he'll have to be the one to find me with the GPS.

That is, if he wasn't hit himself since he's really shit on the ground.

Fuck.

I should've canceled or postponed this operation the moment I felt there was something fucking wrong with this whole day.

A car revs in my direction, and I shoot the tire. It swerves to the side, but it continues approaching me at a maddening speed, so I use my safety net bullet and hit the other tire. It's pointless to aim at the glass since it's likely bulletproof. Besides, it's tinted, so I can't gamble and try to shoot the driver.

The van tilts and hits one of the containers, then rolls over. I grab onto a metal rod on the nearest container then push my weight over to the other side and then on top. I barely miss being shot at by the men in the van.

The moment I rise to my full height, the hammer of a gun clicks at the back of my head.

I let my weapon turn upside down and hang off my forefinger.

So I was the target of this whole operation. Interesting.

"Are you from the Belsky Organization?" I start to turn around.

He hits me across the head with his gun and then kicks me in the back of my knees. I fall to the top of the metal container with a resounding thud.

Red blurs my vision, but I smile. "I'll take that as a yes. I must say, using the shipment day to get me is smart. I bet you meant to ruin the relationship between me and Juan, and that way, when you kill me, it'll be marked down as a dishonorable death. But what to do? I might be one step ahead on this one. You don't get to fuck with me and get out unscathed. That's not how I operate."

He hits me again, and this time, I wince, but I use the small moment to turn around. I get a glimpse of his masked face, but that's the only thing I see before the barrel of the gun is shoved at my face.

"Kirill!" The shout comes first, then the shot follows.

Fuck. Fuck. Fuck!

I would recognize that voice even if I were sleeping. But what the hell is she doing here?

The masked man runs backward, and Sasha's shot hits his chest, but he must be wearing a vest, because no blood comes out and he jumps off the container like a ninja.

For a moment, I consider going after him, but I remember that I don't have any bullets, and he'll probably shoot me on sight.

The fact that he didn't engage with Sasha is weird, though.

Unless he thought she brought backup.

Quiet but fast footsteps stomp across the top of the container before she drops to her knees in front of me, the bottom of her rifle making a loud sound on the metal.

Her hands cradle my face, fingers shaking, and tears shining in her eyes. "Are you okay? Oh my God, is this a gunshot wound…? Did you…"

"Would I be alive if I were shot in the head, genius?"

"No, I guess not…" She's talking to me, but she's barely seeing me as she wipes my forehead and my cheeks with the back of her jacket sleeves.

The tears cling to her lashes before they drop and stain her cheeks. And these tears do unpleasant shit to me.

I reach a hand to her cheek and wipe one away. She pauses and shivers beneath my palm.

Fuck.

It's been a long time since I've touched her, and now that I am, I feel like an addict who's been thrown back into bad fucking habits.

I resist the urge to close my eyes and breathe her in, maybe even try to devour her in the process.

"Why the fuck are you crying?"

She continues wiping the blood diligently, like it's her life's mission. "I thought…I thought you would be hurt like…the other time and…that nearly made me go insane…"

"I'm fine." I stroke my thumb underneath her eyes, but the more I do, the harder she cries. "We need to get out of here."

"No, wait. Hold on…just one moment…let me get rid of all the blood and then…then—"

Her words come to an abrupt halt when I seal my forehead to hers. "I'm fine. This much won't hurt me. Got it?"

Her chin trembles, but she doesn't say anything.

"I'm going to need your reflexes, Sasha. I don't have ammunition, and you're the only one who can get us to safety. Can I count on you?"

Her hand sinks into the side of my jacket as if she's a child who's holding on to someone older, but her expression sobers up.

She offers a sharp nod and then brushes her lips against my cheek. The motion is fast enough that I only realize it after she breaks away. "Thank you."

Fuck me.

I have to internally shake myself to be aware of the current situation and that I can't actually fuck her on the top of this container.

"What for?" I definitely sound more casual than I feel.

"For staying alive." She grins. "And for calling me Sasha again."

I did?

Before I can reply, she clutches me by the arm. "Let's go. I'll get us safely to Yuri."

And this fucking woman does exactly that.

ELEVEN

Sasha

THERE ARE TIMES IN LIFE WHEN EVERYTHING IS uncertain.

Your beliefs.

Your purpose.

Your whole being.

However, in the middle of the blurry ambiguity stands something real. And that's the only thing I currently believe in.

The one person because of whom I found another goal. The one person who motivates me to get out of bed in the morning and work harder on myself.

Even if he ignores me most of the time and only pays me stilted attention.

So I'm glad I let my instincts guide me and followed him after he ordered me to stay put.

When I made this decision, it wasn't only because I insisted on being by his side, or that I'm still desperately trying to prove my loyalty. I truly had a horrible feeling the moment his car left the premises.

Karina came out of her room and celebrated the prospect of the two of us spending time together, but that wasn't going to happen. I didn't bother with an excuse as I fetched my rifle, jumped into the car, and started driving.

I didn't pay Maksim any attention when he banged on the window and told me to at least take him along. I had only one concern at the time—get to Kirill.

Turns out, it was a legitimate concern, because the moment I arrived at the site, it was a full-on war, and he was about to get killed.

It didn't take us long to find Yuri since he was already following the GPS to locate Kirill. The car was shot a few times, but it remained functional.

Instead of leaving immediately, Kirill stayed put until he ensured the rest of the men were also retreating. Then we heard from Viktor that he'd sent the Mexicans back and told their leader, Juan's right-hand man, that Kirill would get in touch about what to do next.

The weirdest thing about the hit is that after Kirill was cornered and I got there in time, it was like the attackers got an order to retreat. They completely disappeared, taking their dead and injured along.

One of our men died, and a few were wounded, but none of them are in a critical condition.

Despite my attempts, Kirill refused to get his head wound looked at because the other men were his priority.

He only complied after both Anna and Karina got involved and basically forced the doctor to treat him.

After he's gotten everyone settled in the clinic and has given instructions to Viktor about the site's cleanup, he starts to leave the annex, then stops.

"You're coming with me, Aleksander."

My spine jerks, but it's not accompanied with the pain I felt whenever he called me by my fake last name. Aleksander is better.

Besides, he did call me Sasha earlier. He touched me, wiped my tears, and brought me down from the overwhelming fear I had when I saw a gun being pointed at his head.

I had gruesome flashbacks from when he was on the verge of death while surrounded by blood and snow in Russia. For a second, I thought I'd lost him for good this time.

All my fears and nightmares played in front of my eyes, and all I could think about was saving him.

Even after the assailant was out of the picture, all I could see was the blood trailing down his temples and cheeks, and I nearly lost it. That high of emotions would've swept me over if he hadn't been there to keep me upright.

Maksim winces as Kirill turns and leaves. I mouth, "What?"

"You disobeyed his order, idiot," he hisses. "RIP."

Yuri looks at me in a weird blank way before he offers a sympathizing tap on the shoulder.

Oh, shit. I completely forgot about that.

My steps are heavy as I follow Kirill out of the annex and try to keep up as he strides in the direction of the main house.

I jog to his side and clear my throat. "About earlier, I—"

"Shut the fuck up."

"But—"

"Not another word." He throws me a chilling side-eye. "I mean it."

My lips clamp shut, but I walk the rest of the way in complete silence. My mind, however, is in overdrive.

How can I convince him to completely forget about what happened without endangering the fragile peace we re-found?

Or, at least, I did. I don't know how he feels about the recent events or if he feels anything at all.

If it's the latter, I would seriously be heartbroken—more than I already am.

Once he walks inside his room, I follow and I try again, "Look at it this way, if I hadn't come, you'd probably be dead—"

One moment I'm standing there speaking, and the next, the breath is knocked out of my lungs when strong fingers wrap around my throat and slam me against the nearest wall.

Kirill's face is inches from mine. The bandage wrapped around his head takes nothing away from the pure fire that devours me in seconds.

It's been a long time since he's been this close, and I find it hard to breathe. That has less to do with his grip on my neck and more to do with the fact that I'm inhaling him and his addictive scent with each intake of air.

"I told you to shut the fuck up, Sasha." His nostrils flare as tension rises from his shoulders to the tendons of his neck, and he clenches his jaw.

I swallow, and he must feel it against his fingers that are holding me in place.

"Did I or did I not ask you to stay put?"

"You did, but—"

"It's a yes or no question. Did I or did I not tell you to stay fucking *put*?"

"You did, but I had a bad feeling and had to follow. Besides, I saved you, okay? If I hadn't been there, you would've died!"

He doesn't like that. Not one bit. His hand tightens around my throat further. "And if there had been anyone else there, they would've easily shot you."

"But there wasn't. It ended well."

"After you disobeyed a direct order."

"I still saved your life. Seriously, you should be rewarding me instead of whatever this is."

"Reward you?"

"Yeah. That's common sense."

"Here's another piece of common sense for you. In cases of disobeying a direct order, you're to be *punished*."

A war of shivers break out over my skin at the way his voice drops when he says that word.

"I…can accept punishment for disobeying orders, but on one condition."

"What makes you think you have the right to make any conditions?"

I lift my chin. "The fact that I saved your life and proved my loyalty to you."

"Debatable. But let's hear it."

"I want to choose my reward."

"I never said I was granting you one."

"Well, you have to. Otherwise, I'll be punished for nothing, and I'm not game for that."

I can almost swear that his lips twitch in what seems to be a smile, but it soon disappears. "It's for disobeying an order, not for nothing."

"I'm afraid that's a dealbreaker for me."

"You…" he trails off, closing his eyes for a brief second, and I wish I could touch his face.

I don't dare to, though. Obviously, I don't have the same confidence I did when I shamelessly kissed his cheek earlier.

Since I was overwhelmed by emotions, I didn't quite think about the consequences of my actions. My only concern was having him there safe and sound.

When his eyes open again, I'm dragged into their world against my will.

"You get your reward," he lets out begrudgingly and then adds, "but only within reason."

I can work with that.

"Right now, however, is the time for your punishment."

My yelp echoes in the air when he uses his hold on my throat to drag me to the bed and then unapologetically throws me on top of the mattress.

I prop myself up on my elbows and try, then fail, to control the chaos that's whirling inside me. It doesn't help that I'm on this bed that I haven't been on in ages. The last time was when I fainted outside and he carried me here.

It used to smell like me a few months ago, but now, it's only him, which is weird since I know for a fact that he barely sleeps.

Kirill stands opposite me and unhurriedly removes his jacket, revealing his white shirt that's molded against his muscles. Red soaks the collar due to his injury earlier, but that's the least of my worries when he unbuttons his cuffs and rolls the sleeves to his elbows.

"What's going on?" My voice comes out shaky despite myself, and I have to clear my throat in order to speak again. "I thought my punishment would be push-ups or physical labor."

"You thought wrong." The whip of his words hits me across the skin, and I suppress a gasp.

"But that's how the others are punished."

"This isn't about the others; this is about *you*." He unbuckles his belt, and my eyes fly to his large veiny hands as he methodically removes it.

Without realizing it, I'm pushing back on my hands toward the headboard. "What type of punishment is this?"

"I think you know exactly what it is."

I shake my head even as a frisson travels the length of my body and pools between my legs.

Holy hell.

Am I wet at the prospect of being punished?

No. It's not about the punishment itself. It's about the fact that Kirill will be the one conducting it.

He wraps the end of the belt around his strong hand, and I feel myself on the verge of hyperventilating. Gone are my attempts to act or remain strong. Isn't it unfair that Kirill is the only one who has this inexplicable effect on me?

He's about to punish me, and my body chooses this exact moment to become sexually frustrated.

"This isn't the first time I've told you not to challenge my orders, but you've done exactly that again." He slowly rounds the bed like a predator who's circling their prey. "And *again.*"

He reaches over, and I flinch, hitting my back against the headboard.

Shit.

Why am I so jumpy? This isn't me.

Kirill effortlessly seizes both my hands, and a shock of electricity rolls through me at the contact. It's been a long time since he touched me this deliberately and this…intimately.

I should probably fight or resist this, but I can't.

In fact, I don't want to.

So I remain still as he pulls my hands above my head and expertly ties my wrists to the headboard using his belt. The leather snaps securely, stretching my arms and forbidding me from moving.

"You think it's fun to challenge my authority, Sasha?" His forefinger slides from my wrist to my arm and then to my cheek.

My lips part, and fire erupts everywhere his skin touches mine.

"Do you?"

I shake my head once.

"That's right. It's not. So now, we need to fix that behavior problem of yours."

He reaches into the nightstand, and the sound is heightened by the unbearable silence coated with thick tension.

It's crazy how hyperaware I am of all my senses. My nostrils fill with Kirill's cedar and woodsy scent but also with my elevated pheromones until I can almost taste them.

I'm fully clothed, but I can still feel the covers and the mattress as if they're rubbing against my bare skin. Not only that, but ever since he grabbed me by my throat, my nipples have been hard and achy, and they've been pushing against my bandages. Instead of being merely uncomfortable, the sensation is downright painful.

My lips part when Kirill retrieves a military knife, but before

I can focus properly, he grips a handful of my collar and lifts me partially off the bed.

I'm surprised my heart doesn't leap out of its confines and melt in his hands.

His dangerous gaze studies the length of me in a slow rhythm that leaves me hyperventilating. "I should've done this a long time ago, and not only for the foolish move you pulled today, but for every-fucking-thing."

"I…didn't do anything wrong."

"Is that so?" He wrenches my shirt out of my pants and cuts it down the middle, using the knife with staggering ease. It's as if it's made of butter. "How do you explain your involvement with that band of mercenaries back in Russia?"

"I…really didn't know, Kirill. I swear—"

My words get stuck in the back of my throat when he cuts off my chest bandages as easily as the shirt. My breasts gently bounce free, but that offers little to no reprieve to my overstimulated nipples.

The fact that I'm bound and unable to do anything adds a perverse pleasure to my throbbing core.

"Whether you knew or not isn't the fucking problem here." He lets the knife hover over my heaving breasts, then down to my stomach before he cuts right through the center of my pants and boxer briefs, his hand hovering too close to my pussy. "The problem is that you not only went back to your lover, but also colluded with him against me."

I shake my head, but I can't find the right words to say. It's impossible when he's shredding my pants and boxer briefs to pieces and throwing them to the side.

I'm lying completely naked in front of him, short of the sleeves of my jacket and my torn shirt beneath me.

"Was that him earlier?"

"W-what?"

He runs the dull end of the knife up my thigh and to my

stomach, leaving shivers in its wake. "The man who cleverly plotted tonight's attack and held me at gunpoint. Is he your lover?"

"N-no! I've never seen him in my life. Besides, would I have shot him if I had any relationship with him?"

"I wouldn't know. You didn't really hurt him, so maybe that was part of an elaborate plan to make me trust you again."

"You think I'd put you in danger again? *Me?*" I can't help the sadness that clings to my words.

I thought we were making progress after tonight, but maybe that was all smoke and mirrors. This is Kirill, after all. He wouldn't simply erase his suspicions, even if I'd died for him.

He'd probably think that I was playing with him in that sense, too.

"I don't know, Sasha. You did it before."

My lips tremble, and I turn my head to the side. If I keep looking at his face, I'll see that he'll probably never give me a chance, and I'll probably cry.

I seem to do that a lot around him. It's ironic that this cold-hearted man is the only one who can trigger the emotional part of me.

He places the dull part of the blade beneath my chin and forces me to focus back on him.

"Look at me when I'm talking to you."

I clamp my lips shut in a hopeless attempt to stop them from shaking, then whisper, "Will you ever trust me again?"

"I never trusted you fully, so the *again* is irrelevant."

"Then would you at least trust that I'm loyal to you, like before I went to Russia?"

"Give me the name of the fucker who was standing beside you that day, and I will forget about the Russia episode."

"I told you that...I can't."

His eyes rage to a frightening blue that stiffens my muscles, but that soon morphs into hot-red desire when he slides his knife down my throat, pauses at my pulse point before continuing his path to the slope of my breast, and then turns the sharp side on my engorged nipple. I feel no pain, but a trail of blood trickles down my breast and stomach and then pools in my navel.

The sight should be appalling, but pure fascination forbids me from looking away.

"Here's how it'll go, Sasha." He continues the knife's path over my stomach, hips, and then to the sensitive spot between my legs. "I'm going to keep torturing you until you tell me a name. So unless you give me what I need, you'll stay here all day…" he trails off, a wolfish smirk tugging on his lips. "What do we have here?"

His fingers slide between my thighs, and a dark look fills his eyes. "Are you wet at the prospect of being tortured?"

"N-no."

"Your pussy doesn't sing the same tune your mouth does." He strokes my opening and teases my clit. "Look how it's soaking my fucking fingers."

I have to physically stop myself from humping his fingers and getting off on them. I've been in this state of hypersensitivity for so long that I can't take it anymore.

He glides his fingers through my folds in a torturous rhythm, offering me stimulation but not enough to get me off.

This is a first from him. Kirill was always about getting me off. Whether with his mouth, fingers, or cock. He had the sole purpose of making me come for him and preferably scream his name during it.

But now, he seems to not want me to get off at all.

His middle finger hovers near my opening, and my hips automatically jerk. It's been such a long time since he touched me, and no matter how much I do it myself, it's entirely different from when he does it.

I don't know if it's the thickness of his fingers, the sheer dominance of his touch, or his delicious intensity, but I'm always left starving for more from him.

Just *more*.

"You want me to fuck your tight little cunt, Sasha?" There's harsh amusement behind his words. "Want me to relieve the ache and make you scream?"

I nod once, my cheeks heating, but I couldn't care less about the embarrassment right now.

"I can do that." He slides a finger inside, and my back arches off the bed.

Oh, God.

More…more…more…

I *need* this.

"I can also add another one." He thrusts the second finger in. "And another. You take three of them like such a good girl. You're my favorite fuck hole, Sasha."

When he rams the third finger in, I think I'll burst. Yes, I used to take three of his fingers, but that was months ago. Being celibate and having only my fingers for company doesn't help.

"You're so tight that you're milking my fingers." He curls them inside, and my nails dig into the leather belt.

"Kirill…"

"What?"

"Please…"

"You're going to have to be more specific with your begging. What do you want me to do?"

"Fuck me." *And not only with your fingers.*

As much as I love the feeling of them inside me, I need something more.

I need all of him pressed up against me and his muscles crushing me while he gives me the most intense pleasure I've ever experienced.

"You can barely take my fingers, and you want my cock?" He thrusts them in a fast rhythm that leaves me gasping. "You're such a greedy little whore, Solnyshko."

I'm supposed to feel offended by that, but I'm not. Not one

bit. If anything, it makes me wetter, until my arousal drenches his fingers.

"I can do that, too," he continues in that deep, sexy tone. "I'll fuck you good. Fuck you hard. I'll fuck you until you forget about all other cocks and worship only mine. You want that?"

I nod several times, completely delirious from his dirty talk. I want to keep looking at him, to get lost in this moment and have no means of return, but it's hard to force my eyes open when intense pleasure is building at the base of my stomach with frightening speed.

Still tearing me apart with his fingers, Kirill lowers his head and whispers hot words near my ear, "Tell me his name first."

My lips tremble, but I murmur, "I can't…"

One moment, I'm on the verge of an orgasm; the next, it's gone. Kirill wrenches his fingers from inside me, leaving me hot, bothered, and with a scream bubbling at the back of my throat.

"What…? Why?"

His expression is now closed off, and if I wasn't so frustrated, I'd be frightened. "This is a punishment. You're not supposed to come when you haven't confessed yet."

"You can't be serious…?"

He thrusts the knife's handle inside me, and I reel from the renewed pressure. Kirill all but fucks me with the knife, and I don't know why it feels so hot. Depraved, yes, but it's so erotic that my earlier intense buildup seems like a joke compared to the wave that's currently sweeping me under.

"Oh, God…"

"I'm the only god you'll ever have." He goes faster, harder, and so out of control that I think I'll faint from the intensity alone. "What's his name?"

At the moment, I forget why I shouldn't be confessing everything. But some brain cells remain functioning and forbid me to.

The moment I shake my head, Kirill pulls out the knife when

I'm a second away from coming. This time, I scream with frustration, and tears line my eyes.

"Stop it, please," I cry out.

Sweat coats my skin, my nipples hurt so bad due to the sexual stimulation, and my core screams for a release that he won't offer me.

And since my hands are bound, I can't do it myself either, so I'm completely at his nonexistent mercy.

Kirill's face turns stone-cold as he teases my clit with his fingers and thrusts the knife's handle inside again. "You're the only one who can stop this by giving me his fucking name. The more you resist, the more creative I become about denying you one orgasm after the other. I know your body, Sasha, even better than you do. I know when you're about to come. Your breaths are faster, your neck flushes red, and your hips involuntarily jerk. I'll let you come close to the peak but never reach it. I'll do this again and again and fucking again until you give me what I want."

And then he proceeds to do just that.

Until I think I'm going to die.

TWELVE

Kirill

I'VE NEVER EXPERIENCED FRUSTRATION THAT'S SO CLOSE to the level of self-fucking-destruction I'm feeling now.

I had to physically remove myself from the room before I did something I'd regret for the rest of my life.

My steps are controlled, but they hide a raging fucking war. Once I'm in the bathroom, I splash my face with cold water a few times, but it does nothing to kill the flames that are devouring me from the inside out.

I stare at my reflection in the mirror and barely resist the urge to drive my fist into it. That would be no different than spiraling back into bad habits.

Namely the younger, less balanced version of myself.

The man who stares back at me overflows with negative fucked-up energy that could be used as ammunition for a weapon of mass destruction.

I had everything I fucking wanted. Not because of privilege. In fact, being born into this family has worked against me all my life. The only reason I got to where I am is because of pure fucking will.

The best way to get what you wish for is to block all other paths so that those against you have no choice but to turn to you.

And I succeeded, again and again.

Except with the fucking woman tied to my bed.

I whirl around and head back into the bedroom. Sasha lies in the middle of her shredded clothes and spots of her arousal. Her skin is sweaty, red, and smeared with droplets of her blood and wetness that I made sure to tease her whole body with.

There are also marks from my knife on her breasts and stomach because I couldn't resist putting them there.

Currently, a toy teases her clit on a low setting, so she's close but will never get there.

Did I get this toy on impulse a few weeks ago? Yes, I did. But maybe it wasn't impulse, after all, since I knew all along that I would be torturing the fuck out of her.

I just didn't know that she wouldn't budge. Not even a little. Not even close.

I used every single method under the sun and denied her more orgasms than should be legal. Yet this little fucking shit only shook her head while sobbing and begging for a release.

Then, when I continued depriving her, she started calling me names and cursing me six ways to Sunday while trying to dry hump my fingers.

Now, she's in the acceptance stage. Her head lolls to the side, sweat coats her skin, and her nipples are as hard as diamond pebbles.

Her expressive eyes are half closed, and her dry lips are parted. Despite giving her water now and again, she's still on the verge of dehydration.

I grab a bottle on my way to her and lift her head. "Open."

She's like a doll in my hands, so weak and light that she could be broken with the snap of a finger, but she still glares and purses her lips shut.

"You feel victimized?" I close her nose, so she has no choice but to breathe through her mouth, then I pour the water in. "None of this would've happened if you'd just given me the fucking name."

She chokes, and water splatters out of her nose, but she does drink most of it.

"Does this fucker mean so much to you that you would go to this length to protect him?"

She purses her lips shut again and looks the other way.

My fingers wrap around her throat, and I have to mentally remind myself that I can't snap it as I force her attention back to me. "I told you to look at me when I'm talking to you."

I retrieve the toy's remote from my pocket and push the setting higher. A whole-body shiver goes through her, and her breathing starts to quicken.

She shakes her head, fresh tears rimming her eyes.

"The more you choose him, the meaner I treat you. The harder you defy me, the colder I become. You should know by now that I always, without a doubt, get what I fucking want."

She lets out a whimper. "Kirill…"

"What? You have that name for me?"

The fucking woman shakes her head and I struggle to remember why she's not six feet under right now.

"I thought you wanted us to go back to before Russia, but that won't be possible if you have another fucking man in your heart, Sasha."

"It's not…" Her voice is small and shaky. "It's not a lover…"

"If he's not, then give me his fucking name."

"I can't…" She shudders, and her hips jerk and lift off the bed.

I wrench the toy out. She sobs and screams, her nails digging into the belt's leather.

Her legs rub together in a hopeless attempt to trigger the orgasm, but nothing comes.

"Do you want to stay tied to my bed for the foreseeable future? Because I can make that happen."

"Just kill me..." she murmurs through tears. "If you can't trust me anymore, get rid of me."

Those words fill my mind with murderous scenarios, but none of them include her.

Only her lover.

"Where's the fun in that?" I tighten my hold on her neck. "You think you can escape me, Sasha? You think there will be a day when you'll be out of my sight and back with him? I'll always find you, and when I do, I'll kill him right in front of your eyes."

"Fuck you..." she whispers, and her lids close.

When she fell asleep the previous times, I woke her up with some form of sexual stimulation. I'm still tempted to do that just because she cursed me for threatening her lover.

But I don't.

One, she's past her limits.

Two, I can't guarantee I won't leave a permanent mark if she continues refusing to tell me the fucker's name.

I tried finding it on my own, both through Viktor's investigation of the Belsky Organization and even digging into her past.

I actually did that after she wanted to come with me to New York, but since she's using a fake last name, it only comes with a fake background that the army believed. Or more like, she bribed her way into the institution, which isn't a surprise considering her previous rich-lady status.

And that leaves only one way to find out about her lover's name. Through her.

It's a problem when she's completely refusing to cooperate.

I remove the belt from around her wrists and massage the red marks left by the leather.

A soft moan leaves her lips, and my cock hardens to a painful degree. Fuck.

I should've fucked her before I came up with this torture method.

Or better yet, fucked her while I tortured her.

I went celibate for months before she came along. Searching for a drama-free hole was a hassle that I didn't want to take part in unless absolutely necessary.

But being celibate after being in Sasha's pussy exactly two hundred twenty-seven times has been pure fucking torture.

What? I didn't mean to count, but I might have grown obsessed with it and done it unconsciously.

My fingers linger on the slits of red on her pale skin. Is it fucked up that I want to put more marks on her so the world can see who she fucking belongs to? Probably.

That doesn't mean the thought disappears, though.

Her head lolls to the side and falls on my chest. Fucking fuck.

For a second, I forget that I'm mad at this woman. No, mad is an understatement. I'm livid and so close to losing my fucking mind whenever I think she has someone else.

Those thoughts make me consider setting the whole of Russia on fire just to weed him out.

Such crazy, completely impossible thoughts haven't left me alone since I heard her telling him on the phone that she loved him and that she'd go back to him.

As if I would ever let that happen.

Add the sense of betrayal and being shot, and I'm spiraling down a path even I don't like.

Not one bit.

I stroke my finger marks on her neck, and she leans her cheek on my palm, snuggling close as if I'm her safe haven.

More like, I'm her custom-made hell.

As I wipe the droplets of sweat off her face, the name of the abyss I've fallen into punches me in the fucking gut.

Obsession.

That's what it's called, isn't it? This is what it feels like to have the need to own someone when I've never thought about that concept before. This is also why I'm plagued by images of complete wrath if anyone dares to take this woman away from me.

And that includes her.

I meant it earlier—if she continues to not choose me, I'll be the cruelest monster in her life. I'll completely destroy her until one of us dies.

And that's dangerous. Not only for her, but for me as well.

Because she's starting to look like a fucking weakness. She's someone who can be used against me to put me on my knees.

And I don't do weaknesses.

I've always been the type to play, never to be played with. I've never gotten too close, never revealed my cards or allowed emotions into my decision-making process. So imagine my fucking annoyance when I realized that the very damn foundations of my being were being shaken by none other than an enemy.

And Sasha *is* an enemy. I might not treat her like I do my traditional enemies—which is usually to kill them or manipulate them, then kill them—but she's not someone I'd trust.

She has relations with the Belsky Organization, and while I have no idea why they want me dead, I know they're after me.

And until I can completely turn her to my side, meaning she'll hide nothing from me, she'll have to stay in the gray area.

Now, if my cock would understand that fucking her is reckless, that would be wonderful.

It doesn't help that her naked body is splayed out in front of me, tempting me to take her and remind her exactly who she belongs to.

Down, boy. We'll have our time.

I lift her enough to remove the damp cover—along with the sex toys, the knife, and my belt—from beneath her, and then I place her on the clean, dry sheet.

She whines in an adorable way that doesn't help with the state of my starving cock, then turns on her side with a sigh.

My self-control has been tested today more times than in my whole fucking life. It takes everything in me to go to the bathroom and place a few towels in a bowl of hot water. When I return, she's on her back again, every inch of her naked skin laid out for me.

I stare down at my cock that's becoming a fucking nuisance. "Really, now? Since when are we into somnophilia?"

The only reply I get is an antagonizing erection.

I think of babies, the faces of people shot in the forehead with a shotgun, and Yulia.

The last one does it.

I sit on the side of the bed and start by wiping Sasha's face, then her neck—lingering for a bit too long on my finger marks. Then I clean the blood off her chest and stomach. After that, I take extra care of cleaning her unsatisfied pussy. She moans when I wipe her folds, and that threatens to wake my cock after I finally put him to sleep, so I move on to her hands. She injured a few of her fingers with her nails during the struggle earlier. I stroke those and then move to the red stripes left by the belt.

After I finish, I do it again, touching every nook, every slope, and the scar the bullet left on the back of her shoulder. She has a few other scars, too—some are on her stomach, but the majority are on her hands and feet.

Such a soft body wasn't made for the military or being a body-guard, but then again, she looks like she enjoys it.

Not so much the military, since she always seemed to be on a mission there. Ever since we came to New York, however, she's more carefree, and I catch her grinning whenever she finishes her perfect sheet—one of the few who manage to do it.

She shivers, and I realize that I might have been at this for way too long.

I retrieve a fresh blanket and cover her with it.

A few seconds pass as I watch her sleep.

You know what? Fuck it.

I remove my shirt and pants and lie on my side to have a better look at her. I don't even sleep, so the fact that I stripped down for that is weird in and of itself. I'm even laying my head on the pillow and shit.

The view is fucking worth it.

I place my hand on her tit and start to tease her nipple just because I obviously have no fucking control. But then I feel her steady heartbeat and a distant episode comes back to me.

It was that time in the car when she sang to me and made me feel her heartbeat. My palm stretches over her breast, and I start to listen. I'm also about to close my eyes.

But before I do that, Sasha turns to her side and glues her chest to mine. Her heartbeat collides with my hyper one as she snuggles her face in my chest and throws her leg over mine.

Fuck.

Now, I won't move even if I have to.

∽

"Help me, Kirill!"

"Don't worry, Kara. I'm here," I say in a broken voice that I wouldn't believe if I weren't here.

I'm hanging by a cord that's cutting through my wrists with every passing second, and the worst part is that Karina has to watch me being tortured for fun by our fucking father's men.

"Kirill!" She screams hauntingly until her voice turns raw and hoarse. But the men who are holding her back don't let her move an inch.

"I'll be okay," I croak and manage to smile, but that triggers the pain in my swollen lips and eyes, and I cough.

The man who was tasked with beating me up slaps me across the face, then punches me in the stomach. I spit out blood as my vision turns blurry.

Oh, fuck. I think I'm going to pass out.

The last thing I see is Karina's shocked expression, her soft face going into shock before she shrieks, "Kiriiill!"

I startle awake at the soft touch of two hands at my cheek.

"Kirill!"

"Kirill!"

"Can you hear me?"

Through the slits of my opening eyes, I see Sasha perching over me, tears clinging to her lashes and her brows creasing in a line.

Two thoughts come to mind.

One, I fell into a deep sleep around her again. In fact, it was so deep that I had a nightmare about a distant memory.

Two, Sasha must've witnessed something that made her this distressed.

Fuck.

This is exactly why I don't like sleeping.

"Kirill?" she asks in a low, haunted voice that's so similar to Karina's that day.

I slowly sit up, and she lets out a breath as she begrudgingly releases me. I want to grab her hands and put them back on my face.

Instead, I stand up and stride to the minibar in my room. I catch the clock in my peripheral vision. Six in the morning. I actually slept for a few hours.

What the fuck is even happening to me lately?

I pour myself a glass of cognac and gulp it in one go, then pour another. There's a rustle from the bed before Sasha wraps the blanket around her and joins me. Her eyes are glittery, but they're more green than brown, so that's a good sign.

"You okay?" she asks carefully.

"Couldn't be better." I start to drink the second glass, but she gently grips my hand, making me pause.

"You thrashed in your sleep and wouldn't wake up no matter how many times I called your name. Was it a nightmare?"

"What if it was?"

"I know how gruesome those get. I don't think drinking helps."

"We'll find out then." I twist my hand free of hers, down the second glass, and pour a third.

This time, she snatches it and gently places it on the table. "I know something better than alcohol."

"Doubt it."

And then the fucking woman opens the blanket and wraps her arms and the blanket around both of us. She's hugging me, I realize. What in the ever...

"You let me hug you when I was mourning Nadia and Nicholas, and that's my favorite form of comfort. I know it's not yours, but I'm giving it to you anyway. Maybe one day, you'll come to appreciate it, too."

My shoulders drop, and part of me wants to throw her away, but the other fucking part wants to cage her in my arms and never let go.

So I just remain still, not giving in to either.

She pulls away slightly and freezes, then runs her fingers over the new scars on my chest, courtesy of her fucking lover.

Scars I wouldn't have if it weren't for her.

I'm about to restart the death circle of rage and anger, but then she stares up at me with shiny eyes and sniffles. "I'm so sorry."

"If you're that sorry, tell me the fucker's name."

"I can't do that, but I can make up for these shots for the rest of my life."

"You'll stay here for the rest of your life?"

"If...you want me to, yes, I will."

A sense of raging possessiveness grabs hold of me, and I pull her close to me with a hand glued to the small of her back. "You will stay."

"I will."

"That wasn't a question. It was a statement."

She smiles a little, but she nods. "As long as you don't erase me."

I never did. Erasing her is nowhere near possible. I did a perfect job at pretending she wasn't there, though.

That was easier than replaying everything that happened in Russia.

"That depends on your performance." I release her, and she pauses before wrapping the blanket around herself.

"Speaking of performance." She clears her throat. "Let's talk about that reward."

"What about it?"

"I want to become your senior guard."

"You *what?*"

"Senior guard. Viktor's current position."

"He will kill you."

"I don't care. You promised me a reward, and I already took your punishment, so you have to give me what I want."

"You'll have to share that position with Viktor."

"No, I want to be on my own."

"Not possible. I trust him more than you, and, therefore, he can't be removed from his post."

Her lips push forward in a scowl or a pout, I don't know which, but I want to lick her lips with my tongue anyway.

"Fine." She lifts her chin. "One day, you'll trust me more than him."

Highly doubt it.

But I give her hope anyway. This might be the best way to have her lower her guard.

THIRTEEN

Sasha

MAYBE I LOST MY MIND.

There's no other explanation to what I told Kirill a week ago after he proceeded to deny me one orgasm after the other in the worst form of torture I've ever experienced.

But when I woke up to find myself enveloped in his arms, all that discomfort vanished. However, the moment I actually felt strongly about making this decision was when he not only let me hug him, but also hugged me back.

Well, he only wrapped his arm around my lower back, but that counts.

Those aren't the only reasons I did it, though. After my grandmother and uncle disowned me, Kirill is the one who gave me purpose. Yes, it came with pain and heartbreak, but it was purpose all the same.

Is it a surprise that I pledged my loyalty to him for life? In a way, no, since that's exactly what I've been doing since I came here with him after he was shot.

And who knows? Maybe in a couple of months when his trust is restored, I can confirm that he has no involvement in my family's deaths.

He's just not the type.

So I scrapped my previous plan that entailed sneaking around his office. From now on, I'll be direct and refrain from using any deceitful methods.

On one hand, I have no clue what else I can do. But on the other, it feels like the best decision I've ever made. Kirill doesn't only make me feel like the woman I yearn to be again, but he also makes me *feel*.

So much, it's painful.

Uncomfortable, too.

Sometimes, I think it'd be better if I just removed myself from his side. Maybe I'd fly back to Russia or a different country altogether and start over again.

But the mere thought of separating myself from him physically hurts and I have to take a few moments to recover from its imaginary impact.

"Move it, Lipovsky."

I stand in front of the car and stare at Viktor, who's been glaring at me ever since Kirill announced that we're sharing the senior guard position.

To say he doesn't like it would be an understatement. He asked Kirill if I'm threatening him with something—as if I could ever do that.

The others, though, took the news well. Actually, Maksim threw a party for me a few days ago and nearly got himself killed by Yuri when he tried to make him dance.

Even Karina showed up wearing the most beautiful lace dress and gave me a gift—a stunning coat that I will only wear on special occasions.

She told her brother that she still hasn't given up on me and will one day have me as her guard.

Kirill, on the other hand, wasn't impressed with the whole party thing and kept glaring at anyone who held me by the shoulder or bro-hugged me—mainly Maksim. He even retreated to his office early and spent the entire night there, telling us not to disturb him.

Viktor, who currently looks like he's plotting my death, barely showed his face that night and only came to shadow Kirill.

Now, we're standing in front of the main car while Kirill, Damien, and Rai are inside a traditional Japanese restaurant for a meeting with the higher-ups of the Yakuza.

Since Kirill will be leaving with Damien in the same car, only one of us gets to ride in the front. Usually, that's Viktor, because he makes everyone follow his order.

"You, move it," I say casually. "You can ride with Maksim."

He steps forward so that he's towering over me. "The fuck did you just say?"

"You heard me just fine."

His eyes blaze as he glares down on me. "Move it. That's an order."

"You have no right to give me orders anymore. I'm in the same position as you."

"Listen here, you little shit. I don't know what you threatened Boss with to get here, but I will find out and get you exiled from the fucking country."

"Are you insinuating that Boss is weak and is prone to be threatened?" I say with a fake alarmed tone.

"I didn't say that."

"But that's the impression I got. I'm sure it's what he'll get, too, if he hears about this after he specifically told you there was no threatening involved. Are you, by any chance, calling Boss a liar?"

"That's not what I said."

"I can't guarantee to keep this bit of information to myself." I pat his shoulder. "But since we've been through thick and thin together, I'll pretend I heard nothing as long as you back the fuck off."

His shoulders tense beneath my touch and I think he'll punch me or something, but his palpable anger slowly subsides.

"This isn't over, you little fuck."

I make a face at his back and go to escort Kirill out of the restaurant. Since this meeting was requested by the Yakuza, there's an army of their guards around the property. We got a copy of their security plan, so we know the best exits in case of an attack.

I nod at Damien's senior guard, Vladislav, and he nods back as we head in the same direction. Where his boss is impulsive and trigger happy, Vladislav is as calm as a mountain. And no, it's not the same stoic mountain that Viktor resembles.

Vladislav is down to earth, wise, and has a silent presence. I'm going to guess he's one of the main reasons Damien hasn't already gotten himself killed.

Rai's guard, Katya, silently joins us. I've always liked her, though I've never shown it due to the obvious animosity between her boss and mine.

Like me, she's a girl who's making her way in a man's world. Rai, who's a huge advocate of women in the organization, personally handpicked her and helped make her this powerful.

The only difference between Katya and me is that she doesn't hide the fact that she's a woman. Yes, she gets shit about it from everyone since she's the only female guard, but she just ignores them and does her thing.

I wish I had that luxury. If I'd met Kirill as a woman, would he have let me be his female guard?

What the hell am I talking about? A leader in this misogynistic organization wouldn't let a woman protect him. He'd be seen as weak and hiding behind her skirt.

It's different in Rai's case because she's a woman herself, so having a female guard isn't as weirdly viewed.

Besides, if I had presented myself as a woman, I probably

wouldn't have met him in the army and none of this twisted fate would've happened.

Once Katya speeds ahead of us, probably to avoid being with us as much as possible, Vladislav falls in step beside me. "How many cars do you have?"

"Two including the main one. You?"

"Same. But we didn't know about this meeting, so we have six men in total."

"Eight for us."

"You have any idea where your boss is taking mine?"

"I have the same information you do."

He stops and fixates me with his blank expression. "I don't like this, Aleksander. I don't like being kept in the dark."

"You think I'm a fan?" All I know is that Kirill received a huge backlash from Juan's cartel after the failure of the last mission.

We're having problems, and as a result, the shipment has been postponed indefinitely. Juan is a very careful man, probably because he's been betrayed more than anyone can count. So despite Kirill's reassurances that the security would be doubled, Juan wouldn't hear of it.

Of course, no one in the organization knows about this. Kirill merely told them that there's a delay in the upcoming shipment, but that it's minor and nothing to worry about.

I'm guessing he has something on Damien and will use it to get him to his side, but I have no clue how he intends to do that or when.

All I know is that it's crucial Damien joins us instead of Rai, who's coming on strong in the race toward the throne, especially since her marriage. It doesn't help that she's been particularly antagonistic toward Kirill.

"Two high-risk meetings in one day isn't something I approve of," Vladislav continues.

"I'm the same." I'm just praying for this day to end already so I can be alone with Kirill.

Well, not in that sense, but I'm his night guard again and I get to sit opposite him while he works, then eventually falls asleep.

This morning, I found myself on his bed while he was getting dressed. I might have pretended to still be asleep so I could watch the erotic show like a creep.

It doesn't matter how many times I see him naked, he still has the same effect on me as he did the first time.

Only now, I get this squeeze of pain whenever I see the bullet scars on his chest. I think I'll have this sense of guilt for the rest of my life.

Vladislav merely gives me a look that says, *This is all because of your boss*, then heads inside. I catch a glimpse of Kirill stepping out of the restaurant with Damien, who's clearly not amused.

Jesus.

How is it possible that I'm only focused on Kirill as if the whole world around him doesn't exist?

All I can see is his impressive physique and his long legs eating up the distance to where the cars are.

I follow the others but stop when I catch something in my peripheral vision.

Rai freezes for a moment in front of a kid with dark blond hair and green eyes.

"Auntie…?" he calls in a brittle voice, but she's completely out of sorts. A look of subtle panic covers her features, but it soon disappears when a man carries the child and apologizes to her as he takes him back into the restaurant.

I walk backward for a moment, my eyes meeting Rai's for a fraction of a second before I look ahead.

There's a story between her and that kid, a story that I could use to protect Kirill if she attempts to tell the others that she caught him with a 'man' or that he's gay.

I catch up with the others as Kirill and Damien get in the back of the car.

Vladislav insists that Damien's driver substitutes for Yuri. Either that or he substitutes for me, so I go with the former, despite the discomfort at having to trust someone else other than Yuri with the driving.

Rai sprints in front of me and starts to shove herself into the back seat before I can close the door.

"What the fuck are you doing?" Kirill snaps at her.

"Take me back with you."

"You have your own car."

"It's broken down. Ruslan is trying to fix it."

"Do I look like a taxi to you?"

"Well, you could be."

"Leave, Rai." Damien takes a sip from the bottle of vodka he brought along. "Kirill and I have a meeting."

"Then do it after you drop me off," she says.

Kirill shrugs. "Or I can just throw you out."

"You just wasted a minute. We would've arrived faster if we'd taken off already. Besides…Abe told me something after you left."

"Who cares what that delusional old man says?" Damien swallows another gulp.

Kirill pauses before motioning at the driver to go. I look back at Rai, then immediately stare ahead. It's better not to get her suspicious.

The car rolls down the street as we sit in relative silence. I'm still uncomfortable about this unexpected change of events. Like Vladislav, I'm wary about anything that doesn't go according to plan. It started after that army mission in which we lost most of our men.

"What did Abe say?" Kirill asks.

"It's about Damien." She peeks at him. "Don't you want to know?"

"I do want to know why you said I'll think about it. You want to marry me off, Rai?"

"If it benefits the brotherhood, why not settle down?"

"Settle down? What are you, my mother?"

"First of all, eww. Second of all, just go with it."

"Just like you went with your own marriage? It's so boring if we're all so sacrificial like you, Rayenka."

"Does that mean you won't do it?"

"I don't see why I should."

"You can't disrespect Abe that way, Damien. He's one of the strongest allies we can have."

Kirill adjusts his glasses. "And he will become our worst enemy if this bull kills his daughter in one of his violent episodes."

"You hurt women?" she all but snaps at Damien.

He continues drinking from his vodka before he whispers something in her ear.

She pushes him away. "You will control that side of you and treat Abe's daughter well, and if I find out you hurt any woman, you'll have me to answer to."

A grin curls his lips. "Will it be kinky?"

So Damien is getting married. Good luck to the unlucky lady.

Maybe one of us should do her a favor and tell her to run away from home or something. That's better than sealing her fate with a crazy man like Damien.

He's in an awfully bad mood and that's been the case ever since Kirill cornered him in the Pakhan's house earlier and told him something that made him agree to accompany us now.

That's probably also why Vladislav has been glaring at me—because I was tasked with keeping him preoccupied while Kirill did his thing.

Rai, however, was never part of the plan, which is why

Kirill is annoyed. He doesn't show much, but I can sense it with the frequent amount he's adjusting his glasses.

I stare at him through the rearview mirror and our eyes meet for a fraction of a second.

It's brief, nearly unnoticeable, but my whole world catches fire and I can feel the heat creeping up my cheek.

Shit.

How can he look at me in the same intense way he does during sex? It's no different than being naked in public.

Not that everyone recognizes that look, but still.

It's a major distraction in a possibly dangerous situation.

I clear my throat and stare ahead to concentrate better.

Which is kind of impossible, considering I'm sexually starved. Aside from that stupid torture session where he fucked me with all the objects in his nightstand and denied me the pleasure that comes with it, he hasn't touched me again.

Yesterday, I came out of the shower dressed only in a towel and he looked at me as if he was angry.

No shit. It was like he hated seeing me that way or something, and I wordlessly headed to the closet and changed as fast as I could while biting back my frustration. My things are in the room I share with Yuri, but recently, Kirill has been allowing me to bring a change of clothes when I'm stationed as the night guard.

He doesn't like to look at me, though.

Maybe he doesn't want me anymore.

Maybe the sense of betrayal he has toward me is overshadowing everything else.

All of a sudden, the car swerves and comes to a screeching halt. The force is so strong that Rai bumps against the back of my seat.

"What is it?" Kirill asks the driver in Russian.

"Don't know, sir. There's something in the road—"

His words cut off when a shot hits his chest—straight through the bulletproof glass.

I don't think about it as I pull out my gun.

We all rush out of the car as bullets fly everywhere.

I meet Vladislav's and Viktor's glances with the same thought.

We're under attack and we need to protect our bosses.

The three of us and Maksim rush to the front line, facing soldiers who look like an army of ants. From their words and the orders shouted, they're Albanians.

They're the last thing we need at the moment.

Yes, we have disagreements with them, but I didn't think they'd go as far as ambushing us in the middle of the road.

I catch a glimpse behind me, and after I make sure Kirill is taking cover behind one of the cars with Damien and Rai, I run to the front.

"Don't be a fucking martyr." I hear him screaming in my head like he did a long time ago, but I don't stop.

I told him I'd offer my life in return for the shots he took because of me, and I meant it.

My priority is to protect him at any cost.

The bad news is that we're outnumbered. Hugely so.

And because of that, we have to count our bullets. We hit a few, but I'm not as good with a handgun as I am with a sniper rifle. I still injure or kill anyone I shoot. Better than Viktor anyway.

He runs out of bullets first and jumps behind a nearby car for cover.

It's only Vladislav and me now, but we're running out, too.

Shit.

Shit.

This situation is a lot more dire than I originally thought. If they get us, it'll be child's play to kill Kirill and Damien, who I'm sure are the reason behind this whole attack.

With a battle cry, Vladislav and I eliminate seven of them combined, but that leaves me without any more bullets.

My shoulders drop as I stare back at Kirill, who's shooting his own gun.

The world pauses for a moment. There are no more screams, shouts, or sounds of guns being fired. It's just me and him suspended in the middle of nowhere. I promised that I'll protect him with my life, but I just failed miserably.

"Forgive me," I mouth in Russian.

"No!" he roars.

The palpable emotions ring in my head and I want to stop him. I have to, because he's running toward me and he'll get himself killed.

But before I can move, something hard hits my head.

Everything turns black.

FOURTEEN

Sasha

SOMETHING DRIPS ON MY FACE.

I blink my eyes open and they fill with a red mist.

Blood.

Blood...

And more blood...

No, no, please.

A pool of it surrounds me while I lie on the ground and the stench of death fills my nostrils. I look up and a scream bubbles in my throat at the sight of bodies hanging from the sky.

"Sasha..." a haunted voice calls.

"Sachenka..."

"Malyshka..."

My mom.

Oh, God.

"Mama? Where are you?" I shout as loud as possible. I try to get up, but it's like I'm strapped to the ground with invisible wires. I thrash and kick, but my limbs don't move.

"Malyshka…" she calls again, her tone growing more haunted. "Malyshka."

"Mama!!" I scream until my voice turns hoarse. "I'm here, Mama! I'm down here!"

"Sachenka…"

"Papa?" I choke on my tears. "Is that you, Papa?"

A shadow falls over me and I sob as his face perches over me and then my mother's follows. "Malyshka."

"Mama! Papa!" I try to reach a hand out, but I can't move.

Mama drops to her haunches beside me and strokes my cheek. "You've grown so much, Malyshka."

"Yeah, I have…" I choke, unable to articulate words or all the emotions I want to blurt out.

"I'm so proud of how well you've survived."

"Mama…"

"Find your brother, Sachenka," my father says faintly, almost as if he's speaking from underground. "You need Anton and he needs you."

"But I have no clue where he is. It's like he completely disappeared off the face of the earth."

"Find Anton!" he orders in a harsh tone and I flinch.

Mama smiles with tears in her eyes, but they soon turn to blood. A slit appears in Papa's neck and then his head falls to the side, grotesquely dislocated from his body. My mother's eyes shoot out a fountain of blood and then they both explode into a foam of red mist.

"Nooo!" I screech as I'm jerked down to the pool of blood.

My eyes shoot open and all the red disappears. I don't relax, though. I still can't move. At least, not like I usually can.

If it were any other time, I'd be able to jump to my feet and inspect the situation, but right now, I can barely turn my head to the side or lift my arm.

I'm lying on my stomach, and the fractured concrete beneath me freezes my limbs despite my layers of clothes.

Gray stone walls surround me, and the smell of urine reeks from the corners.

On the other side of the room sits an old rusty bed that's covered with a yellow sheet that could also be the source of the pungent smell.

There's a metal door with thick bars. If I can get to it, I should be able to pick the lock with my knife. Only, I don't feel its holster strapped to my calf, which means I was searched for weapons before I was thrown into this fucking hole.

But even if I had my knife, I'm unable to move, let alone pick a lock.

The only explanation for this loss of strength is that I was also injected with something.

As my unfocused eyes move around the room, I'm shocked to find a woman lying next to me. Although her face is covered by her blonde mane of hair, I can tell by the familiar dress that it's Rai. Damn it. This means both of us were kidnapped by our attackers—the Albanians.

A sense of terror grips hold of me and I find it hard to breathe properly. Did they possibly reach Kirill after they hit me?

I internally shake my head. There's no way in hell he let them get him. It's Kirill, after all, so he must've gotten out of it alive. No, not only alive, but also unscathed. They couldn't have killed him.

He has to be safe.

Using all the strength I can muster, I push myself off the floor but soon sag into a sitting position against the wall.

Something burns in my arm and when I look down, I see a tear along the sleeves of my jacket and shirt. I must've been grazed by a bullet. But that's not what has me panicking.

It's that I only have access to ten percent of my energy, and most of that is being used to breathe and try not to swallow my tongue that feels too big for my mouth.

I tap my pockets and, as expected, don't find my phone.

My chin trembles and I think I'll turn into a crybaby again, as is usually the case whenever Kirill is involved.

What if he was shot during the attack today, and this time, I'm not there to help him?

It was only days ago that I promised to be by his side and protect him with my life, but I'm here, alive, and he's not.

I stare at the door. I need to get out of here, but how will I do that when I can barely move?

Besides, why did they kidnap me? It makes sense for them to take Rai since she can be used to threaten the Pakhan, but what about me?

Did they do this to threaten Kirill with me?

That theory doesn't make sense for two reasons. One, Kirill is known to have no weaknesses—except his alleged homosexuality that Rai is threatening him with. Two, he is not close with anyone in his family—except Karina—but they don't know that.

It's not possible that they'd use me to threaten him when I'm just a guard. Unless they had someone watching and reporting his daily life to whoever is the leader of these guys?

That doesn't make sense.

But still, that's the theory I want to believe. I loathe the prospect of being used to twist Kirill's arm, but if they kidnapped me to threaten him, then that means he's alive and I should stop thinking about the worst-case scenario.

A moan of pain comes from Rai before she struggles to get up like I did earlier. Her hair that's usually very well put together has several strands escaping on the sides. Her makeup is highly recommended, though, because it's mostly stayed in place except for some smudges of black beneath her eyes.

"It's useless," I say in a quiet voice.

Rai startles before she looks up, weariness covering her expression.

"They injected us with something," I continue. "I don't know what it is, but it's robbing me of energy."

She attempts to stand up, only to fall back again with a resounding thud.

"Better save your energy, Miss." I speak in my polite 'male' voice.

"Shit," she heaves.

"Shit, indeed."

She glimpses at me in that inquisitive way in which she watches everyone and everything. She's known to be heartless, and while I don't really like her due to the threat she poses to Kirill, I respect her no-bullshit personality.

She motions at my arm. "Did you lose a lot of blood?"

I look down to see what she's talking about. In my overthinking about Kirill's state, I actually forgot I was wounded. "No. This should be fine."

"How did you end up here, too?"

"They took me in place of Boss."

"Kirill?"

My lips start to tremble at the renewed thought of him getting hurt, but I clamp them shut. "Yes."

"Why would they want to take Kirill?"

"I'm not sure. I just knew I had to protect him."

She pauses, looking at me peculiarly for a second before a bright gleam covers her eyes. "We need to come up with a plan to escape."

I nod. "Our best option is if one of us causes a diversion and the other escapes."

"I will do it."

"No. You're the Pakhan's grandniece. I'm disposable, so I'll do it."

"Even though you're Kirill's guard, you're not disposable. None of our men are, even if you hate me."

That catches me completely by surprise and I have to swallow a few times before I speak. "I don't hate you."

"Your boss does."

"That's because you're threatening him, Miss."

"Only to protect myself. I won't cause any of you harm if you don't cause me harm."

"Does that mean you're not..." I clear my throat. "You know, against his preferences?"

"Why would I be? They're his preferences and no one's opinion matters. As I said, I will only use his sexuality against him if he threatens me. I would rather not, but that's the only thing I've got on him, considering how closed off he is. If you tell me something else...I can ditch it."

"Nice try, Miss." My lips twitch in a smile. This woman really deserves to be on the board and within the inner circle.

"Doesn't hurt to try." She mirrors my smile. "Let's escape first, then we'll talk."

I attempt to come up with a way she can create a diversion. The pins keeping her French twist in place can help me in picking the lock—

The door is thrown open, hitting the wall with a bang. Rai and I both go still. As an unspoken agreement, we don't attempt to escape. We need to preserve our energy for when we have a real chance.

Five muscular men with angular features waltz inside as if this is their show and this god-awful room is their stage. They're wearing black leather jackets and pants, as if they're part of an MC club.

A bald guy with a scar that slashes down his head to his eyelid—definitely their leader—heads in Rai's direction with a sleazy look in his eyes.

"We should start with this one. You'll scream for your uncle and husband, won't you, kitten?" He has a thick accent that's more East European than Russian.

Two of his men pounce on Rai, each grabbing her by an arm. She thrashes and kicks, but due to whatever drug they injected us with, she does little to no damage. They laugh at her, speaking among themselves in Albanian.

I jerk in her direction, kicking one in the shin but the other two men push me to my knees and one of them applies pressure on my injury. Pain explodes through my arm and I sink my teeth in my lower lip to stop the sound that's attempting to escape.

"Get her on her knees," the leader orders. "I want those lips around my cock."

Shit.

The man pushes Rai into position, and one of them even adjusts his crotch like a pig.

The leader waltzes toward her while unbuttoning his pants, then he pulls out his short, thick dick and jams it against her pursed lips.

Rai glares up at him as if he's nothing more than the dirt beneath her shoes.

His eyes bulge red and he motions at the men holding me. One of them drives his fist into my stomach and it feels like he's rearranged my guts. A groan escapes me as I drop to the floor. Then the two assholes push me upright and the other one digs his fingers into my injury.

I grunt as it pulses with intense pain.

"For every second you don't suck me off like a good whore, that girly faggot will be punched." The leader speaks with sickening arrogance. "How long until he dies, I wonder?"

The men punch me again and again. Blood explodes from my mouth and I feel like vomiting my guts out.

A feeling of frustration whirls through me like a storm. Just why the fuck did I have to lose my energy now? I'm virtually useless.

"Wait a second." One of the men crouches in front of me and slaps his palm to my chest.

No, no...

Otherworldly energy grabs hold of me and I use everything I have to buck and try to kick them away.

While his friend holds me in place, the one in front of me pulls down my pants and boxers.

Please no...

I catch a glimpse of Rai forcing herself to look at me. Pain lingers in her eyes, but she wants to offer me any form of consolation, even if she's also on the verge of being assaulted herself.

I go crazy in my attempts to stop them from undressing me. I kick and thrash. I try to bite, too, but it's impossible to cause any form of injury when I barely have any strength.

Before I know it, I'm half naked in front of their greedy eyes.

"Fucking shit. Jackpot, Boss." The man who undressed me grins. "It's a woman."

I make eye contact with Rai, who can see the evidence of my actual gender, then lower my head, a tear escaping my eye.

I've screwed up everything. Me. Kirill. The whole of the Morozov carefully built influence.

"Have fun with her while I have fun with this one." The leader smiles and turns his attention to Rai.

The two guards push me down on the floor. One stands by my head and hold my hands and the other parts my legs.

Fuck them. No one but Kirill will touch me. No fucking one.

I stare at Rai, only to find her searching my gaze.

Now.

She opens her mouth, but once he stuffs his dick inside, she bites down so hard, the leader howls as blood explodes on her face.

The guard kicks her, so she releases the boss as I try to fight the one who's hovering over me and pushing his rotten dick against my mouth.

A sense of panic floods my throat as reality sinks in. I'll never forgive myself if I don't stop this assault.

Rai kicks the one who's on top of me and snatches his gun. I hit the other one, then pull him down in a headlock and steal his gun as I break his neck with my arm.

Fuck you, asshole.

A rush of energy surges through me as Rai and I shoot whoever we can. She gets the leader in the dick—I should've done that with the other bastard.

I pull up my pants and zip them up. Once I'm decent, we cover each other on the way out.

Once we're out of the room, which appears to be in a huge basement, we head down a long hallway, looking back at any intersections in case one of them followed us.

Rai wipes the blood off her face with the back of her hand and steals a look at me. "Is your name Aleksander? Do you prefer I call you that?"

"It's Aleksandra." I lower my eyes.

"Thank you for helping me."

"Anytime."

We run as fast as we can down the hall. The drug is definitely starting to wear off, and the adrenaline helps, but we're nowhere near our full strength. In fact, it takes a lot of effort for me to stay focused while still running.

I have to shake my head now and again whenever the floor gets blurry.

A noise comes from upstairs and we hide on either side of a hallway that intersects the main one.

We shoot at the soldiers following us, and despite my dizzy state, I manage to kill two. However, I find myself in the same predicament as prior to my kidnapping—I'm running out of bullets. Rai wouldn't be any better.

And we need to get the hell out of here before they catch us again, because this time, with the damage we inflicted on their leader, they'll kill us, no questions asked.

Boom!

We freeze when what sounds like a bomb explodes near the stairs leading to the basement. Then a hail of gunfire follows.

The guys who were behind us disappear, and soon after, we hear Russian words and orders.

Oh, God.

I mirror Rai's smile when she looks at me. *We have backup.* Or she does because she's the Pakhan's grandniece.

Still covering each other, we slip out from behind the wall and head toward the commotion.

A lot of our, Damien's, and Kyle's men are shooting the whole place down. Even Damien has a machine gun with the ammunition slung across his body as if this is some sort of toy war.

But that's not what gets my attention.

It's Kirill.

He's on the front line, wearing a vest and leading Viktor, Yuri, Maksim and the guys I've grown to consider my family.

Kirill looks regal in his suit, despite the fact that it's a bit disheveled and droplets of blood smear his forehead.

He's here for me.

The fight leaves my shoulders and I want to fall to the ground and cry. No, I want to hug him and cry.

I run to him, ignoring everyone and everything in my path.

"Kirill," I call, but my voice is drowned out by the chaos.

He hears me, though, because his attention flies in my direction immediately. He sprints toward me, killing a man on the way. Blood splatters on his glasses and face, but he doesn't even blink as he continues jogging until he nearly runs into me.

"You okay?" he breathes the words out as if they're a prayer, and I want to close my eyes and listen to his voice all day.

I nod and lift a hand to touch his cheek, then I remember we're not alone and let it fall to my side. "You're alive."

"No one will be able to kill me. Or you. Hear me? No fucking one."

I swallow my tears.

I want to cry. I want to say how happy I am that he's here, but if I say that right now, I can't guarantee that I won't break down in sobs.

So I remain silent and concentrate on the battle.

Soon after, the Albanians are wiped out in droves, mostly by our men and Damien, who went completely rogue.

I only managed to shoot two before I was out of ammunition, so Kirill shielded me from the bullets. He physically pushed me behind him as if he were the bodyguard and I was under his protection.

As I took cover, I could only watch his back as the muscles contracted with each shot he fired.

"Stay beside me," he orders as he tells the others to clean up.

"That was over too soon," Damien complains. "They couldn't put up more of a fight or something?"

I try to help with the cleaning, but a glare from Kirill keeps me rooted in place. I look at Rai and she smiles.

I walk to her as her husband, Kyle, hugs her to his side. "Thank you."

"Likewise, Aleksander."

Warmth fills me at the way she respected my apparent gender. I was terrified she'd certainly use this information—that Kirill hired a female guard who's pretending to be male—to threaten him with, but she proved me wrong.

In more ways than one.

Maybe Rai isn't as bad as I initially thought.

"You can call me Sasha, Miss." I offer her a bow of respect. When I lift my head, my eyes clash with Kirill's icy ones. He's wiping the blood off his glasses and glaring at us.

I jog to his side, or as much jogging as I can do under the

circumstances. The last thing I want to do is spur some sort of war between Kirill and Rai because of me.

When I stop beside him, he gives Rai an 'I'm watching you' gesture, then slips his glasses up his nose.

"You don't have to do that—"

"Shut the fuck up and walk." He nudges me in front of him not so gently and I stumble but then regain my composure.

What's wrong with him now? I would almost swear he's mad at me, but why would he be?

I didn't do anything to warrant this...or did I?

FIFTEEN

Sasha

KIRILL AND DAMIEN ARE CALLED IN BY THE PAKHAN to report back on what happened with the Albanians. I follow them to the car, limping slightly and without much energy. My arm wound isn't bleeding anymore, so that's a good sign. Before I can open the door, Kirill whirls around and fixates me with his signature stare. People downright tremble when he looks at them in this cryptic manner that can only translate to possible trouble.

"Where do you think you're going?"

His tone is so harsh that even the others, namely Yuri, Viktor, and Maksim, stop a safe distance away and stare at the scene.

I clear my throat despite the tinge of pain bursting through my chest. "With you. To the Pakhan's house."

"You'll do no such thing." He stares behind me. "Yuri, Maksim. Escort Lipovsky back to the house and make sure the doctor takes a look at him. If I find out my orders weren't met, you'll be the ones who face punishment."

"Yes, sir," both say at the same time.

I start to speak, but the words get stuck in my throat when he glares down at me. It's not a good idea to provoke Kirill when he's in this unpredictable state. It's worse that I don't know what made him this mad.

Is it because I got myself kidnapped? Or is it the fact that I couldn't protect him?

His shoulders are tense, causing his jacket to strain against his strong muscles. His lips part as if he wants to say something, but they soon clamp shut again, and he slips into the car without a word.

Viktor moves to the front, and I intercept him. "Make sure he's safe."

The mountain of a man looks at me as if I were an alien. "I don't need you to tell me the obvious."

"If anything happens, call us."

"I know that," he says with a note of frustration.

"Make sure your phone is on you the whole time."

"What the fuck, Lipovsky? Did you get your head hit in there?" He pauses as if he doesn't want to say the next words, but then he speaks in a lower tone, "Worry about yourself first."

And then he's also gone. Soon after, the car that Damien, Kirill, Viktor, and Vladislav are in leaves the premises, followed by a few others.

I instinctively walk for a few paces as if I could run after them or something, which is entirely impossible, considering how weak I am. The fact that I'm standing upright is a feat in and of itself.

A familiar, safe arm holds my shoulders and pulls me into a headlock. Maksim ruffles my hair. "You scared us, you little shit."

I tap his arm, wheezing. "I can't breathe—"

Yuri pushes him with a surprisingly strong shove, and once Maksim releases me, he kicks him in the back of his knees. Then

Yuri wraps his arm around my shoulder. "The fuck, Maks? Can't you see he's been drugged?"

"Oh, right." Maksim scratches the back of his neck, looking apologetic. "My bad, Sash. Should've thought of that."

"I'm completely fine. Look." I duck from under Yuri's arm, spin around, and punch the air. The moment I do, the whole world turns blurry.

I'm about to hit the ground when Yuri catches me, holds me upright, and says in a soft voice, "Don't push it."

"Yeah." Maksim hugs my shoulder. "Take it easy. And I swear to fuck, if you scare us like that again, I'll kill you."

I can't control the smile that lifts my lips. It's hard to imagine that I only met these guys a year and a half ago. It feels like I've known them forever, but I guess that's what true friendship should feel like.

"You did scare us," Yuri offers.

"Even Boss lost his shit," Maksim says.

I swear my heart is about to jump out of my chest and flounder on the ground. "He...what?"

"Fucking *lost* it, Sasha," Maksim repeats slowly as if he thinks I didn't hear him the first time.

"What did he do?" I really, *really* hope the heat rising to my cheeks isn't externally visible.

"Let me see." Maksim releases me, jumps in front of me, and starts to count on his hand. "He ran in your direction when you were knocked out and would have gotten himself killed if it weren't for Viktor, who jumped on top of him and protected him with his body. Then Boss punched him for it. Can you believe that?"

"Kirill punched Viktor?" I ask, looking between my two friends.

Yuri nods. "I know. I wouldn't believe it if I hadn't seen it myself."

"But why? He protected him, no?"

"Yes," Yuri says. "But Boss said that if it weren't for Viktor meddling in the situation, he could've gotten to you before they took you away. So in a way, he blamed Viktor for that."

My lips part. "But...that's not true. Viktor was only doing his job."

"I agree." Maksim nods. "I don't like that dick most of the time, but Boss's actions were uncalled for. But listen, listen! That's not half of it. We managed to capture a few Albanians alive. We tortured them on the spot, but when they didn't answer Boss about where they took you, he killed them. It was like a mass execution in some concentration camp. Of course, Damien was mad about not being allowed to participate in the action. We were close to losing our last chance at getting a lead, but thankfully, Kyle managed to use a different tactic and got the location from the last one alive. It didn't end there, though. Oh, no, it didn't. Did you notice that he brought almost all of our guards, even those who are supposed to remain in reserve? He only left a few behind to protect the house and Miss Karina."

My jaw nearly hits the ground. Did Kirill really do all of that? *For me?*

No, he must've been under some sort of order from the Pakhan to save Rai.

But there's only one problem with that logic—the Kirill I know wouldn't put all his resources into saving someone he dislikes, even if he were ordered by the leader himself.

It takes me a few moments to compose myself and be able to speak in a moderately normal tone. "Did he explain why he was doing that?"

"Seriously, Sasha? Do you know Boss to be the type who explains himself?"

"Oh, right." *He's definitely not.*

"It's obvious why he did it," Yuri tells me in a strangely agitated tone. "He was worried about you."

"No..." I laugh it off, but neither of them is joining me. So I clear my throat. "I'm not important enough in the grand scheme of things for him to do all of that."

"You didn't see him lose it and threaten to rape the Albanian with all objects available, so shut it," Maksim says.

"He...what?"

"His exact words were"—Maksim clears his throat and mimics Kirill's apathetic tone—"listen to me, cockroach, if you don't tell me where you took him, I'm going to have you raped. I'll assault you with every object available until I fucking break you. Maybe then you'll know how it feels, yeah?"

I can almost imagine the unhinged look on Kirill's face when he said those words. A part of me wishes I had been there to witness that side of him.

I must be wrong in the head.

"Besides," Maksim continues. "Boss is not the type who leaves a man behind. If getting you back had meant going through more trouble than this, I'm sure he still would've done it."

That's certainly true.

When I was shot during that special operations mission, we weren't that close, but he still carried me to safety. It's not Kirill's modus operandi to leave a man behind.

"Don't get into shit again." Maksim slaps my cheek with the back of his hand, teasingly. Almost lovingly.

Yuri's face hardens. In an instant, he grabs his wrist and twists his arm behind his back, looking at him with a weird type of tension. This is actually not the first time he's done it. Whenever Maks starts acting too familiar with anyone in his immediate surroundings—as in being himself—Yuri would become surprisingly violent. I haven't thought much of it before, but I think this isn't just part of Yuri's methods to keep Maksim under leash.

It feels like...more.

"The fuck?" Maksim struggles against Yuri. "Let me go."

The latter releases him with a jerk as if just realizing that he might have done something he shouldn't have.

Maksim rotates his wrist, frowning. "I didn't know you could be this…strong."

"You were being an idiot." Yuri's wise mask slips back in place and he pushes me in the direction of the car. "Let's get you home, Sasha."

Home.

I like the sound of that.

After all the hell I've been through today, it's comforting to know that I have a home to go back to.

Now, if the reason I consider that place home—Kirill—would tell me why he's so angry, it'd be great.

⌒

Thankfully, the drug doesn't have a permanent effect, and it almost entirely wears off an hour after I get to the house.

I can move my limbs voluntarily, and my strength slowly returns to its usual level. My arm's injury is shallow and doesn't even need stitches. It'll add another scar, though.

One more battle scar, Sasha.

I stopped counting all the scars I've gotten, especially in the army. That was when I officially stopped being a sheltered young lady.

After the doctor finishes bandaging my arm, Anna brings me a tray of food and stands there like a statue until I'm finished.

She doesn't have to say a word. Her silent presence is enough to order me around. Sometimes, she feels like the female version of Viktor with her tunnel-like vision about protecting and ensuring Kirill's well-being.

I guess, lately, I'm also turning into another version of them, because protecting Kirill has become my top priority since Russia.

After I finish, she fetches the tray. "Stop getting yourself in trouble, young man."

And then she's gone.

I'm ready for this day to finally end. Alas, both Karina and Konstantin barge inside next. Yuri and Maksim, who were playing the role of my caretakers, have to push to the side to make room for them.

"Oh my God, oh my God…" Karina grabs onto my good arm, her eyes filling with tears. "Are you okay? Look at all the blood!"

She motions at the red smearing my shirt, and her expression falls further. She's in some of her fluffy sleeping pajamas that she doesn't usually wear outside of her room.

"I'm fine. It's just a little graze. Nothing to write home about."

"But you were shot!"

"There's no bullet. I didn't even need stitches."

"Promise?"

"Promise."

"I'm glad you're all right." Konstantin studies my surroundings. "Where's my fucker of a brother? Shouldn't he pay a visit?"

I suppress a smile. Konstantin wants to ask if Kirill is okay, but he vehemently refuses to say it out loud, so he chose this route as middle ground.

"He was called in by the Pakhan."

"Is he okay?" Karina asks point-blank, definitely not as concerned about saving face as her brother.

"Yeah, don't worry."

She and Konstantin release a breath, and I exchange a look with both of them.

Karina clears her throat. "I don't want anyone other than me to kill him, you understand, right?"

"I certainly do."

"I'm just asking because if he died, you could easily become my guard," Konstantin says.

"Dream on."

The whole room grows silent at the newcomer's voice.

Despite my best efforts, I can't stop my heart from doing that slight jump or forbid my body temperature from rising.

Will there be a day when Kirill Morozov won't flip my world upside down by merely existing?

He strolls inside, one finger hooked in his jacket that's thrown over his broad shoulder while his other hand rests in his pocket.

It's unfair that he's effortlessly the most charismatic, beautiful man I've ever seen, and that includes actors and models.

The only difference is that they have nothing of his breathtaking intensity.

"Kirill!" Karina sprints in his direction, then stops short in front of him and hikes a hand up on her hip. "Since you're obviously unable to protect Sasha, you should give him to me."

"And you will protect him how, exactly?"

"I'll hire other bodyguards!"

"That's the most illogical thing I've heard today. Go back to the drawing board and let me know when you actually have an actionable, pragmatic plan." He faces his brother. "And you. Stop asking Lipovsky to become your bodyguard."

"He's wasted on you."

I wince and jump down from the bed. I'm not sure what to do or even if I could do anything to kill the tension between the two brothers, but I would rather act than watch it unfold and regret it later.

Maksim and Yuri silently slip out of the room to join Viktor outside. The traitors.

So it's only me with siblings who have entirely different personalities, they might as well be considered polar opposites.

"The fuck did you just say?" Kirill glares at his brother, who glares back.

Now that they're standing toe to toe, there are some similarities, but they're not as blatant as, say, how much Karina looks like Kirill at first glance.

"You heard me." Konstantin speaks in a calmer tone. "You'll

eventually drive him to the point of no return. It's your modus operandi, to destroy everyone around you, no?"

"I swear to fuck, Konstantin, if you don't stop talking, I'm going to make it my mission to actively destroy everything you and your dear mama have been building."

Konstantin goes still, and a cruel smirk lifts Kirill's mouth. "You think I don't know what you two have been up to behind my back? If you think planning a coup to throw out Yulia's family members who chose to help me will do me any damage, think again. Just because I'm letting you do your thing doesn't mean I'm in the dark. I'm just waiting to see how far you go before I destroy you. After all, the higher the rank, the steeper the fall. If I choose to, I can end you both." He snaps his fingers in front of Konstantin's eyes. "Just like that."

The younger brother's face tightens and turns deep red. He lunges forward, but I step over to block his path and shake my head at him.

If he gets physical, he'll give Kirill the incentive he's been looking for.

It's not that Konstantin is easily provoked, it's that Kirill riles him up more than anyone else, and he finds it hard to control his emotions when it comes to him.

Kirill strides toward the door and orders without looking back, "We're leaving, Lipovsky."

I offer Konstantin a reassuring nod and a smile at Karina, who's been fidgeting during the entire exchange. After she hesitantly smiles back, I limp to catch up with Kirill.

His long legs cut through the garden at supersonic speed, making it nearly impossible to reach him.

I release a breath when I finally fall in step beside him. "You didn't have to say that just now."

"The way I deal with my family is none of your fucking business."

The weight of his harsh words hits me in the chest, and I

have to swallow a few times to recover from the metaphorical punch.

"Well, I'm giving my opinion anyway, since everyone else is so scared to voice theirs out loud."

He glances down at me. "And what opinion is that?"

"You were a jerk just then. Nothing Konstantin said warranted such treatment."

"That's where you're wrong. Konstantin keeps wanting to add you to his fucking band of incompetent fools, and unless he stops, I'm going to keep crushing him until there's nothing left of him to be recognized."

"It's not like it's going to happen, so I don't see the problem."

"That's where you're wrong. There are multiple problems, not only one. Now, drop it."

"But—"

"I said. Drop. It."

I clamp my lips shut even as I fume from the inside out. Sometimes, I truly wonder why the hell I like this man so much, to the point where I'm ready to offer my life to save his.

He's such an asshole, and they're nowhere near my type.

Why did he have to be the exception?

It doesn't help that he saved me. *Again.* At this point, he's protected me more times than I've protected him, and that's just so backward, considering I'm the bodyguard.

One more problem. If we keep going at this rate, I'll probably never be able to pay him back, and I'll be indebted to him for life.

We walk silently to his room. Once we're inside, he motions to the bathroom. "Take a shower."

"You go first."

He subtly pushes me. "You need to seriously stop the martyr act before I find an unorthodox way to extract it out of you."

"I was only being nice…" I trail off when he glares at me. "What?"

"You're not moving."

"Fine. I'm going, I'm going." Jeez, could he bring down the intensity a notch or something? It's not so good for my overworked heart.

I close the bathroom door and lean against it to catch my breath. Then I remove my jacket and shirt, wincing every time I cause discomfort to my injury.

My hands tremble when I lower my pants and boxers.

Images of those men stripping me assault me. I can almost feel the repulsive thickness of that cock at my mouth. The strong smell of alcohol, cigarettes, and disgusting male musk. My skin revolts and a sandpaper-like sensation explodes at the back of my mouth.

Nausea fills my throat, and I nearly retch. I have to grip the wall for balance, or else I'll collapse on the floor.

I was sure I was strong-minded enough not to be affected by the incident, but I clearly overestimated myself.

The feelings of being powerless and unable to stop their advances beats beneath my flesh, making my skin crawl.

I slide to the floor, entirely naked, and pull my knees to my chest.

Breathe.

You need to breathe.

It's all over, I know that, but my brain doesn't seem to have caught up.

A part of me is trapped in that dirty basement, unable to defend myself as they overpowered me, stripped me down, and—

"Sasha?"

I startle at Kirill's voice coming through the door, but I can't seem to move. "Y-yes?"

"What's going on?"

"N-nothing."

"You stuttered twice. You don't stutter."

"I'm fine. I just…need a moment."

"Fuck that." The door opens with a bang.

Kirill stops short to view the scene of me naked on the floor and probably looking hideous.

His expression is neutral, though, as if it's a normal occurrence. He's always had a strong mentality that I've often been envious of. Nothing fazes him, not the loss of men who were with him his whole life, his father's death, or even his mother's irrational hatred toward him.

Sometimes, it feels as if I'm looking at a robot in the form of a man.

A few seconds tick by as he watches my chaotic state, and then he crouches in front me. "What's the problem?"

I shake my head.

"I swear to fuck, if you don't start talking—" He cuts himself off and softens his voice, or as much softening as Kirill can do. "You can tell me, Sasha."

"I…" I choke on my own words, and I have to blurt them out. "The men earlier stripped me and found out I was a woman, so they held me down and tried to…to…rape me."

His face tightens, but his expression remains the same. "Did they?"

"No. I thought…I was going to be assaulted for sure, but then Rai helped me, and you came and…this is stupid. I shouldn't be affected this way."

"It's not stupid," he says with deceptive calm. "What do you need me to do? How can I help?"

He's asking.

Wow. Kirill is asking how he can help.

I suppress a smile. I know he's not the type who comforts others and that the concept is alien to him.

So the fact that he's doing this is a huge deal, and I certainly don't take it for granted.

"Can you…stay here?"

He sits beside me on the tiles, his back against the wall, and stretches his long legs out in front of him. "That's it?"

"Can I hug you?"

"Since when do you ask permission for that?"

I throw myself in his arms, and all the shivering and fear from earlier fade away by his embrace.

And just like that, I know everything is going to be okay.

SIXTEEN

Kirill

To say today was a clusterfuck would be an understatement.

Just when I thought it was finally coming to an end, it turns out, not really. Not even a little.

Not even close.

Sasha shivers against me as her arms wrap tightly around my waist and her nails dig into my back.

She sniffles, the soft sound highlighted by the silence in the bathroom. I lay my palm on the middle of her back, making her sniffle louder. The sound is like a constant shrill ripping at my eardrums.

Her naked body feels so small in my arms, so weak and defenseless. The contrast against my fully clothed one doesn't escape me and I have to remind myself that she's distressed and I can't attempt anything my cock is currently suggesting.

"I thought something had happened to you," she murmurs

between sniffles. "When I woke up in that basement, I thought I'd failed you. That I didn't keep my word, and they kidnapped me and then killed you. It made me go crazy."

"Do you have such little faith in me?" I say in a lighter tone, trying to salvage the mood.

"No, but…but I made a promise to protect you for life, and at the first test, I didn't keep it."

"You did everything you could."

"Did I, though?" She lifts her head to stare at me with her watery eyes that mirror the color of the earth.

"Why ask that question when you know the answer?"

"Just tell me."

I lift a brow. "Do you want my validation, Sasha?"

She nods once, and it takes everything in me not to take advantage of this moment for nefarious ends. Such as devouring her on the spot or something inappropriately similar.

"You did do your best. In fact, you went above and fucking beyond."

"Then…why are you mad at me?"

"What makes you think I am?"

"You glared at me earlier when we left the Albanians' nest."

"I could've done that because you were unnecessarily conversing with Rai."

"If it was only that, you wouldn't have been distant and cold since then."

"I'm always distant and cold."

"You're not right now." The little shit smiles a little as if she said something to be proud of. "Point is, there's something else to it."

"How can you be so sure?"

"I just know it. Besides, you're clearly evading the question right now."

"Maybe I'm just trying to understand the situation better."

"Ugh, there's obviously more to it. You just won't reveal it unless it's on your terms."

My lips twitch despite having the urge to snap her neck not too long ago. I never thought there would be a day when someone would have a deep understanding of the way I operate. My men, especially Viktor, have a basic understanding and know when to back off if they sense something isn't adding up.

Sasha is the only one who's always closely studying me for tells. Sometimes, she comes up empty, no matter how observant she is, but other times, like now, she hits the nail on the fucking head.

I should be angry that she even has this much of a read on me, but I'm strangely not.

Far from it.

"If you know that…" I slide my fingers up her back, enjoying the tremors that break out on her skin and the slight parting of her lips. "Why are you still asking?"

"I won't understand if you don't tell me. Is it something I've done?"

"What do you think?"

"I think it is. I just don't know *what* I've done. No matter how many times I replay the events in my head, I come up empty. Besides, you said I did everything I could, so I'm lost here."

"I said. You went fucking beyond."

Her eyes widen, and I can see the exact moment she seems to understand the entire situation. "Oh."

Fucking oh.

My hand slides from her back and I wrap it around her throat, feeling her frantic pulse point beneath my fingers. "What did I say about being a martyr, Sasha?"

"I wasn't…I was there with Viktor and Vladislav…"

"What the fuck did I say?"

"That I shouldn't be one, but I wasn't. I was just doing my duty of being your bodyguard."

"Fuck that nonsense. If you were so serious about such duties, you would've listened when I ordered you to stay by my fucking side."

"But I had to cover you!"

"Viktor did that."

"How is Viktor different from me? He can throw away his life, and I can't? We share the same position, so I shouldn't be scrutinized for performing the same actions he does. You're being unreasonable right now."

"I'm unreasonable? What about being kidnapped, assaulted, and nearly raped after having your true gender revealed in front of Rai? Is that perfectly *reasonable?*"

"How…did you know she figured it out?"

"I suspected it when you were talking and disgustingly smiling at each other, but I confirmed it just now when you mentioned she helped you. I'm going to take a wild guess and say she witnessed you being stripped down."

She swallows. "She called me Aleksander afterward. I think she'll keep the secret."

"If you believe Rai won't use this information against us, you're sorely fucking mistaken."

She shakes her head, and the sad part is that she seems to actually have faith in Rai. Maybe I should plot her assassination anyway. She has a lot of elements to threaten me with, and while that's a disadvantage to me, it's a ticking bomb to her life.

If I fall, I'm handcuffing her with me on the way down.

I'll start with the secret she's been trying to hide from the organization.

I might have to take drastic measures for this. All because fucking Sasha decided that she would be at the front line of the action and get herself kidnapped.

"We helped each other down there," she argues. "She's not as bad as we originally thought—"

"She wants to get to the top at any cost, and if that means exposing both of us, she'll do it. Whether now or down the line doesn't matter."

"But—"

"Shh." I place a finger on her mouth, and her lips quiver against it. "Unless it's to promise to never, and I mean *never*, be a martyr again, don't speak."

A moment of silence stretches between us, and I find myself studying her face. The color has returned to her cheeks despite the dried tears staining her face. Short of the bandage wrapped around her arm. She's fine—physically, at least.

When she whispered that she was sorry during that attack, I thought that was the last time I would see her. I didn't think about it as I ran in the middle of that rain of bullets just to get to her.

Due to my upbringing, I always had a plan A, B, C, and sometimes D before I took any action. Running toward Sasha was the first time I've acted without a plan.

And that's fucking disturbing, to say the least. I could've gotten both of us killed without meaning to.

Sasha slowly removes my finger from her mouth. "I can't promise that, because our definitions of a martyr are different. If I have to protect you, I won't hesitate, even if you try to stop me."

"Sasha—"

"You can't change that. I'm afraid it's final."

This little fucking shit.

She holds my hand in both of hers. "In return, I promise to be more careful. I can't exactly protect you if I'm dead. We'll agree to disagree on the execution method."

"No, we won't. As I'm your boss, you're under obligation to follow my orders."

"That's not how it works."

"That's exactly how it works. Have you seen any of my other men challenging my orders?"

"No, but they're fake bodyguards sometimes. I can't believe they don't intervene whenever Yulia starts being a bitch and tries to slap you."

"That's because I ordered them not to. And did you just call my mother a bitch?"

"Well, she is." She winces. "Sorry, I shouldn't have said that in front of you. That was completely out of line."

She sounds sincerely apologetic, and I can't help the smile that lifts the corners of my lips.

Sasha taps my chest. "See? You also think of her as a bitch."

"No, I don't. That woman is everything nefarious and soulless. Calling her a bitch is putting it lightly."

She inches closer so that her body warmth mixes with mine. "Have you…always had this strained relationship with her?"

"She's hated me since the beginning. When I was an infant, she refused to take care of me and attempted to kill me a few times. The only reason she didn't succeed is because she didn't get the chance. My father shadowed her as if knowing her exact intentions. And I think he did. When he was mad at me once, he told me I should be thankful to him for keeping me alive. Apparently, he locked her away and tied her up during most of her pregnancy with me after she threw herself down the stairs and attempted to stab her belly—and me, in retrospect. After her continued efforts to kill me, even post-birth, my father entrusted me to a nanny and three bodyguards who were ordered not to allow Yulia and her murderous shit near me."

She shivers, and fresh tears gather in her eyes. Why would she cry for me when I never cried for myself?

"No one should be treated like that by their mother. I'm so sorry."

"Don't be. I accepted the fact that she has some sort of vendetta against me."

"Do you know what it is?"

"Don't know, don't care."

"I'm sorry," she repeats. "I won't pretend I know how you felt growing up without the affection of the woman who was supposed to love you unconditionally."

"Does that mean you had an affectionate mother?"

She hesitates for a beat, then nods. "She was so kind and pure and always busy."

"Now I know where you get that trait from."

"I'm not always busy."

"You definitely are. You're also a nosy busybody who doesn't follow orders."

"I don't respect irrational authority, okay? It's what Mama taught me. She had time to tutor me and check on my educational progress while also taking care of the house. I swear she did more in a day than I do in a month. Despite having helpers, she couldn't stay still." A nostalgic smile covers her lips. "I used to drive her crazy with my antics. I would return to the main house with a dirty dress, hair, and shoes because I was playing football with my cousins, and she'd be like, 'Malyshka! What did I say about dirtying your clothes? At this rate, you'll never be a lady!' If only she knew how right that statement was."

Interesting. For many reasons.

One, she chose to talk about a part of her life I'm unfamiliar with without much pushing from me.

Two, not only was she a rich young lady, but apparently, she lived in a big family mansion, because she referred to her home as the main house and they had helpers.

Three, her mother is dead, because she talked about her in the past tense.

Actually, she's never mentioned any family members until now. Are they in Russia? Why does she never call or visit?

"If you hate being a man, why don't you return to being a woman?" I ask.

She blinks. "And stay as your guard?"

"That probably won't be possible, but I will find you another position."

My woman, for instance.

I pause. What the fuck was that thought all about? Did I just think of Sasha as my woman? Yes. Yes, I fucking did.

Despite all the question marks buried around her like a deadly minefield.

"I can't," she lets out with a small sigh. "It's dangerous to be my original gender because...well, I'd be a target."

"To whom?"

She shakes her head. "I don't even know anymore."

So that's the extent of what she'll reveal.

For now.

One day, I'll know everything there is to know about her.

I slowly remove my hand from hers and stand up. "If you're better, go take a shower."

She's caught off guard and seems to only now realize that she's actually entirely naked. Her face turns a deep shade of crimson as she uses the wall to stand up.

"Do you need help?" I ask.

"What? No, no, why would I?"

She remains there, probably waiting for me to leave, and only after I make sure it's out of embarrassment and not actual weakness, I exit the bathroom.

And that, ladies and gentlemen, is on the list of the top five hardest things I've ever had to do, right below not fucking her a week ago when she was splayed out naked on my bed.

There's nothing I'd love more than to help her shower, but that would mean touching her. It would mean being intoxicated by her nearness, smell, and presence, which seems to overshadow the whole fucking world.

And if I did that, I'd succumb and fuck her without a second thought.

I'd take out all of today's complex emotions, frustrations, and failures on her body, and I can't do that when she's traumatized about nearly being assaulted.

So I choose to deal with that part instead.

I text Viktor to wait for me downstairs with Yuri and Maksim, then I change into a fresh suit. After making sure Sasha is actually showering, I step out of the room and softly close the door behind me.

I find my best three men in front of the house.

"What's up, Boss?" Maksim asks, yawning. "I thought we were all praying for this day to be over."

Viktor hits him upside the head without even looking at him.

Maksim clutches the spot and shouts, "What the fuck was that for?"

"Your insolence."

"I'm just voicing what everyone is thinking. The fuck?"

"We'll only be done after we burn down all the Albanians' nests."

Yuri's lips lift in an uncharacteristic smirk. "Are we going after their other branch?"

"Yes, we are."

Viktor's brow creases. "The Pakhan told us to take care of them in our own time."

"Tonight is as good a time as any." I head toward the car, and Viktor makes way for me. I stop in front of him and grab his shoulder. "I shouldn't have punched you earlier."

"I've forgotten about that."

"I haven't." I meet his dispassionate eyes that mirror mine sometimes. Viktor is more unfeeling than I am and uses the loyalty he has only for me as his driving force and occasionally allows it to influence his entire personality.

He was brought up by a single father, who worked as Roman's head of security and died during a mission when Viktor was around twelve. He had no other family, and since he was always a grumpy asshole who's a fan of pointing out other people's shortcomings, no one liked him.

I was the only one who sat beside him during meals and practiced martial arts with him. I did it because I liked his silent company and pragmatic personality. As time passed, he became my shadow and grew to be my most loyal man.

I squeeze his shoulder. "But I'm warning you, Viktor. Don't get in my fucking way again."

His expression doesn't change, as he says in his robotic voice, "I won't. Unless it comes to your safety."

He sounded exactly like Sasha just now. What the fuck are they? Telepathic or something?

"I've gotta say." Maksim opens the passenger door. "I love the idea of getting rid of them once and for all. I can sacrifice sleep for this."

Yuri pushes him and covers his mouth with his palm.

Yes, the day should be fucking over already, but not until every last one of Sasha's assailants has paid the price.

I might not have been there to stop it from happening, but I'll take care of the aftermath.

I will annihilate each and every person who attempts to harm Sasha.

She might be peculiar, and I still don't know much about her past, but she's mine.

And no one touches what's fucking mine.

SEVENTEEN

Sasha

THE SHOWER LASTED LONGER THAN USUAL.

Not only did I scrub clean every inch until it turned red, but I also stood under the streaming water for twenty minutes so it could cleanse away those assholes' filthy touch.

It didn't help much. I feel like no matter how much I clean myself, there's something dirty inside that I can't reach.

Why do women have to deal with this everywhere we go? The whole outdated victim-blaming speech about 'what you were wearing' is laughable in this case. I was dressed as a damn man, but even that didn't stop them.

During the entire process of cleaning and hating myself, I expect Kirill to either bang on the door or come inside to inspect what's taking me so long, or both.

Surprisingly, none of the above happens, even though I've been in the shower for over forty minutes.

Kirill might have let me use his company for comfort, but

he's not a patient man, and he certainly doesn't react well to any bursts of emotion.

I was surprised that he not only sat next to me earlier but also let me hug him and cry against his chest like a baby.

That's not the Kirill I know, which made the gesture have more of an impact. I'm not sure anyone else would've been able to calm me down or wrench me out of those self-destructive thoughts.

I slip on a bathrobe that swallows me whole and stops right above my ankles and make sure to wrap the belt around my waist.

I can't believe I threw myself in Kirill's arms while I was completely naked. Talk about embarrassing myself.

Truth is, I've never been the type who's comfortable with being naked, even before I had to disguise myself as a man.

Since the army, I've become so careful about that in order to protect my identity. So to say what happened earlier was normal would be a giant lie. The other day, too, after his nightmare. I willingly opened the blanket and hugged him while I was in the nude.

I'm almost certain it's only because it's Kirill. I don't think I'd have the same reaction if it were anyone else.

It's both fascinating and terrifying that he's my first in many things—first crush, first sex, first heartbreak, and now, first—and only—person whose presence I feel comfortable and safe in since the massacre.

He's slowly but surely occupying so much room in my life, and if he's somehow removed, the gap will be too big to control.

I internally shake my head to chase away those thoughts.

On my way out, I catch my reflection in the bathroom mirror and freeze. My cheeks are red, lips puffy, and my eyes shine with an unfamiliar light. It's almost as if I look...radiant.

What the hell?

I want to deny those thoughts and shove them where no one can see, but as I step out, my heart thunders louder, harder, and with so much intensity, I think I'll faint.

After trying and failing to control my illogical reaction, I head to the sitting area opposite the bed.

My shoulders drop when I find no trace of him.

Did he go to the office? But it's late, and I'm sure that even he needs some downtime before he gets back to business.

Sometimes, I wonder if he's a machine. It feels as if he was trained to always give two hundred percent of his attention and energy. That if he gives anything less, it's an insult to his intelligence and capabilities.

But surely, he realizes how damaging that rhythm can be long-term. I don't think he cares, though. I'm the only one who does.

I grab my phone from the nightstand and check my messages. My heart nearly leaps out of my throat when I find his name at the top of my notifications.

> **Kirill:** I'm out on an errand. Get some rest. You're off tomorrow.

I let myself fall on the mattress, chest inflating with the heavy weight of disappointment.

What type of errand could he have this late in the evening? He already had his meeting with the Pakhan, so what is this, and most importantly, why am I not part of it?

I pace the length of the room for what seems like an hour, then stare out of the window at the main entrance for another half an hour. When the car doesn't show up, I text Maksim and Yuri but get no reply.

Does that mean they're on whatever this *errand* is?

I glare at the phone. Why do they get to take part in it and I don't? Besides, how could Kirill throw himself in danger's way again after we barely escaped this day's predicaments?

The fear I had when I woke up in that damn basement creeps back in me from all directions. If Kirill gets hurt and I'm not there to protect him, I'll never forgive myself.

I lie down on the bed and try to expel those thoughts, but they continue haunting me in the form of gruesome images.

Shootings. Bombs. Snipers.

Stop it.

I lunge into a standing position and do over a hundred push-ups. Then I shower again, but this time, I let the cold water turn my skin blue. It does nothing to quench the fire inside me.

And Kirill is still not here.

My attention is divided between the door, my phone that has no new text messages, and the clock on the wall that's now ticking past two in the morning.

Just when I think I'm going insane, the door softly opens. I jump up at the same time Kirill walks inside.

A low gasp leaves me when I catch a glimpse of blood splashed on his shirt, his neck, and face. Some form a blurry red smear on his glasses, probably from when he wiped them.

He strides inside with his usual leisure, not paying attention to all the blood that's been the theme for the night.

Upon seeing me, he pauses and narrows his eyes slightly. I run to him and force myself to stop before I hug him or do something equally idiotic.

"What...what happened?" I can't look away from the blood. I really, *really* hate that fucking stuff. Call me superstitious, but whenever I see it, I get a horrible feeling.

I probably shouldn't have been in the army or the mafia. In hindsight, those two are terrible career choices.

But then again, I only get this hectic when those I care about are injured, specifically Kirill.

"Nothing much." He casually removes his jacket and throws it on a nearby chair. "I only took care of some unfinished business."

"What unfinished business?"

"Whatever remained of the Albanians' nests. What are you doing up? I specifically told you to rest."

"As if I could do that when you disappeared in the middle of the night. And don't change the subject. You went after the rest of the Albanians on your own?"

"That's what I said. But I wasn't alone; Viktor, Yuri, and Maksim came along. I invited Damien, too. And while it was tedious to witness him laugh like a maniac the entire time, including him in action, it makes him owe me. We blew up their hideout and killed whoever didn't die."

"But why would you do that? Their other branches might come after you."

"Let them. They'll meet the same fate."

"That's not how it works, Kirill! You're not the type who starts wars without a reason."

"That's where you're wrong. I have a perfectly solid reason."

"And what is that, I wonder?"

"They hurt you, and that's enough incentive for war. I couldn't be there to stop them. What I could do, however, is finish every last one of them."

I think my heart is about to explode. That, or I'm having some form of heart issues that need to be checked.

How can he…render me speechless with a few words? Just how can he make me feel so cherished with a small sentence?

My voice softens. "I'm thankful for that, but as I said before, being the reason behind your problems brings me no joy. I don't want you to collect enemies just because of me."

"I only hear that you're thankful. Everything else is redundant."

"But—"

He jams his index finger against my mouth, causing me to shut up mid-objection.

"I don't want to hear whatever you have to say, because it'll only piss me off, and, considering the amount of anger and adrenaline in my system, I might react drastically toward that." He releases a charged breath and removes his finger. "Today has been a long fucking day, so why don't you go to sleep?"

"What about you?" I whisper.

"I'll go through a few reports."

"You should rest, too."

His eyes darken as they fall on my chest before he slowly slides them back to my face. "Just go."

I look down and find that the opening of the bathrobe shows a hint of my breasts.

Is that what made his eyes darken and caused his demeanor to stiffen? I don't really get my answer, but a strange compulsion pushes me to stare at him even as my cheeks catch flames. "I'm not tired."

"Sasha…" The warning in his deep, somber tone strikes me in my bones. "If you don't move this instant, you can only blame yourself for what I'll do."

My limbs shake, and tingles erupt all over my body, but I refuse to move. If anything, this place right here feels like the best place to be.

A second passes.

Two.

On the third, Kirill grabs me by my nape, fingers digging into my skin, and crashes my body to his.

Just like that, his hungry lips capture my starving ones.

I release a long breath that feels like relief. I've been starved for so long, and now that I have his intense touch again, it's like I'm being struck by lightning.

He threads his fingers in my hair as the hard muscles of his body overpower my softer build. No matter how much I train, I could never measure up to the way his body is built like a weapon.

"Just so you know…" He wrenches his lips from mine and tears away his shirt.

The buttons fly everywhere before the blood-soaked material hits the ground. I'm rewarded with the view of his beautiful tattoos splayed across his rock-hard abs and chest.

His hands travel down, unbuckling his belt. "I'm going to fuck you, Sasha, and I'm going to do it so hard and fast, it'll hurt."

Electricity strikes my whole body, but I refuse to move. In fact, my body melts, waiting for his touch. I even undo the belt of my bathrobe.

It should be disturbing that I yearn for someone who not only doesn't trust me but could also be involved in my family's death.

But that's the thing. I don't think he is.

Kirill is a monster, but he's not that type of monster.

A lust-filled look passes through his gaze as he removes his belt and pushes his pants and boxers down. His animalistic eyes never sway from me the entire time. He wants to watch me watch him.

It's a small detail, but the fact that he always insists on maintaining eye contact during sex is one of the reasons why I've always felt we have more than a mere physical connection.

There's an intimacy in the gesture, and, for a moment in time, it's only the two of us.

I'm lost in the eternal beauty of his naked body. He also has a few tattoos on his thigh that he got a few months ago. There are ravens flying toward his groin. The first time I saw it was when he was getting it, and I had to stand there and stop myself from getting hot and bothered.

My personal favorite, however, is the newest one he got a month ago on his right thigh. A satanic skull surrounded by a beautiful sun.

Kirill throws his glasses aside and wraps the belt around my throat, then he uses it to pull me in his direction. I gasp, but it turns into a moan when his lips devour mine again. Earlier, he was abrupt, but now, it's more intense, as if he's sucking the life out of me.

Kirill kisses without a filter. He's not flirty or gentle, and he's certainly not trying to pursue me.

No.

He's simply conquering me.

But he's passionate and pours all his energy into it, giving two hundred percent like in all other areas of his life. The hard pebbles of my nipples rub against the toned ridges of his chest, causing painful friction.

But none of that matters.

My mind is filled with only one thing—Kirill is touching me again. After months of torture in its worst forms, he's finally looking at me like I look at him when he's not paying attention.

The twisted desire that burns inside my chest is reflected in his arctic wolf eyes.

He rids me of my bathrobe so that we're skin to skin. Heartbeat to heartbeat. Though mine is crazy compared to his. I wish I had the mental ability to control the sheer amount of emotions I have for this man.

Still holding me with the belt around my neck, he lifts my leg to his waist and then pushes. I stumble as my back hits the mattress.

His mouth leaves mine, but the agitation still lurks on his set jaw and stiff muscles. When he speaks, his words are deep, charged, almost completely devout of the control he's so good at maintaining. "I meant to leave you alone tonight, I really did. But you're a greedy little whore for my cock, aren't you, Solnyshko?"

My heart bursts.

I'll agree to anything if he calls me by that nickname. Absolutely *anything*.

I honestly thought he'd never use it again, and I almost forgot just how ethereal it feels to be called his sun.

The earth revolves around the sun. But my world is starting to revolve around him, and I'm not sure how I feel about that.

"You belong to me," he lets out against my ear and then bites down. He releases the belt and thrusts three fingers inside my starved pussy in one go.

My back arches and everything bursts—lust, longing, and... even gratitude.

It hits me then. He has a hold on my mind, and I think, my heart, too, because it's beating like crazy.

"Your cunt is mine to do with as I please. I'm the only one who can control your pleasure or the lack thereof. This is fucking mine."

He thrusts in a maddening rhythm, curling and scissoring his fingers. I push off the mattress, writhing, and moaning the loudest I ever have.

Unlike a few days ago, Kirill isn't punishing or torturing me. This isn't orgasm denial.

Not even close.

He's touching me with the sole purpose of pushing me to the edge as soon as possible.

He's proving that he's the only one who has this much control over my sexual appetite. The only one who can make me this animalistic for his touch.

Sure enough, a few strokes later, I'm screaming. The waves engulf and swallow me whole. The release is so intense that I cease breathing for a few moments.

"Everything about you is mine," he says in dark words as he pulls his fingers from inside me and replaces them with his cock.

It's so huge and hard that I go into a mini-shock, but for some reason, more wetness coats my inner thighs, and my pussy tightens around his girth and length, demanding even more inside me.

Kirill drags me to the edge of the bed while he's standing. My legs are bent on either side of his sculpted waist as he uses the strength of his thighs to thrust into me.

He's pure power. Absolutely maddening in its form and impossible to keep up with.

But I place my palms on his strong abs anyway. I need the connection, the feel of his skin on mine, the reminder that he's actually touching me again.

He wants me again.

I never stopped wanting him, so to have that feeling finally reciprocated is like floating on clouds.

So I don't care that it hurts with each thrust. I don't care that I will probably walk funny tomorrow.

As long as I can have him all to myself like this.

"Even your pussy knows it belongs to me. Do you feel how it's welcoming my cock home?"

I nod.

"No one but me will touch you, own you, hurt you. No fucking one." He leans down, grabs the ends of the belt that's still around my throat, and pulls in opposite directions. "You're my fucking property, Solnyshko."

I can't breathe.

Oh, fuck. I *can't* breathe.

But even as I think that, I can feel the orgasm swallowing me. My mouth opens in a wordless scream as warmth fills my insides.

Kirill pulls out, loosens the belt from around my neck, and tugs me to a sitting position and thrusts his semi-hard cock in my mouth and finishes coming down my throat.

"I want you to lick every drop like a good girl."

I cough, but I dart my tongue to suck his cock and my lips. My eyes remain on his the whole time, enjoying how they darken by just watching me.

And just like that, I completely forgot about today's violation.

Kirill is right.

I only belong to him.

EIGHTEEN

Kirill

I'M LOSING CONTROL.

I can sense it seeping beneath my skin, clinging to my bones, and destroying every shred of discipline I've maintained over the years.

The sole reason for such a blasphemous change starts and ends with the woman lying in my arms after I fucked her until she couldn't take it anymore.

Until she cried and sobbed and finally begged in that soft voice that does shit to me. "I really need to sleep, and so do you. Please?"

I certainly can't fucking sleep.

One, it was distracting when she hugged me in her sleep and even threw her leg over mine in some sort of territorial ownership.

My Sasha might seem naïve, but there's an animal inside her, too—like in all of us—and that animal needs to stake a claim.

I might have marked her skin red and left bruises and hickeys all over her tits, stomach, and inner thighs, but she left her own marks. They're invisible and lurk beneath the skin, but they're so powerful in their softness, so…irritably persistent.

Sasha didn't have to physically cockblock me for these past months, but my cock still refused to touch any other woman but her.

That's probably why I nearly broke her earlier. I had to remind myself that she was kidnapped and nearly assaulted yesterday. My negotiating skills with my cock's beastly side came to a staggering halt when she submitted to everything I dished out to her.

I warned her that I wasn't going to hold back, but she stood there, looking at me with the same desire that twisted my guts.

It doesn't matter how much I try to stay away from her, if she gives me that look, all my resolve vanishes.

I stroke my fingers through her hair, then pause.

What the fuck am I doing?

There's always this need to touch her, whether during or outside of sex, and I'm not the type who does any sentimental shit. I fuck, and only to satisfy a physical need. I don't get off on wooing women or landing a pussy, but all of those principles have changed drastically since this particular woman came into my life.

Not only do I want to keep her, but I also have this urge to pursue her.

I don't even know what the fuck that means.

Courting women doesn't happen in our world. Most of our marriages are arranged for an alliance or some strategic shit, and the union has to be approved by the Pakhan himself.

The real question is, why do I want to pursue Sasha when I already have her?

Due to the fact that she's not yours and might leave.

That fucked-up demon in my head is right.

Yes, Sasha hugged me to sleep, her lips parted in a small smile, and her arms and legs enveloped me as if she was scared to let me go, but she's also not one hundred percent here.

She has roots in some other place, and unless I completely weed those out, she'll never be mine.

I release her hair and peel her arm and leg from around me. Sasha nuzzles her face in my chest, refusing to let me go even in her sleep, but I gently push her until she's lying on the pillow.

Fucking her was the most logical—or illogical—solution to my dick's unresolved issues, but it's not the best one.

Especially after the one-on-one talks I've had with the Pakhan. He knows of the problems we're encountering with Juan's shipment and the attack that happened, probably due to intel from Vladimir. Since I'm no closer to resolving it or bringing the perpetrator's head to Juan as a form of peace offering, the Pakhan is taking matters into his own hands and will talk to Juan leader-to-leader.

I don't like that idea. In fact, I dislike it enough that I considered getting Adrian involved in this issue, but I soon voted against it. Not only would I be giving him incentive against me, but I might lose the one thing that's keeping me strong on my way to the throne.

And I will get there one day.

Once Sergei is out, I'll be the next Pakhan. No doubt about it. I just need to think of a way to do it without sacrificing Sasha's identity, considering that Rai knows about it now.

I wash up in the bathroom. Once I'm done, my immediate course of action is decided. I text Viktor with instructions about what to do while I go to the Bratva's meeting.

After I get his confirmation, I step into the closet and put on a suit. I'm in the middle of doing my cuffs when a soft moan reaches my ear.

I head to the bed and stop at the sight before me. A deep frown creases Sasha's face, and sweat beads on her upper lip and forehead. Her delicate features are caught in a symphony of pain as she thrashes. Her legs kick away the blanket, and her nails scratch the sheets. The shirt she threw on after the shower we had—my shirt—crumples and rides up her thighs.

She whispers intelligible words in Russian, so I silently inch closer. I'm not the sentimental type, but seeing Sasha in pain is no different than being shot. I've been there, and it hurts like a motherfucker.

Once I'm near, I opt not to wake her up.

Considering how closed off she is about her life, this may well be the only way to find out more. So I crouch beside her head and listen carefully.

"Mama...please...Papa...no...it's not...Mishka...I don't... can't...Babushka, please...no...no...I don't want to die...no... Mama! Anton...Anton...I...miss...you...please come back..."

Without my realizing it, my hand has already balled into a fist, and I have to release it before I do something I'll regret.

Who the fuck is Anton, and why does she miss him?

She has parents and a grandmother, and a Mishka, who I assume is her brother, considering she gave him the endearment of a little bear.

And this fucking Anton.

Was he the one who was beside her that day on the cliff? The lover because of whom she shot the phone so I wouldn't be able to find him?

All evidence points in that direction.

I still don't have a last name, but a first name is enough to start. If I have to search the planet for everyone named Anton, then so fucking be it.

Her words turn intelligible—not even words anymore, but more like cries of pain and distress.

I grab her by the throat and squeeze, but not hard enough to cut off her air supply. Sasha's body jerks, and she opens her eyes.

In the beginning, they're more brown than green, unfocused, and without a spark. But the turbulent energy soon transforms into panic as she lunges into a sitting position. I loosen my hand enough to allow her, but I don't release her.

"What...what's going on? Are we under attack...?"

"We're not. Breathe." I squeeze a bit further, and only then does she relax.

So I let my hand drop from her neck because I was just contemplating stroking her cheek like some doting asshole that I absolutely am not.

"You had a nightmare," I announce the obvious. "What was it about?"

She sinks her teeth into her swollen bottom lip, and my eyes follow the motion, imagining my own teeth there, like I devoured her last night—or, more accurately, early this morning.

Sasha slowly releases it and clears her throat. "I don't remember. Just something random, I guess."

Liar.

Something random doesn't include her family or this certain Anton.

But if I push her about it, she'll only get defensive. It's better that she thinks I didn't hear anything just now.

"Did I...say something?" She gauges my eyes, hers careful, fearful, and on guard.

There'll be a day when she'll lay out everything about her life to me. I'll make sure of it.

"No, but you were thrashing."

"I'm sorry. I hope I didn't wake you up."

"You didn't." *I wasn't sleeping in the first place.*

I stand, ready to get on with my day. Sasha, however, gets on her knees and grabs me by the arm. "Please tell me you slept."

When I don't reply, she swallows. "Not even a little?"

"Sleep is overrated."

"That's not true. This situation is getting serious and will have a huge impact on your health if you keep going at this pace, Kirill. I can help if you let me."

"You need to call me something else when it's the two of us."

She pauses, her expression frozen for a second too long. I love how she looks when caught off guard, but what I love more is the slight narrowing of her eyes when she realizes I'm diverting the conversation in a direction she doesn't approve of.

Sasha is a smart cookie and the only one who can keep up with my fast-paced mind.

"You're not changing the subject, Kirill."

"As I was saying, you need to call me something else."

"What's wrong with Kirill?"

"Too impersonal."

"It's your name."

"Still impersonal. You're supposed to be born and bred in Russia, so you, of all people, should know the importance of a familiar name."

Her lips part. "I...can't call you by the diminutive form. You're older than me by a whole eight years."

"I don't want that either. A diminutive form is weird all over. What I want, however, is a pet name, like the one I gave you."

"But why...?"

"I just want one."

She pauses, swallows once and then again before she clears her throat, her cheeks becoming a deep shade of red. This view of her, all bashful and looking absolutely fuckable in my shirt, is an image I need to engrave in my head for life.

New resolve—make her wear my shirts more often.

Her colorful eyes flicker to more green than brown as she whispers, "Solnste?"

"That's just lazy. You can't just choose the masculine form of the pet name I gave you."

"Well, that's the first thing I thought about."

"Think harder then and put some effort into it."

"As if you put any effort into Solnyshko," she murmurs almost to herself.

"I will have you know that I did."

"What type of effort is that? You just picked the first one you thought of back then."

"Not true, but that's not our topic of discussion right now."

"I just need time to think about it. I haven't done this before, okay?"

So she didn't give her lover a pet name? *One-nil to me, motherfucker.*

"You have until the end of the day."

"Gee, way to put pressure on someone," she mutters under her breath again.

"What was that?"

"Nothing, nothing." She smiles sweetly, and I completely forget why I should be mad at this woman for more reasons than one.

"Where are you going?"

"To a meeting at the Pakhan's house."

She stumbles out of bed. "You should've woken me up earlier. I'll be ready in a minute."

I'm the one who grabs her by the wrist this time before she reaches the bathroom. Sasha whirls around and stumbles in my embrace. "Have you forgotten what I told you in the text last night? You have a day off."

"I'm fine now. I don't want a day off."

"You're getting it anyway."

"But—"

"That's an order, Sasha."

"I'm going with you, Kirill."

"No, you're not."

"Either I accompany you in the same car, or I follow in a separate vehicle. You choose the method."

"How fucking dare you give me an ultimatum?" I sound angry, but I'm actually proud of this little shit. She's come a long way from being an inflexible, weak soldier to this strong, assertive guard.

"I'm just informing you of my actions, sir." She straightens against me, and that only causes her hard nipples to brush against both our shirts.

The little fucking tease.

"You can come along." I squeeze her wrist. "But I swear to fuck, if you do something out of order, I'll tie you the fuck down and send you back here faster than you can blink."

She grins. "Yes, sir."

And then she runs to the bathroom.

~

About two hours later, we're done with the brotherhood meeting, so it's time for my own plan.

During the entire thing, I had to physically stop myself from shooting Rai because she smiled at Sasha.

The worst part? The fucking traitor who claims to only be loyal to me smiled back.

Despite yesterday's debacle, Rai is put together. She even hid the scratches on her face with makeup and looked like some sort of politician. She's currently lost in her own thoughts while manically checking her phone. I'm going to take a wild guess that she's distressed because her husband isn't around.

Good. I hope he dies and she becomes a widow and then decides to become a nun.

But since that option isn't on the table right now, I look at her stone-faced guard and then at Sasha. "Leave us. I need a word with Rai."

She lifts her head from her phone and nods at her guard, who obediently leaves. Sasha, however, steps to my side, body full of tension. I don't give a fuck that she became Team Rai overnight. The woman sitting opposite me is a threat that needs to be dealt with sooner rather than later.

Sasha's lips part. "Boss—"

"What part of fucking leave do you not understand?" I don't look at her as I cast the harsh command. I can feel her going rigid behind me, unease drifting off her in waves. When I lift my head, she nods at me and follows the other guard, but not before glancing at Rai.

As if she wants to warn her or something.

Sasha needs to be hit upside the head with a clear definition of loyalty and private lessons from Viktor.

"I didn't realize we were close enough to sit for tea after breakfast, Kirill." She sips her coffee and glares at me.

"We're not. Fortunately."

"Fortunately. So to what do I owe this honorable meeting?"

"I've been wondering."

"About?"

"When are you going to tell Sergei and the others about what you saw?"

"What I saw?"

"In the club. You remember now, don't you?"

"Oh, you mean your sexual preferences? I told you, I don't want to use that against you unless you force my hand."

"I'm forcing your hand, then." I adjust my glasses with my middle finger. "Tell them."

Her brow furrows in clear bemusement. "Why would you want me to tell them?"

"Don't you want to destroy me? You have your chance, so fucking seize it."

"No," she says with force.

On one hand, I take this strong opposition as an indication that Rai probably never meant to use that bit of information and only wanted to hold it as ammunition.

On the other, being outed as gay would be the only way to protect Sasha's real gender. If they know she's a woman, she might get killed just for having the audacity to lie to the Pakhan.

Knowing her character, she'll probably say I didn't know, and I'll get out of it unscathed, but I made an internal vow to protect her gender in the army until she's comfortable revealing it herself.

So I glare at Rai. "I said. Do. It."

"No, Kirill. What the hell is wrong with you?"

"If you don't, I'll kill your sister."

She freezes and swallows, but she soon regains her composure. "I don't know what you're talking about."

"Reina Ellis. Though she's Reina Carson now, yes?"

She chokes on her mouthful of coffee, sending splashes flying all over the table. "How…"

"Did you really think I wouldn't find out about her with you holding something over my head? You hid her well, but I have my ways."

"Kirill," she warns.

"She's been married to her childhood sweetheart for seven years now, right? He's a lawyer and works for his father's firm. They also have a beautiful little boy who was named after your father. Should I start with the child first? Would that give you a good enough incentive?"

She lunges up, grabs her gun from her bag, and points it at my forehead. "I'll spill your brains here and now."

Checkmate.

After Rai caught me with Sasha, I made it my mission to have her followed wherever she went. That's how I knew she has a twin sister that she barely keeps in touch with due to not wanting to drag her into our mafia affairs.

I've kept that secret for a long time, but today, I'll make use of it.

"Kill me, and an unfortunate gas accident will blow up their house. And since it's the weekend, they're all home today. Can you picture the headlines talking about the tragic event?"

Her hand shakes until she's barely holding the gun. "What the hell do you want?"

"I'll pretend I know nothing about Reina's existence if you tell the brotherhood about me."

"Why don't you come out yourself?"

"That's none of your fucking business. Just do as you're told."

I stand and button my jacket. "You have a day before the bomb goes off."

Could be less, depending on how fast Viktor works.

I ignore her and the gun, then step out of the dining room. Sasha, who has been watching the door like a statue, falls in step beside me. "What happened in there?"

"None of your business."

"I'm your senior guard. Your business is my business."

"Not on this particular issue since you're obviously a Rai convert and I don't trust you to be unbiased."

"She's really not that bad." Sasha leans over to whisper so only I can hear her, "She promised to keep your alleged homosexuality to herself."

"Doubt it."

"I mean it, Kirill." She comes to an abrupt halt in front of me, forcing me to stop. "You need to give people some leeway sometimes."

"I haven't been given any, so why should anyone else benefit from it?"

Her expression softens, and her shoulders drop. "I've lost so, so much in my life. You have no idea how much. But I don't think that just because I have nothing, no one else should."

"You do you. I'll do me." I pause. "That sounds sexual. Are you up for it?"

She suppresses a smile. "Up for what?"

"You doing you and me doing me, preferably in front of each other and possibly at the same time to preserve energy. Or better yet, I can, say, do you."

"How about *I* do you?"

"Not even in your wildest dreams." I pause. "Do you want to do me? Is that a kink?"

"No." She clears her throat. "I actually like not having to think about at least one thing in my life."

"You just lie there and be a princess."

She glares up. "I'm not a princess."

"You're the definition of a princess."

"No, I'm not."

"We'll agree to disagree."

"I'm just saying—"

I place a finger on her lips, then realizing we're in a semi-public place, I let my hand fall to my side.

Fuck. If someone were passing by, they would get ideas.

I need to get better control of my need to touch her at all times.

"Don't worry your pretty head about that, and start thinking about that pet name."

"I already found one."

I straighten. "Oh?"

"Yeah. It's Luchik."

"Another variation of the sun. Are you even putting in any effort?"

"I actually did, and this one is different. It's sunray. As in, the only beam of light in the darkness."

"Am I your beam of light in the darkness? *Really?*"

"I don't know. Am I your sun?"

You are.

I almost say that out loud.

The worst part is that I believe it.

Fucking fuck. I'm truly and irrevocably fucking doomed.

NINETEEN

Sasha

TODAY IS KIRILL'S BIRTHDAY.

I know because Karina has roped me into planning a surprise party of sorts. My role is to get him back to the house at a reasonable hour so he can at least eat a slice of the cake she ordered a month ago.

And while that sounds easy in theory, it's harder in reality. Kirill usually spends most of the night at the club and only goes back during the ungodly hours of early morning.

The weirdest thing about his birthday is that it happens to be one day before mine. *Just one.* Well, separated by eight years, but anyway.

He doesn't know that, though, because my birthday in the army files is fake. Last year, he asked me if I wanted a day off for my birthday, and I told him that one wasn't real. He asked for my actual one, but I said that I don't celebrate anyway, so there's no need.

And I don't. At least, not since my family passed away.

The thought of celebrating without a party, presents, dinner, and games with my cousins makes me sick to my stomach. It's better to think that chapter of my life is long over.

The new me doesn't have a birthday. Just duties.

However, like Karina, I want to make Kirill's birthday special. He's always plotting or executing a plan and barely has any time for himself or his family—not that he holds that in high regard. He only cares about Karina's well-being.

The problem is getting him home. Viktor refuses to cooperate and has only been following whatever Kirill asks him to do. Yuri said he has no power to convince Kirill of anything, and Maksim was like, "He doesn't like celebrating his birthday. Does he even know it exists?"

I wouldn't be surprised if he doesn't, considering the strained relationship he shares with his mother. His sister said that she always wanted to offer him different memories about the day he was born but didn't know how—which is where I come in.

Ever since the kidnapping episode by the Albanians two months ago, things have evolved between us.

Countless events have followed, mainly a war with the Irish and a lot of drama in Rai's life, but eventually, the organization reached a careful downtime.

It can be seen on the men's bored faces, and their restlessness can be felt in the air. And I don't mean only our men, but every soldier in the brotherhood.

These men are so used to violence and war that peace makes them uncomfortable. I'm somewhat the same, and the only reason I haven't been getting antsy is because Kirill tires me every night. He either ties me up, straps the leather around my throat, or bends me over the nearest surface so he can fuck me like an animal.

It's precisely that animal side of him that's been giving me the stimulation I need. And I think he needs it, too, because our nightly endeavors have become more intense with each passing day. Sometimes, I think I'll die in the throes of pleasure. Other times, I keep up with him stroke for stroke until we're both spent and satiated.

But most of the time, there's this twisted need for more and *more*. I crave his savagery, how he dominates, bites, and bruises my skin. He doesn't hold back or treat me like a delicate flower. Far from it.

Kirill gives me exactly what I need, and in return, he takes what he wants.

I've started to hate daytime because I can't touch him. At least, not when everyone is around.

As much as I hate to admit it, Kirill has better control than I do. While I often catch myself staring at him and recalling whatever fuckery he did to my body the night before, he usually doesn't pay me attention and acts professionally.

Which I'm thankful for because the last thing I need is for the men I'm supposed to be leading to think that I'm having sex with their boss.

Sometimes, however, he sends me these sexy texts out of nowhere that leave me hot and bothered. The worst part is that they usually happen when we're surrounded by others.

It's things like:

You look tense. Want me to loosen you up with my cock?

I can still taste your greedy little cunt on my tongue. I'm coming back for more tonight.

You better not be tired, because there'll be no sleep until you're all choked up with my cum.

Are you sore? You look uncomfortable. Should we ghost my cock and let my tongue take care of you?

Be in my room in ten. Naked. Lie on your back, legs apart. If I don't have a clear view of my pussy when I walk in, you'll be punished.

It's hard to remain as unaffected as he is when I get those texts. And the asshole smirks at me as if he knows the exact effect he has on me.

I can't help feeling a sense of relief at the routine Kirill and

I have fallen into. I don't think he completely trusts me yet, but I never expected that anyway. The most important part is that he looks at me as if he can't get enough of me, like he can't wait to kick everyone out just so he can have me wholly to himself.

He can be a bastard about it, too, not bothering to be amicable to the men who respect him a great deal.

But with this strange stability comes the fear that it's only a matter of time before the shit hits the fan again. And I don't mean about the Bratva wars or the rocky relationship with the cartels. I can handle shoot-outs and chaos.

What I can't handle, however, is the possible implication of my family and having Kirill find out about everything I've been keeping neatly tucked behind my ribcage.

It's been months since the Russia incident, and nothing else has happened since. My uncle hasn't gotten in touch, and there have been no clear attempts on Kirill's life except during that drug shipment episode. Or…the other month when some of the Irish soldiers specifically targeted him. Or a few weeks ago, when someone attempted to assassinate him while we were getting out of the club.

But…those are normal, right? The first two were gang wars, and the third could be because he offended someone—which is more common than not.

At least, that's what I choose to think of them. I don't believe that Uncle Albert or Babushka sent men here for these particular missions. If they did, my uncle would've warned me to abandon Kirill's ship.

Not that I would've listened.

I often wonder how they're doing and how much Mike has grown since I last saw him. Whenever I miss him, I call Uncle Albert, but it never goes through. Sometimes, I think about visiting them, but the image of what happened to Kirill the last time I was there quickly erases that idea. Besides, they disowned me. I don't think they care about what happens to me.

It doesn't help that I constantly have this doomsday feeling about the possibility of a disaster happening in the near future. I've been extra jerky and might have been too violent toward anyone who's attempted to get close to Kirill, let alone touch him.

Maybe I'm reading too much into this, or I'm being paranoid for no reason.

But that's the thing, there is a reason. I know deep in my heart that it's only a matter of time before something happens. And maybe that's why I've been on edge.

"You need to relax," a deep voice whispers in my ear.

That only manages to make me stiffen more. One, it came out of nowhere. Two, feeling Kirill's hot breaths in my ear makes me shiver and brings back erotic images of flesh against my flesh and low words growled against my skin.

We're leaving the Pakhan's house after a long afternoon meeting. It's already nighttime, so he'll head to the club now, and I need to figure out a way to make him go home.

"I'm relaxed," I murmur, watching our men head to the car.

Viktor offers me a knowing look, but he doesn't insist on being by Kirill's side all the time anymore. I think, and I'm not sure, that he softened up a little after I was kidnapped. He's still a stubborn, unmovable mountain, but he doesn't make it his job to be an asshole for shits and giggles anymore.

"Could've fooled me." Kirill's lips twitch in a smirk, and I swear my heart is about to burst from its confinement. How do I resist Kirill's charm—as twisted as it is? The answer is I can't, and it's not for lack of trying.

It doesn't help that he's become more intimate in recent months. Unlike in the past when it was clear that we were strictly using each other, now, he lies beside me, and sometimes falls asleep. While holding me to him.

My favorite time of the day is sleeping in his arms, listening to his heartbeat, and being surrounded by his warmth. And maybe I'm thinking too much, but I want to believe that there's more to us now.

He even made me give him a pet name that I rarely use, because it's just too embarrassing.

So now, whenever he's teasing or being casual, I find myself reacting sentimentally and out of character.

"I really am," I say defensively.

"You couldn't be relaxed to save your life." He pats my shoulder, and although it's a simple, innocent gesture that he'd do to anyone else, I can't help the temperature that rises throughout my body.

"That's not true."

"You still act like a soldier outside the army, Sasha. Maybe we should get into the sauna later and relax those *muscles*."

I don't miss the way he stresses the word muscles, and I can't help thinking about the first time he touched me in that sauna and how he devoured me alive until I fainted.

"Stop it," I hiss under my breath.

"What? You do need some relaxation."

"I'm afraid your methods only add tension."

He steps closer to my side, and I inhale his cedar scent. When he speaks in low, dark words, my whole body trembles. "Is that why you were asking for more while you were bouncing on my cock last night?"

"Kirill!"

He pushes back, his expression entirely nonchalant, which can't be said about my heated cheeks. "What?"

Rai comes out of the house, followed by her two guards, and physically barges between him and me, a hand to her hip. "You're an asshole, that's what. Leave Sasha alone."

I clear my throat and rub the back of my neck. Ever since we were kidnapped together, Rai has been trying to convince me to leave Kirill and become her guard, because, in her mind, not only does he not deserve me, but he also doesn't know how to treat me.

She was also the one who told me about what Kirill planned to do with her sister. Thankfully, she promised not to threaten him about his sexuality or reveal my gender, and the whole thing blew over—or I hope it did.

"His name is Aleksander," Kirill says in a hard tone, all his humor vanishing in a split second. "And you have no business telling me what to do with what belongs to me."

"Sasha is a person, so you better treat him as such, or I'll claw your eyes out."

"I'd like to see you try."

"I'm not joking, Kirill."

"Neither am I. Now, step away from me before I blow your head off."

"What if I say no?"

"Miss." I smile and stand in front of her. "It's nothing, really."

She faces me with a soft expression. Rai has certainly changed her tone with me ever since she saw my vagina. But then again, she was always the women's advocate in this man-centered organization.

"How could it be nothing? Your face was red just now. Was he scolding you? Giving you a hard time?"

Shit. "No, no, it's not like that—"

"What if I was?" Kirill cuts me off and speaks in his closed-off tone. "I'm warning you, Rai, get your nose out of my and Aleksander's business, or you'll regret it."

"Show me your worst. If I catch you abusing Sasha again, I'll deal with you." Then she flips her hair in a pure diva move and leaves, the sound of her heels echoing behind her.

"I'm going to fucking kill her," Kirill announces casually.

"Please don't."

"Are you defending her?"

"No. I'm just saying that she…means well."

"Fuck that." He strides toward the car. "We're going to the club."

Ah, damn.

How will I convince him to go home now? I check my phone and wince when I find ten missed calls and fifteen texts from

Karina. There's even a text from Anna with a picture of the dining room that she decorated herself.

Okay, desperate times, I guess.

I run in Kirill's direction, then yelp and throw myself down the stairs leading to the circular driveway. I roll down several flights and use my hands to protect my head. The thud is much stronger than I anticipated as I lie on my side at the bottom.

Maksim runs toward me. "Fuck, Sasha! You okay?"

As he helps me sit up, Kirill starts to push him, then stops. Because Yuri, Viktor, and a few of our and the Pakhan's men are watching the show.

A muscle tightens in his jaw, but he thrusts both his hands into his pockets. "What the fuck happened?"

"I…fell down the stairs," I offer from between clenched teeth because my side and the back of my thigh hurt like hell.

"Who pushed you?"

"No one."

Kirill and even Viktor narrow their eyes. *Shit, shit.*

"I wasn't watching where I was going." I struggle to a standing position with Maksim's help. "I'm fine."

"Nonsense." Kirill watches me for a few silent seconds. "We're going home."

"Isn't the club our next stop?" Viktor asks, threatening to ruin my plan.

Kirill doesn't reply and heads to the car. Which means we have to go home.

Yes.

I start to follow and stumble. Yuri catches me by the arm at the last second, and I could swear he glares at me for a moment before his expression returns to normal.

Did I imagine that?

"I know you promised Miss Karina to bring him home, but don't you think you went a bit extreme on this?" he asks in his usual wise tone.

I grin even as I limp to the car. "I don't know what you're talking about."

"You sound so happy about something you don't know."

"Who? Me?" So, yeah, maybe I'm a bit over the moon because Kirill canceled the club altogether just because I got hurt.

It was a slim chance, and I didn't think he'd actually do it. But then again, it goes against his territorial nature to send me back with Maksim or Yuri while he goes to the club.

So let's say I'm a tiny bit happy.

Or a lot considering I can't stop grinning like an idiot. But my good mood gradually disappears when I sit beside Kirill in the back of the car. As soon as we start moving, he rolls down the partition, cutting us off from Yuri and Viktor.

"What the fuck do you think you're doing?" His deep voice swishes in the air like a whip.

My back snaps into an erect position. "N-nothing, I just tripped."

"You want me to believe that nonsense? I would've bought that when we first met in the military, but now, you have better balance than almost anyone, so why don't you tell me the actual reason you pulled that fucking stunt."

Okay, it was a long shot to fool him.

"I just want to go home."

"You could've simply asked for that like a normal human fucking being."

"And you would've granted it?"

"Why wouldn't I?"

"Oh, I don't know. Because you distrust everything?"

"Watch that fucking tone, and if you think this show will make me trust whatever you're up to, then you're in for a wake-up call." He reaches out to me, and I grow still.

Kirill is intense on good days. On bad days, however, he's a force to be reckoned with.

I feel stomped on in his path and can be either destroyed or discarded. Or both.

Kirill grabs my side, and I wince.

He lifts up my shirt and inspects the bruise that's turning purple on my skin.

"You fucking—" He cuts himself off to breathe heavily. "If you hurt yourself for whatever reason again, I swear to fuck, Sasha…"

"I won't."

His light eyes taper as they watch me closely, intently, almost like he wants to cut my head off. But then he shakes his head and tucks my shirt back into my pants gently to avoid causing me any discomfort.

I don't know what's come over me.

He's still carefully putting the shirt back in place when I lunge at him.

"What the fuck are you doing—" His words are cut off when I slam my lips to his.

I've never been the first to kiss Kirill, have never found the courage to do it, because I've always been insecure about the enormity of feelings I have for him.

It started in the army and has never dwindled. If anything, it's been growing stronger and more dangerous until I couldn't control it anymore.

But now, I don't care if he knows how much I like him. No, *like* is too mild a word and describes nothing of the overpowering intensity my heart holds for him.

It hits me then as my lips find his.

I probably love the asshole.

Kirill is stunned for only a moment before he threads his fingers in and fists whatever length of my hair he can grab as he devours me. My kiss is tentative, emotional, and vulnerable. His is the epitome of destruction.

And you know what? I might be fine with that, after all.

His beastly side is part of who he is and I wouldn't have him any other way.

The car comes to a halt and we break apart—or I do.

Kirill still has his hand fisted in my hair, and he uses it to force my attention back to him. "Care to explain what that was for?"

"We're at the house," I whisper.

"That doesn't answer my question."

His face is close. It's so close that I can count the tiny flecks of black in his light eyes through his glasses. So close that I can smell the whiskey on his breath from the drink he had earlier.

I can also taste it on my tongue. So strong and such a damn turn-on.

I clear my throat. "You kiss me all the time. You don't see me asking you why."

"It's different when I do it. My purpose is to claim you. What's yours?"

I lift my chin. "Maybe it's to claim you, too."

A smile lifts his lips—it's gradual and big and so gorgeous, I wish I could take a picture of it so I can stare at it whenever I please.

Viktor knocks on the window, and Kirill finally releases me and steps out of the car, but not before he gives me a weird look.

My leg is better, though the limping isn't gone. The moment we're in the house, a huge confetti bomb pops and Karina shouts, "Happy Birthday, Kirya!"

Viktor, Yuri, Maksim, and Kirill all stop. Though Yuri and Maksim were in on this and helped Karina and me with the preparations, they're still Kirill's guards and will abandon the ship if he so much as hints at any form of disdain.

The man of the house stares at the festive-looking table and the decorations on the walls, the ceiling, and even the floor. Anna went all out and prepared dishes that could feed the entire house for a few days. To the side of the feast, a huge birthday cake with Kirill's name on it sits majestically on a wheeled cart.

"I had it specially made," Karina chatters on when he shows

no sign of approving or disapproving the situation. "They almost ruined it on the way here, but it was saved last minute! Anna made a lot of food, and we can invite everyone if you want, except for Yulia since, you know…"

She trails off when I limp to her side and hug her by the shoulder. She's wearing a cute pink dress with tulle and matching nails and pumps. She even had her hair done up as if it were her own birthday party.

"Karina went to a lot of trouble for this," I offer in a careful tone. Because he's looking a bit displeased, and I can't have him break his sister's heart.

"Sasha, too," Karina says. "And Anna. We wanted to surprise you."

A moment of silence falls over the hall before he strides to his sister. She stiffens for a moment, but then he kisses the top of her head. "Thank you, Kara."

She grins like an idiot. "You're welcome!"

He side-hugs Anna as a form of thanks, and she smiles like a proud mama. Kirill merely pats my shoulder on his way to the head of the table and leans in to whisper, "So this is why you wanted to come home."

I nod.

"As I said. You could've told me."

I could've?

Has he seen himself in the mirror? Who would dare disturb His Majesty about something as trivial as a birthday?

I don't get to say anything as he pulls his chair out. The rest of us follow, and Maksim calls the rest of the guys after Kirill allows it.

Chatter and laughter echo around the table, even though Kirill says little to nothing and only when Viktor, who's sitting at his right, engages him.

Karina is on his left, and I'm beside her, listening to how excited she is and that she couldn't sleep last night.

The entire time, I steal glances at Kirill. I don't know if he's okay with this or just pretending for the sake of Karina and Anna.

The general laughter and clinking of plates stop when Yulia and Konstantin walk into the party. She's wearing black today as if it's a funeral and stomps her foot on the floor upon seeing the guards at the dinner table.

"What's the meaning of this?"

Karina turns and clears her throat. "It's...uh...you...see... today is...well, Kirill's...birth..."

"Get it together, you idiot. Don't you know how to form sentences?"

Tears gather in Karina's eyes before they stream down her delicate face. Her lips clamp shut, and all her carefree energy disappears.

"Mother, no." Konstantin shakes his head.

"What? She *was* talking like an idiot."

"You're the one who turned her into what she is." Kirill rises to his full height and holds Karina by the shoulder. "If you talk to her in that tone again, I'm going to throw you out of the house."

"What did you just say to me?"

"I have full ownership of this place. If you don't respect my people in it, you'll be out in a fucking instant and I'll make it my mission to burn each and every one of your designer bags." He stares at his brother. "Take her away from here. I don't want to see her face."

Konstantin's jaw clenches, but he starts to drag a fussy Yulia away. I could tell he was extremely uncomfortable with the way she spoke to Karina, too.

"How dare you kick me out? I'm the one who gave birth to you, you insolent piece of trash—"

The door closes behind them, and Kirill smiles down at Karina. "Don't believe anything that woman says. Just because she gave birth to us doesn't make her a mother, okay?"

She nods twice, smiling back, and even hugs him.

Then she pulls back to run to the other side of the room and brings back a huge black box wrapped in white ribbons. The present is a tailored tuxedo with gorgeous matching shoes and a dress shirt.

Did she spend a fortune on this? Definitely.

Anna also gives him her gift, a scarf that she knitted herself. The guys offer him cards with services he might ask of them on their days off—as if he can't do that already.

Kirill smiles at that, but it disappears when he finds a similar card from me in the pile.

So I kind of had to do the same as the others in order to not stand out. Only Karina and Anna gave him personal gifts, after all.

There's also a third gift, a luxurious watch that Karina swears isn't from her, but she's the only one in this house who's rich enough to be able to buy it.

While they're busy arguing about the watch and Maksim calling Karina humble, then Viktor hitting him and Yuri scolding him, I slip out of the dining room and head to the bathroom with a huge smile on my face.

Not to jinx it, but I think this birthday is a success.

After I finish my business, I wash my hands and freeze when I catch Kirill's reflection in the mirror. He's leaning against the doorframe, legs crossed, as he toys with the card I slipped him with the ones from the other guards.

"So this is all I get for a huge birthday that you nearly broke your leg to have me attend?"

I let the water drip from my hands into the sink for a minute, then face him while I dry them with the towel. "That card can mean many things. Use it wisely."

"I have so many cards. What if I lose this *special* birthday gift?"

I grin. "Stop being an asshole. I actually got you another gift, but I couldn't show it to you in front of everyone else."

He raises a brow. "Another gift? Where is it?"

I bite my lower lip, then I unbuckle my pants. The sound of

rustling clothes is so heightened in the silence that I nearly chicken out.

In one go, I lower my boxer briefs so that he can see the black ink surrounded by redness right above my pussy.

Kirill straightens, his expression turning into one of bewilderment as he walks up to me, grabs me by the hip, and gently touches his fingers along the Russian word.

Luchik's.

"Fuck," he lets out in a voice filled with awe. "When did you get this done?"

"This morning."

"When you were supposed to be with Karina?"

I nod.

He narrows his eyes, and his grip tightens on my hip, his fingers digging into it. "Did a man ink your skin, Sasha? Did you let a man look at what's fucking mine?"

"No, you caveman. It was a woman."

"Name? Credentials? Location?"

"So you can cause her trouble? Absolutely not. But anyway. You didn't tell me what you think? Do you…like it?"

"I love it. Should've engraved my name on you a long time ago, but it would have been done sloppily with a knife."

I roll my eyes. "You're such a romantic."

"I know."

"That was sarcasm."

"I know." His gaze is still lost in the tattoo as he traces it back and forth.

I'm such a wimp. I had to take three strong painkillers before I could let the girl ink me. I'm never getting a tattoo again. I can't understand how Kirill and the others have managed to have maps inked on their bodies.

"Now, I want to see it up close and personal while I'm fucking your brains out." He grabs me by the arm. "Let's go."

"No." I try to pull my hand free and fail. "We can't."

"Why not?"

"There's a party for you, remember?"

"Party is over then."

"Kirill, no. Everyone will be so sad."

"Not my problem."

"Okay, wait. Wait! If you stay for at least two hours, I'll tell you my real birthday."

He raises a brow. "One hour."

"One and a half."

"Deal." He pauses. "When is your birthday?"

"Tomorrow."

"Really?"

I nod.

He reaches into his jacket, then grabs my hand and clasps a stainless steel bracelet on my wrist.

"How…" I trail off.

"I've had it since last year and was only going to give it to you when you told me your actual birthday."

"Have you…been carrying it on you all this time?"

"Maybe."

Oh, wow. I think my heart is melting at his feet as we speak.

"It has a sniper rifle on it." I touch the engraved image and then gasp at the writing in Russian. "And Sasha!"

"It's also unisex."

I hug him. "Thank you! Thank you!"

His arm wraps around the small of my back. "Happy Birthday, Solnyshko."

Tears rim my eyes. I thought I would never celebrate my birthday again, but Kirill has proved me utterly wrong.

I want to celebrate all my upcoming birthdays by his side.

TWENTY

Kirill

THERE'S A HITCH IN MY PLAN TO TAKE OVER THE WORLD. It's not small or negligible, and it certainly can't be ignored. The problem, however, is the solution I have to use to bypass this hurdle.

It's been six months since the attack on me right before the drug shipment, and Juan has never fully trusted me again. In fact, he asked for another contact within the Bratva, and the Pakhan assigned Igor.

The in I got with the cartels that was supposed to be my ticket to the top has to be shared with Igor because he's Sergei's oldest and wisest companion.

Igor's history with the Bratva is curious at best. Yes, he's old, but he's served under two different Pakhans who liked and appreciated him equally.

He's also the one they like spending their personal time with, which I'm sure he's used to give himself and his brigade more power.

It's no secret that he's one of the main reasons Sergei became the Pakhan after his brother's death. He could've put himself in that position if he'd chosen to—my old man and the others would've voted for him—but Igor is playing the long game.

He had the organization's best interests in mind when he nominated another Sokolov for the position, and as a result, he secured another powerful tool—Sergei.

The Pakhan is growing old, and he's not as sharp as he was in his younger years. So guess who he consults with before making any decisions? Igor.

It's a soft power that keeps growing with every passing day.

I'm almost sure he truly doesn't want to be Pakhan, though, because after Nikolai's death, he announced that he has no interest in the position and prefers to offer support instead.

Now that same Igor is strongly in my business. In fact, he's been in my business since I got back to New York.

The reason for that became clear after the meeting he arranged for both of us at his house two days ago. No guards were allowed inside. Just me and him, and, later, the Pakhan himself joined.

The three of us sat there for hours. They laid out their conditions, and I put mine forward.

It wasn't just words—we had to sign a contract in blood so that if one of us backed out, he'd be outed in front of the entire organization as a coward who doesn't keep their word.

It'd be career suicide, basically. Sergei and Igor might be old, but they've spent decades in the Bratva, and they consider its values sacred.

Me? I want to be at the top. No matter what it fucking takes.

Even if it means selling my soul to the devil. If I'm at the top, I can bring that devil to his knees in front of me. I will be able to do whatever the fuck I please, and no one would dare hurt those close to me.

I sit behind my desk in the club, building the dozenth house of cards in the past hour.

Viktor is opposite me on the sofa with a laptop on his lap, probably watching some security footage. He likes to show small clips to the guards and remind them how sloppy they are.

It's no secret that they prefer Sasha over him. She's compassionate, more attuned to their needs than they are, and often goes out of her way to do their job if they're feeling under the weather.

The air in the house has become lighter since the birthday party a couple of months ago. And it's all because Sasha puts in the effort and gently pushes everyone else to do the same.

She even took Karina out to the nearby park for a whole fifteen minutes. She brought her back after she had a numbing panic attack; however, my sister was smiling soon after and talked to me about the air and the bees and even the children she saw there.

I still don't like that Sasha is close to Konstantin. He's an asshole who might use her against me, but the stubborn little shit doesn't seem to think that's the case and says nonsense like:

"I think he's deeply misunderstood."

"Have you ever thought that maybe he's being corrupted by Yulia? Or that, when you left, you didn't only abandon Karina but also Konstantin?"

"Can you consider giving him another chance? Or at least listen to what he has to say?"

"At this point, threatening and antagonizing him every time you see him is doing more damage than good. Can you try not jumping down his throat the moment you see him?"

I said yes to the last one if she'd think of him as invisible and never talk to him again. To which she glared and said, "No."

I'm often tempted to grab her by the throat and drag her into the nearest dark corner whenever she does that. Her defiant side can be such a fucking turn-on.

Her whole presence is. I don't know the reason, but she's been becoming more and more beautiful. To the point where I often have these dark thoughts about locking her up where no one can see.

To the point where I'm on the edge whenever she's not here.

Like right now.

She and the others are doing the rounds downstairs, but I couldn't be bothered to show interest in that. Tonight, the Pakhan is throwing a party that no one knows the reason behind.

Everyone is expected to be there, though, including our families, and if anyone misses it, there will be repercussions.

So I actually have to put up with Yulia's presence. The look on her face after everything falls in place might be worth it, though.

"Boss." Viktor's voice breaks the silence as he stares at me.

"Hmm?"

"Are you still not going to tell us what went down in the room with Igor and the Pakhan two nights ago?"

"No."

"Since when do you hide things from me?"

"You're not my wife last I checked."

"That's nonsense. You don't have to tell your wife everything. But you have to tell me."

I smile, but I don't say anything.

"Boss."

"What now?"

"Remember when you told me Lipovsky likes men?"

The card I'm holding remains suspended in midair as I lift my head and look at Viktor. "I do. What about it?"

"I think the man he likes is you."

It takes superhuman strength to stop my lips from curving into a smirk and, instead, speak in a casual tone. "Oh? What made you come to that conclusion?"

"He watches you all the time."

"You watch me all the time, too. Does that mean you like me, Viktor?"

His solemn expression doesn't change. "This is different. He has this weird look on his face, and he does it when you're not paying attention."

Interesting.

"I'm sure it's nothing." I place two cards together.

"Or it is something, and you need to be careful."

"Me? Careful of Lipovsky?"

"Well, he's the night guard. Maybe I should take over for now."

"Nonsense." I wave him away.

Just in time, the door opens, and Sasha walks inside with Yuri and Maksim on either side of her.

Would it be possible to send those two on a holiday for the next two years?

Actually, make that ten years.

"We should go back to the house so you can get ready for tonight's party." She speaks in her calm 'manly' voice.

Her hair is growing longer again and reaches below her ears. It's like she does it on purpose to feel like a woman again, but then when she starts looking too feminine, she cuts it off.

"Everyone but Lipovsky out."

Yuri and Maksim nod and step out. Viktor, however, narrows his eyes before he does the same.

Once the door closes behind them, Sasha releases a breath. "You really need to stop doing that, or they'll suspect something is going on."

"I don't give a fuck what they think." I tap the desk in front of me. "Come here."

She sighs and turns the lock before she walks in my direction. Ever since that time Rai caught us, she doesn't take any chances.

Once she's within touching distance, I clutch her by the wrist and pull her so that she's caged between my thighs and her back is against my desk.

Her hands instinctively fall on my shoulders, and she inhales deeply. I love how her neck becomes a light shade of red whenever she's embarrassed or horny. Right now, I'm going to bet on the second.

I start to slowly remove her pants, and she grabs onto me harder. I'm being a tease, and she hates it as much as she loves it.

My hand slides up her inner thigh and stops right above her core as I whisper, "Besides, Viktor already suspects you."

Her face falls, and she stiffens. "W-what?"

"He told me you look at me weird, and since he knows you're gay, he thinks you like me."

"Wait. How did he assume that I'm gay?"

"I told him that over a year ago when he warned me that you might be a threat to Karina."

"You told him I'm gay?"

"I told him you're attracted to men, which is true. He concluded the rest on his own."

Once I rid her of the pants and boxer briefs, I lift her so that she's sitting on the desk, then I throw her legs over my shoulders.

"Kirill! How can you think about sex when we have this situation?"

"It's nothing."

"But—"

"He's Viktor. So when I say it's nothing, I mean it." I slap her inner thigh when she starts to wiggle free. "Now, stay still so I can have my dinner."

Her whole body stiffens, but it soon loosens as I stroke my fingers over her folds and clit. "So wet and ready for me, Solnyshko. Your cunt sure knows how to welcome me home."

And then I'm diving in. I tongue-fuck her fast and hard the way she likes.

Her moans echo in the air, and she slaps one hand on her mouth while the other holds her steady on the desk. I stop now and again to look up and see the ethereal view of her head thrown back in the middle of the ruined house of cards, legs shaking and lips parted.

The symbolism of the picture doesn't escape me. Sasha is the ruin of my house of cards, and there's nothing I can do to change that.

Not even a little.

Not even close.

And maybe, I've finally come to terms with that.

My fingers dig into her thighs to hold her in place as I bite down on the *Luchik's* right above her mound, adding one more mark to the bruises and hickeys I've left there since she got the tattoo.

I've never liked my birthday. It's always reminded me of how Yulia tried to kill me and the black dresses she wears on that particular day as if she's mourning the event of my birth.

But that was before this fucking woman celebrated it with me.

Her fingers clench in my hair as her pussy contracts over my tongue, and then she's coming all over my face.

Fuck.

She's the best thing I've ever tasted.

I pull back, and she gasps when I bite her tattoo again, but her face is a masterpiece of undeniable lust.

My own masterpiece.

She's leaning on both hands, her shirt crumpled and her legs still shaking from the orgasm. However, she watches my every movement as I let her legs fall, then stand up and unbuckle my pants.

She swallows when I fist the belt over my hand and run the metal tip between her thighs, over her stomach, and then wrap it around her throat.

I pump my already hard cock twice, and her lips part, lust and desire shining in her green eyes.

This isn't the first time she's done that. Sasha loves it when I'm touching myself. I might have started to do this regularly just to trigger that look.

"You're going to take my cock like a very good girl, aren't you?"

She nods, her chest rising and falling in a frantic rhythm. I part her legs further, fingers digging into the sensitive flesh of her thighs, then I ram inside her in one go.

Sasha moans, "Oh, fuck."

"You're welcoming me home again, Solnyshko. That's it. You're swallowing my cock so well."

Her face is tinted red, even though I'm not applying much pressure on the belt.

"More," she whimpers. "More, Kirill."

"Not Kirill. Call my other name."

She bites her lower lip and then whispers in the most erotic voice, "Fuck me harder, Luchik."

I'm a goner.

There's no way I can last when she calls me that.

I throw the belt aside, lift her in my arms while still inside her, and slam her against the wall.

I fuck her as if I'll die without her. I fuck her harder and faster, in rhythm with her moans and screams of pleasure. Then I shove a palm over her mouth and nose. "Shh, you're too loud."

She moans against my grip, even as I suffocate the shit out of her. Thing is, I'm not the only one who enjoys breath play. The more I take away her oxygen, the harder her cunt clenches around my cock.

But the part I love the most?

It's the way her gaze remains on me, trusting me not to actually kill her.

Her pussy tightens, milking me for my orgasm, and her eyes start to go out of focus. I remove my palm, grab her face with both hands, and force her eyes to meet my own. They're more green than brown, glittery with tears.

These are her pleasure tears, her 'give me more' tears. The tears that I want to see on her face for eternity.

I pump into her harder. "Tell me you're mine, Sasha."

"I'm...yours."

"No matter what happens?"

She shudders, her heels digging into my ass as she holds on to me for dear life. "No matter what happens."

"You can't change your mind later. You can't take these words back, and you certainly can't, under any fucking circumstances, leave me. Do you understand?"

She nods a few times. "I won't... Oh, God!"

Her head falls on my shoulder, and she sinks her teeth into it as she comes with an erotic moan that triggers my own orgasm.

I fuck her through it before I empty my load inside her. It lasts so long that I'm completely spent.

We remain like that for a few minutes, breathing harshly against one another's necks.

Sasha pulls back, her big eyes watching me with...fear.

What the fuck?

"I love you," she whispers, the sound so low that I almost can't hear it.

But I do.

And my chest feels as if it's grown wings and is currently flying among the fallen angels.

"You can't take that back either," I say with more authority than necessary.

She smiles a little. "I won't."

"I mean it, Sasha. Your feelings for me are not allowed to change. Not even a little, not even close. If you feel they will for whatever reason, take the words back right now."

"No, I won't." She strokes my hair, my cheek, and my lips. "No matter what."

My lips find hers, and she whimpers as I kiss the living shit out of her.

They're not allowed to change.

No matter what.

Especially after the storm that's coming our way.

TWENTY-ONE

Sasha

The party at the main Bratva's mansion is in full swing.

Everyone is here, and I mean *everyone*—including our allies from the other organizations. The Yakuza, the Triads, and the Italians.

Juan even sent his son over after Igor suggested it. I don't think he trusts the older man more than he does Kirill, but he seems more at ease now that Igor is in the game. Maybe that's because they're around the same age and are secretive to a fault.

Aside from the different factions, the leaders' families are also accompanying them tonight, but no children are allowed.

Not that they would bring them. I can't imagine, say, Adrian shoving his son at such an event.

The risks of these gatherings are colossal. If we're attacked, we're sure to lose all the precious allies everyone, and especially Kirill, has been working hard to secure.

Needless to say, it's a security nightmare for bodyguards. We've had to cooperate with so many guards, and some of them are on the fanatic side when it comes to protecting their bosses. They're almost as hotheaded as Viktor, Vladislav, and Kolya—Adrian's senior guard.

Well, and me.

Kirill's safety is a nonnegotiable concept in my book. The other day, I choked a girl for daring to step into his path, and he had to order me to back away before I killed her.

Sometimes, he reacts to my bursts of protectiveness with a smile, and other times, he just sighs and shakes his head as if he thinks he'd have better luck trying to tame a lion.

It's a problem that I'm working on. I know full well that I shouldn't be acting like that, but I'm still traumatized by the scenes of him surrounded by blood on that hill and then lying in a hospital bed with lifeless eyes and bandages covering his body.

I will never allow such a thing to happen again. Never.

So what if I'm being a little bit too crazy about this? Viktor does it all the time, and he's not seen as abnormal…at least, not much.

At any rate, I think I'm being perfectly reasonable, and no one, not even Kirill, will convince me otherwise.

Earlier, after he fucked my brains out in his office and I blurted that I loved him like an idiot, he told me not to come to this party.

He mentioned something about keeping Karina company and taking the night off. I thought he was joking, but he was perfectly serious.

I said, "The possibility of me not accompanying you tonight is on the same level as you allowing me to spend time with Konstantin."

He didn't seem happy with my decision to come along.

It did hurt a little to have him think that way. Maybe he took my feelings for him badly. Maybe I made a terrible mistake by voicing them. Isn't there some sort of rule that you shouldn't express your feelings during or right after sex?

That's when I feel the most vulnerable, which is why I couldn't control those overwhelming emotions or the need to let him know about them. And now…well, now, I'm plagued by this horrible feeling that I did something wrong.

Kirill is not an emotional man, and any outbursts like that could backfire. I knew that, but I stupidly brought up emotions related to whatever we have.

Is it wrong that I want more of him? And I don't mean his body and intense dominance. I don't mean his protectiveness and care, either. I need…something deeper.

I want to wake up in the morning and know that he'll be there for the rest of my life. I don't want to think that this is a phase that will eventually fade.

I'm being a sappy idiot right now, and Kirill can't, under any circumstances, find out about these thoughts, or he might distance himself from me.

Desperate much, Sasha?

I wince at that but straighten when Damien leans against the wall beside me, hands in his pants pockets. He's supposed to be wearing a suit, but I saw him throw off the tie earlier and then slam his jacket on the ground, so now, he's only in a crumpled shirt with the first two buttons undone and surprisingly pressed pants. His hair isn't a disaster like usual, though, but he's definitely run his fingers through it a few times.

I'm more presentable than he is, but he still looks great, even when he's dressed worse than anyone here. People with superior genes like him and Kirill manage to look like supermodels in whatever they're wearing.

"Aren't you supposed to be mingling around with the others?" I ask. "This is a guards' area."

"Fuck mingling." He glares at the crowd. "That Yakuza old

geezer is trying to corner me for a drink, and the worst part is that he doesn't even do vodka."

I smile. Ever since Damien was arranged to marry a Yakuza princess, he's been more irritable than not, especially with Rai and Kirill, who helped arrange it.

In their minds, it's simple. They need a strong alliance with the Japanese, and to accomplish that, a marriage has to happen.

It's so common in these circuits that it's become normalized. I still see the concept as a little disturbing, mainly because women don't get a say in it. They're just traded like stock between men.

"What the fuck you smiling at, pretty boy?" He narrows his eyes. "You find this amusing or something?"

I stand tall, my expression going back to all seriousness. "No, sir."

"You obviously do. No wonder they say the quiet ones are the scariest. You're a fucking sadist, aren't you?"

Try the opposite.

My cheeks start to feel hot as erotic images from earlier barge into my head. It takes me a few moments to dispel them.

I clear my throat. "If you're against this marriage, why don't you pull out? Surely you have the power to."

Okay, so maybe I'm trying to save the poor Japanese girl from Damien.

His lips curve in a smirk. "Who says I'm against it?"

"You…want to get married?"

"I didn't think so in the beginning, but now, I'm sure I do."

Wow. I feel more sorry for the girl. I can't imagine what it's like to have the attention of someone as unhinged as Damien.

He's been doing all sorts of things to fight Kirill and has been failing for so long that anyone else in his position would've given up.

Not Damien.

"Her father is a fucking nuisance, though." He clicks his tongue. "Question. Do you think she'd still marry me if her father was somehow removed from her immediate surroundings...say, for good?"

"You can't kill your future father-in-law, who happens to be the head of the Yakuza, Damien...I mean, sir."

"I'm not going to kill him, I'll just remove him for a while."

"That's still unacceptable."

"Even for maybe a month?"

"No."

"Fine. I'll do it after the marriage."

"You can't do that either—"

"Fuck you, Sasha. You can't do this, and you can't do that. What are you? My mother?"

Damien's words end in a yell when Rai kicks him in the shin with the toe of her shoe. He grabs his leg and raises his fist to punch whoever assaulted him, but he stops when he sees her face.

"The fuck was that for?"

Rai cradles her pregnant belly and glares at him. "Don't speak to Sasha that way again or I'll break your leg next time."

"What do you mean that way? I was just telling him how useless he is at giving advice. He kept telling me that I can't kill and all of the boring nonsense."

"That's because he doesn't want you to get in trouble. If you don't appreciate his advice, don't ask for it again." She strokes my arm. "You okay, Sash?"

I rub the back of my neck and nod. Jeez. It's almost unbelievable how much warmth I've found in Rai ever since that kidnapping.

She's tough to outsiders and even some on the inside, but she has a heart of gold, and I'm so honored to be on the list of people she cares about.

"Why don't you ask how the fuck I'm doing? I've known you longer than pretty boy Sasha." Damien tries to step between us, but she shoos him away.

"Sorry, but this position can't be given to just anyone."

"The fuck? I disapprove of this."

A tall, lean, and darkly handsome man steps to Rai's side and places a possessive hand on the small of her back. It's her husband, Kyle.

No one should be fooled by his good looks. This man is the top sniper in the organization. Even better than me. He's an ex-hitman, so it makes sense that his skills are on a different level.

Rai's eyes turn glittery as she looks up at him with so much love, it makes my heart squeeze. And Kyle—the man who used to be a killing machine? He looks back at her as if she's the reason he breathes.

His hand rests on her belly, and he holds her tighter. I can't help watching them whenever he does these subtle ownership gestures in public. Even Adrian, the man who's rumored to hate his wife, was grabbing Lia possessively earlier.

Why does my heart hurt at these images?

Because you'll never be able to experience them.

Kirill and I can't go public with our relationship unless I stop being a man, and even if I do that now, there'll be more repercussions about the fact that I was hiding my gender.

Not that I want that or anything.

I know it's impossible, and there's nothing that can be changed about it.

"Fuck off, Damien," Kyle tells him in a distinct British accent.

"You fuck off." He smiles at Rai. "I'm up for that affair anytime you wish."

"I'll spill your brains out right here and now," Kyle says point-blank.

Damien grins. "I'd like to see you try."

Rai places a palm on Kyle's chest. "Ignore him. He's just being antagonistic due to being bored. Why would he think about an affair when he was demanding that his marriage be brought up?"

"That was…" Damien trails off, lost for words for the first

time ever. "A *tactical* move. Not my fault you don't know what that means."

"Do you even know what it means?" Kyle jabs at him. "Or did you use it because you think it's fancy?"

"Fuck you, you fucking fuck. Also, as Kirill said, arranged marriages are for power, and only fools wouldn't take advantage of that. Point is, I'm no fucking fool."

Rai and Kyle egg him on, saying that he's just a bit too desperate.

I, however, am thinking about Kirill after the simple mention of his name. I instinctively find myself searching for him in the crowd.

The hall is packed with people, chatter, and the smell of expensive perfumes mixed with premium alcohol. Men are clad in their best suits, and women are in their most beautiful cocktail dresses, including Yulia, who's been holding on to Konstantin's arm the entire evening.

Classical music is being played by a quartet in the corner, the tunes nearly overwhelmed by the chatter and laughter.

Kirill, however, is nowhere to be seen.

He assigned Viktor to be the one who follows him everywhere today, and while I was a bit disappointed by that, I couldn't exactly protest since we have a day-to-day agreement and today happens to be Viktor's.

Still, it's weird that Kirill hasn't inserted himself between me and Rai and Damien. He's always annoyed whenever they talk to me, because Rai is trying to recruit me to her side, and Damien is often attempting to grill me for information.

He's probably in a meeting with the Pakhan. That's the only reason he wouldn't be witnessing this situation. Otherwise, he'd be here to explicitly tell Rai and Damien that my name is Aleksander, not Sasha.

I listen to Rai, Kyle, and Damien's bickering while offering a few smiles or nods. Even though I speak my mind with Kirill, I'm not that talkative with everyone else.

I guess he's the only one who brings out the best and worst in me.

He's also infuriating most of the time, so it's effortless to disagree with him and try to show him the other side of a coin.

The music comes to a halt, and then the tapping of a champagne glass echoes through the hall. Everyone grows silent, including the three surrounding me.

The Pakhan stands on the stage with Igor and Mikhail on either side of him.

Adrian and Vladimir are close by. Even though Adrian used to be so appreciated by the Pakhan, his popularity and position have taken a huge hit in the past couple of months due to some behavior issues that the Pakhan doesn't approve of.

The one who managed to somehow get him back in favor was none other than Kirill. He will cash in on that sooner or later, but it's still a gesture that gets him in Adrian's favor, and that's a good place to be.

Sergei waits a few moments before he starts in a composed, wise tone, "Thank you all for attending this gathering and bringing your loved ones along. In this organization, we believe in family values and lifelong prosperity. We believe in shaking our allies' hands and bringing them to our table." He raises his glass in the direction of the Yakuza leader, then the Luciano family's head, and then to the Triads. "To allies."

"To allies," everyone else echoes, then drinks.

Damien snatches a glass of vodka from his guard's hand and nearly chugs all of it down.

Kyle drinks from his champagne, and Rai sips from a mocktail.

That's when I finally spot Kirill. He's standing in the front row along with Yulia, Konstantin, and Igor's wife, daughter, and son.

Viktor is on the opposite side, close enough to interfere but far enough to not get in their space.

I frown. Since when has Kirill been close with Igor's family? Well, yes, he does business with Igor and his eldest son, and we even go to their house sometimes, but that doesn't mean he'd be too familiar with his extended family in public, right?

"Because we believe in family," Sergei continues. "We also believe in joining together for the greater and prosperous future of the brotherhood. I'm happy to announce that two of our greatest families and leaders, the Petrovs and the Morozovs, will now be joined by marriage. This banquet is to celebrate the engagement of Kirill and Kristina." He raises his glass. "To the future."

"To the future!" everyone, including Kirill and Kristina, Igor's daughter, echoes as they raise their glasses.

Then he grabs her hand in his and leads her to the stage. She's dressed in an elegant black dress, her blonde curls falling to her shoulders with so much sophistication it's nauseating.

I think I'm dreaming.

This has to be a nightmare, right?

But then Kirill smiles charmingly and lifts her hand, showcasing a huge diamond ring on her finger.

She has Kirill's ring on her finger.

The man to whom I confessed my love for after he fucked me into oblivion not two hours ago is engaged to another woman.

A beautiful, elegant, and absolutely stunning woman.

And everyone is here to celebrate it.

"Sasha?"

I blink the blurriness in my eyes away and robotically focus on Rai. She's touching my arm and dragging me away from everyone.

"You're crying," she whispers. "I assume you don't want anyone to see that, right?"

I don't reply. I can't.

I've lost my voice and…every part of me that made any sense.

Once we're in a hall that's hidden from all the attention, she grabs me by the shoulder. "Are you okay?"

I stare at her numbly. "Please tell me what we just heard was a joke or a play of my imagination or...or simply not true."

She winces. "I'm afraid it's real, Sasha. Granduncle just announced Kirill's engagement to Kristina. Honestly, I don't even know how he accepted her when she was Adrian's fiancée six years ago. I guess Igor is ready to sacrifice that poor girl for whoever he sees fit of his support...oh, God. Why are you crying? Don't tell me...oh no, do you actually like that cunning fox?"

"I...I need to go. I have to...to..."

"Sasha..." She softens her voice. "He's no good for you. Or anyone, for that matter. He's an opportunist, and if you have feelings for him, he'll just use them to reach his end goal. It's not too late to remove yourself from his side."

It is too late.

So, *so* late.

"I need to go." I forcibly remove her hand and run outside.

She calls my name, but I'm not hearing her.

The cold air hits my face, and then the rain. It's raining hard and heavily, but I don't stop as I run and run.

I get soaked in seconds, but I'm thankful that the rain camouflages my tears.

But nothing can mend my heart that's currently shattering to pieces.

TWENTY-TWO

Kirill

THIS NIGHT IS GOING WORSE THAN I PREDICTED.

Yes, I knew Sasha wouldn't like the news of my engagement, but I didn't think she'd cry in public.

If Rai hadn't dragged her away, I have no fucking clue what she would've done.

Would she have done anything? Or would she have stood there crying and then I would've been the one who drew unwanted attention?

I'm overthinking at this point with no concrete plan or course of action.

Fucking liar.

I welcomed the deal both Igor and the Pakhan offered me a few days ago.

If it were just Igor wanting me to marry his daughter for some sort of families' union, I would've comfortably said no.

I'm not Adrian. Where he was previously engaged to Kristina

for the mere purpose of an alliance with the secretly most powerful family in the brotherhood, I'm doing it for higher purposes.

That's why I only accepted this deal once the Pakhan gave me an offer I couldn't refuse.

Kristina gives me a reserved smile as we stand side by side to accept everyone's congratulations. She's a woman made for this role. She has no character, no opinion, and no purpose other than being her father's trump card.

She's as beautiful...as a lifeless doll. Expressionless in private and an actress in public.

Yulia and Stella, Igor's wife, are on either side of us. Now, this whole thing is a pain in the ass, except for one part. The look on Yulia's face when she realized that I'm playing the long game and that whatever she has planned will fail miserably once I'm in my future position.

She does have to put on a show in front of the world, though, so as not to embarrass herself.

I'm going to make this woman watch every moment as I stomp on each and every one of her grandiose dreams. I'll crush her hopes and plans, so she'll really wish she'd killed me when I didn't have the strength to fight back.

Konstantin, however, fucked off to God knows where as soon as the engagement was announced. If I wasn't imagining things, I'd think Kristina stiffened, too, but she didn't look at anyone but me and her father tonight.

My eyes keep filtering back to where Sasha disappeared with Rai earlier. A few minutes later, the Pakhan's grandniece came back alone.

I pull out my phone and type a text.

Kirill: Where's Lipovsky?

Viktor meets my gaze from the other end of the room before his reply comes.

Viktor: Seriously? You think I have the time or energy to focus on that little fuck?

I'm going to fucking kill Viktor. For a very irrational reason. Of course, he's in no frame of mind to focus on her when his top priority is to ensure my safety, but that doesn't seem as important right now.

Kirill: Find him. It's urgent.

He goes erect at that and nods before he disappears from sight. I track his movements and discreetly take inventory of the crowd. There's no sign of her.

Did she leave?

Adrian stops before me, a hand secured around his wife's lower back. She stares at Kristina, pauses, then forces a smile. "Congratulations."

My fiancée, who I'm starting to suspect is a robot, smiles as she's done with everyone. "Thank you."

This woman doesn't even care that Lia actually took her previous fiancé. Not only that, but she also accepts Adrian's half-assed congratulations with another smile.

Lia tells Adrian she's going to the ladies' room and the crazy asshole actually motions at one of his guards to follow. His wife merely shakes her head and teasingly hits his arm before she disappears.

Adrian follows her with his darkening gaze long after she's no longer in sight. I've always found it amusing how an unfeeling man like him has this level of affinity for another human being.

You say that as if you're not in the same boat, motherfucker.

Adrian grabs me by the shoulder. "I'm going to borrow Kirill for a minute."

He doesn't wait for anyone's reply as he pushes me onto a quiet balcony. The cold penetrates my suit, and my jaw tightens but for an entirely different reason than the change of temperature.

I barely have access to the hall and, therefore, can't see if Sasha has returned.

"Make it quick," I say absentmindedly. "Besides, why are you acting so friendly all of a sudden? Didn't you pierce my little black heart by telling me not to get in touch unless absolutely necessary?"

"Do you have any fucking idea what you're doing?" His body is tense but only for a moment before he releases a breath. "You're playing with fucking fire."

"My, Adrian. If I didn't know better, I'd say you're worried about me."

"*Focus.*" He drives his fist against my shoulder, knocking me back a step. "This is dangerous."

"And how do you know what *this* is?"

"It doesn't take a genius to figure out you've always been after the highest position. I suspect that Igor promised to get you there and Sergei agreed to renounce to you when his health condition worsens."

"The cat's out of the bag, huh?"

"This might backfire any moment if you don't commit to your side of the deal."

"Why wouldn't I?" I grab his shoulder and squeeze. "Now, real talk. When it's time for the elections, you'll vote for me, right? You know no one can drive this organization better than me."

"That's all you care about?"

"What else is there? Unless…you're thinking of running yourself?"

"Unlike you, fucking idiot, I have a family I need to protect, and to do that, I won't put myself in the limelight. I prefer to work in the shadows."

"And you'll keep doing that. In fact, when I become Pakhan, you'll be my favorite."

"You really don't see the danger you'll be exposed to when you're at the top, do you?"

"The benefits outweigh the danger." I grin. "No one will be able to touch me once I'm there."

"I have one piece of advice for you, Kirill. Walk the fuck away before it's too late."

"There's no going back now."

"Right. Igor will kill you if his daughter is stranded again."

"No thanks to you. Don't you regret not taking this chance while you could? If you'd married Kristina, Igor would've made it his mission to get *you* to the top."

"There are a lot of regrets in my life, but marrying Lia was never one of them." He pushes me with his shoulder on his way out. "Enjoy the craziness."

He calls it craziness, I call it power.

And I'll soon have it all at my disposal.

My phone vibrates.

> **Viktor:** Lipovsky is not on the property. One of the other guards told me he saw him leave.

Fuck.

My hand tightens around the phone, and I take a few calming breaths. I'm barely stopping myself from ditching the party that's being thrown in my honor and going to search for her.

> **Kirill:** Find him, Viktor. I don't care about the method.

I swear to fuck, if she does something stupid...

My thought trails off when Rai intercepts my path and tries to push me back onto the balcony. I consider tripping her, but since I'm not in the mood to kill the infant in her belly, I follow the motion and thrust myself back into the cold.

"What the fuck is this? Corner Kirill Day?" I let my lips pull in a smirk. "Are you perhaps mad that I'm getting more power, Rai?"

"Oh, fuck you and your egomania," she spits out. "How could you do that to Sasha?"

My humor disappears. "Do what?"

"She was a mess, Kirill! Didn't you see her crying, or are you so far up your own ass that you didn't notice the suffering you caused her? You're a damn monster!"

I want to snap Rai's neck, but then again, that would ruin the evening and my deal with her damn granduncle. So I inhale calming breaths. "What did she tell you?"

"She didn't tell me anything, but I could see the heartbreak in her eyes. If you'd shot her in the chest, she wouldn't have looked like that."

My jaw tightens. "Do you know where she went?"

"No, and even if I knew, I wouldn't tell you. I said it before, and I will say it again. You're a cunning fox and an unfeeling monster who doesn't, under any circumstances, deserve someone as pure as Sasha. The only decent thing you can do in this situation is to let her go."

Not in this lifetime.

I leave Rai outside and return to the party, ignoring her curses. She's obnoxious on most days, but she's especially irritating today.

My expression is welcoming as I step back into the engagement parade.

Anyone who's watching from the outside would think I'm ecstatic about this. We even take pictures for the press and everything in between.

Deep down, however, it's a raging volcano, and it's all because of one damn girl.

By the time the evening is over, I'm ready to turn the earth upside down to find her because Viktor and even Yuri and Maksim couldn't locate the little shit.

Before I do that, however, I have to take part in a private meeting with both Igor and Sergei and an extremely displeased Vladimir.

From what I know, he doesn't want the position either, but at the same time, he doesn't want *me* to have it.

But since he agrees with the Pakhan on almost anything, I

don't imagine he'll give me any trouble. If he does, I'll deal with it accordingly.

After we're done, I leave and take a rain check on a drink Igor invites me to.

Since Viktor confirmed Sasha isn't on the premises, we go immediately to the house.

Apparently, she's not with Karina as I expected her to be.

Where else could she have gone? Sasha's world has always revolved around the mansion and my protection. She has no friends, relationships, or places she can turn to outside the house.

Naturally, her phone is turned off, so I can't track her through that.

Fucking fuck.

My men spend a whole hour flipping the mansion and the guards' quarters upside down, but they find no trace of her.

Viktor calls off the search after they do it twice because, according to his words, "It's a wasted effort."

I'm really in the mood to waste his life now.

But he's right. If I keep insisting on overworking my men, this might backfire and not necessarily against me. They might take this out on her when she comes back.

And she *will* come back.

I step into my room for a change of clothes. I'll take a run around the mansion's premises just in case they missed a spot.

That fucking irritating woman better be safe, or I swear to fucking fuck—

My thoughts halt when I walk into my closet. The automatic lights go on, and the stench of alcohol hits me in the face.

Sasha sits on the floor, her jacket thrown to the side and a bottle of vodka nestled between her hands.

Tears streak down her cheeks, and her eyes are too brown, too lost, as if they murdered all the green and are currently mourning it.

Relief washes over me. Here I thought she was doing something stupid somewhere I couldn't find her, but she's been in here.

In hindsight, I should've checked my room, but I didn't think she'd be here, of all places.

I stand in front of her, and she slowly looks up at me with wrenched eyes.

"You done dropping your fiancée off at home?" A slur interlinks with her words.

Sasha never, and I mean *never* gets drunk. Not even during her off days. When everyone else gets hammered, she's more concerned about driving back here safely or making sure none of them commits a mistake they'll regret.

So to see her like this is…strange, to say the least.

She always called me an emotionless vault, but she's closed off herself. Even though she's warm and friendly with the guards, she has this reserved quality that's fairly hard to read.

"I didn't." I speak as calmly as I can muster. "As a matter of fact, she went back with her family."

She laughs, the sound loud and unhinged before it ends in a hiccup, and she chokes on a tear. "You're not even going to offer any excuses?"

"There are no excuses to offer." I crouch in front of her. "Kristina is nothing but a business transaction. She's only a step I'm using to reach the top, and she knows it."

"And…you think that's okay? You think that makes it any better?"

"Don't be irrational, Sasha. You know that my goal has always been the sky, and this is a perfect method to accomplish that."

"Irrational…yeah. I guess I am, right? I'm irrational for thinking about you with her, for seeing you holding her hand in public and putting a ring on her finger. You're going to marry her, too. You will also have to put a baby in her to make sure this thing works out, no? It'll be like a fairy tale."

"Sasha—"

"I'll never have that with you," she cuts me off in a voice so pained, so broken, I want to kick myself in the balls. "I can't be your woman in front of everyone."

"That's not a choice I made. *You* did."

"I know…I know…I made myself into a man, and I have to live with the consequences. I have to…stay like this." She sniffles and takes another sip from the bottle. "But if I…if I become a woman again, would you end it with her?"

I slowly close my eyes, and when I open them, she's looking at me with so much expectation, the fact that I have to turn them black sickens me. "I can't do that. You'll be killed by the Pakhan and Igor."

A sob rips out of her throat, and she hits my chest with the bottle of vodka, sending splashes all over my shirt and jacket. "And you don't think you're killing me right now?"

"It's temporary. Once I become the one who rules everyone, you can be a woman all you want. No one will dare defy me."

"And what am I supposed to do until then? Be your guard while you court Kristina? Watch you marry her? Kiss her? Bring her here? I can't do that, Kirill!" She sobs. "I just can't!"

My jaw tightens. "If you prefer to stay with Karina for a while, I will allow it."

"No! I'm still in your space that way. I will still hear about you and your future wife, and I can't…I can't…"

"What do you suggest then?"

Her lips tremble. "End it with her. Choose *me*."

"I told you I can't do that."

Fresh tears stream down her cheeks, and she lets her hand that's holding the bottle fall to her side. "Then let me go."

My hand flexes, about to turn into a fist and choke the fucking shit out of her. "*No.*"

"You can't have us both!" She punches me in the chest. "I won't be your damn mistress!"

"You'll be whatever the fuck I want you to be, Sasha." I grab her by the throat. "You owe me, remember? You also told me you love me and wouldn't leave me only a few hours ago. Do you re-member that or did you already forget about your promise at the first test?"

"I didn't think you'd have another woman, or I would've never said that!" She pushes at my chest. "Please let me go. You'll have your wife, duties, and stupid power, and I'll have my own path. Do it for both of us."

"No. You already pledged your life to me."

"I want out, Kirill. If you…make me watch you with her, I'll run away, and you'll never find me."

"Who are you running to, hmm?" I squeeze my fingers tighter around her throat. "Your lover in Russia? Are you using this chance to reunite with him?"

"What if I am? What if I fucking am!" She pushes me so hard, she actually manages to make me loosen my grip, then she frees herself and knocks me on my back.

I let her straddle me, tears clinging to her eyes, but her ex-pression is that of a warrior. "You have a damn fiancée, so you have no fucking right to talk to me about a lover or a hundred of them. Fuck you, Kirill! Fuck you! Fuck you!"

Her tears drip onto my cheek, my nose, and I taste them on my lips.

My fingers bunch in her shirt. "You'll never leave me, Sasha. *Never.*"

And then I tug her down and slam her mouth against mine. She tries to resist, but I flip us over so that I'm on top and she's beneath me.

I kiss her, and she kisses me back, but she soon bites my lower lip, then wrestles me so that she's on top again. A metallic taste explodes in my mouth, and I'm not sure if it's her blood or mine.

Turns out, it's both of ours. When she pushes back, her lips are bloodied, her eyes full of tears, and her face is a map of destruction.

"You'll never keep me, asshole. You made your choice, and I'm making mine." She grabs me by the shirt and then punches me in the face. "Fuck you!"

And then she pushes off me and runs to the entrance.

My lips pull in a smirk. Does she think she can leave me?

She must've underestimated what I really meant by *never*.

There will never be a day when Sasha is no longer mine.

TWENTY-THREE

Sasha

I SLOWLY OPEN MY EYES, AND A STRONG HEADACHE SPREADS from my temples to my forehead.

A burn explodes in my lower lip, and my body feels like a heavy brick.

I prop myself up on my elbows and groan when nausea assaults my throat. Damn it.

I'm not a drinker, so why the hell did I consume so much alcohol…?

Memories from last night hit me in my already-fried brain.

The party, the engagement, the…way Kirill so easily suggested that it's normal that he has Kristina and me.

I bit and punched him and was so determined to leave, but then a few steps later, I collapsed outside of his bedroom due to the amount of alcohol I consumed on an empty stomach.

He must've carried me here. That's the only way I would've ended up in his bed.

I look down at myself and release a breath when I find my crumpled shirt and even my chest bandages intact.

If I'd let him have his way with me after swearing never to go near him, I'd never forgive myself.

The pain that I didn't even manage to numb with alcohol resurrects from the ashes, and my bleeding heart nearly bursts from the pressure.

My hand balls into a fist, and I hit the center of my chest, but it's still hard to breathe or even find a reason to breathe.

I start to get out of bed. I can't stay here where I'm surrounded by his scent. He's not mine anymore. He's Kristina Petrova's.

He was never yours, idiot.

That reminder brings tears to my eyes, and I stumble out of bed so fast, I fall in a heap of covers.

My knees take the hit and I cry harder. Right then, moments from when he carried me back here last night come to me in small bursts.

I grab the edge of the mattress in horror and recall the epic breakdown I had. I should've ended it after I punched him, but when he carried me here and laid me on this very bed, I held on to his neck and begged him to be with me.

Oh, shit.

"What does she have that I don't? Why can't you be with me?"

"I chose you over my family, so the least you can do is choose me over her."

"Is it because I'm not feminine enough? Do you hate that I'm like this? I can abandon that, too. I might get killed, but who cares? You certainly don't, you fucking asshole!"

"I can't believe I dedicated my life to you, and you so easily replaced me with some beautiful blonde. I'm a blonde, too, by the way. But I have to hide that or else those people will find me."

Oh, no.

Shit.

Fuck!

I cradle my head between my hands. I can't believe I said all of that out loud. I was crying, too, and hugging him. Then I pushed him away and cursed him in all the languages I know—including French. When he tried to lay me down on the bed, I punched him in the chest. He let me do whatever my intoxicated brain thought of.

That's so damn embarrassing.

I really shouldn't have been allowed to drink. At all.

Especially when I'm heartbroken.

But then again, that's the reason I started drinking in the first place. I couldn't stop replaying the image of that woman, his *fiancée*, hanging on to his arm, and I needed to make it disappear.

Even if only for a moment.

I didn't know I would make a fool out of myself in the process.

I rack my brain for what else I could've said in that hyper mood. It's a disaster that I mentioned leaving my family. If I also revealed their identity...

No, I don't think I did.

There was a lot of crying and cursing, though, which contributed to my epic headache.

I touch my forehead and freeze when I recall Kirill's lips on it last night before he murmured, "You can hate me all you want, curse, hit, and take all your emotions out on me, but you're not allowed to leave me."

I think that was around the time I finally fell asleep.

My gaze filters back to the clock. Eleven a.m.

Fuck.

A small knock sounds on the door, and I freeze. If it's Kirill, I don't know how the hell I'm going to deal with him. It's hard enough that he thinks this whole thing is okay. How can he possibly think that he can have the best of both worlds and I'll be okay with it?

I secretly took pride in how he never looked at any other

woman the way he looked at me. Hell, he's never even looked at other women, and I was the sole object of his desire.

I was even fascinated by how he couldn't get enough of me. How he made an effort and made me feel like it wasn't just about the physical connection.

But then, not only did he get himself another woman, but he's also going to marry her.

The knock comes again, and I release a breath. It can't be Kirill. He doesn't knock.

Anna steps inside, holding a tray, and pauses when she sees my state. I stumble to a standing position and wince when pain explodes in my temples.

She hastily places the tray on the nightstand and sits me back down.

"Don't force it," she says in a soft voice. "You okay?"

I nod.

"Kirill said you weren't doing well and could use some breakfast." She motions at the tray she bought, which is similar to one she'd make for Kirill.

Anna warmed up to me after she found out I saved him in Russia and again after that cartel shipment incident.

I think I got her seal of approval for having the ability to protect Kirill. And for what?

I dedicated my life to him, but he gave me the middle finger in return.

"Thanks, but I'm not hungry."

"Nonsense. Look at your malnourished face." She brings me a bowl of what looks like soup. "Here, have this. It'll help with the hangover."

I start to protest but stop when she raises a brow and hikes a hand on her hip, silently saying, 'I dare you to try.'

Clearing my throat, I grab the bowl and drink it in one go.

Anna doesn't leave until she gets me to eat a piece of toast with jam and butter and two boiled eggs.

After she's gone, I take a shower and head to the closet. My heart shatters all over again, and I burst into tears as I put on my clothes.

This part of the closet will belong to his wife now. Everything will. His bed. His body. His last name.

I hit my chest over and over again.

Why the fuck does this hurt so much? No one told me about the pain of having a broken heart.

After the wave subsides, I lift my chin and stare at my face in the mirror. Even though it's tear-streaked and my eyes are bloodshot. I make a vow to myself that I won't ever be this weak again. *Never.*

And in order to do that, I have to remove myself from Kirill's immediate surroundings.

A sob fights to break through, but I swallow it down even as a tear clings to my lower lid and then streams down my face.

I can do this. I've survived worse.

My movements are mechanical as I pack what I can fit of my things into a duffel bag. I stop at the room's threshold and cast one last look behind me.

Every corner of this place is filled with memories of us. He fucked me in every nook and on every surface. He held me as I slept on that bed and sofa. He carried me in his arms to the bathroom and even offered me a shoulder to cry on after a hard experience.

He was there for me, until he wasn't.

Until he ended us so cruelly that the wound is still gaping and bleeding all over the ground.

I wish him all the unhappiness in the world. I'm not much of a selfless person. I won't wish him and his new fiancée well. I wish for them to suffer every day. I wish that he'll see my shadow in every corner of this room and have nightmares about me.

"I hope you never forget about me and that the thought of me haunts you for eternity," I whisper, then close the door and go down the hallway.

I don't even know where I'll go now. If I fly to Russia, will Babushka and Uncle accept me again? Will they make me kill Kirill now?

No. I can't do that, no matter how much he hurt me.

But where else can I go if not Russia?

"Lipovsky."

I stand tall and slowly turn around to be greeted with Viktor's dispassionate gaze. He studies me from head to toe. "Where do you think you're going?"

"I'm quitting." My lips curve in a bitter smile. "Good for you, huh? You can finally go back to being the only senior guard."

"That won't be happening."

"What do you mean by that? I want to quit."

"That's not how it works. There's no such thing as quitting the Bratva. This is for life."

"Surely there are exceptions?"

"Only if Kirill allows it."

Shit. He clearly said no to that last night.

"Well, you can convince him of that." I start to turn around. "I'll go say goodbye to Karina and the guys."

Viktor strides ahead and steps in front of me, and I stop when he narrows his eyes on me.

"What?" I whisper, not sure what to make of his expression.

"Is this why you left your post and disappeared last night?"

I purse my lips.

"You're not the type who leaves their post. Ever."

Yeah, well. That was the last thing on my mind after I was metaphorically hit in the face by the news of Kirill's engagement.

"Listen." He grabs me by the shoulders. "I know you like Boss, but he can't be with you in that sense. He's expected to get married and have kids. Especially if he's shooting for the Pakhan position. You understand that, right?"

My neck heats. Can the earth just swallow me now?

I forgot that Viktor thinks I'm gay and crushing on Kirill. But for some reason, the fact that he's attempting to comfort me—or as much comforting as someone like Viktor can offer—makes me want to cry.

"I don't know how hard it'll be, but try to stay," he continues.

"I can't do that. I'm not as emotionless as him and won't possibly be able to watch him with her every day."

"I don't think it'll be every day."

I smile, but only because Viktor sounds weird in his attempts to offer support.

"Just let me leave, Viktor."

He shakes his head once. "I can't do that. Boss asked me to bring you to him as soon as you wake up."

My lips purse. Of course he'd want to make the wound deeper. It's already ugly. Why does he have to rub salt in it, too?

"If you let me go, no one will know, and I'll be out of your hair."

His expression doesn't change. "You can either come with me willingly or by force."

"Is there a third option where I walk out this door, and you erase the security footage?"

"No."

I release a long sigh. "You're like a damn wall."

He doesn't react to that and starts walking in the direction of the basement.

"What is he doing down there?" I ask to distract myself from thinking about the doomsday-like feeling of having to see Kirill.

Viktor, however, doesn't answer. The heavy weight of his steps contrasts with my lighter ones, and I grab the duffel bag's strap tighter.

Kirill usually comes down here when he's either in the mood to torture someone or for the home theatre.

I really hope it's the second option.

Viktor stops in front of Kirill's underground suite. I've been here before, and it looks a lot like his room upstairs, minus the balcony and the view.

"Are you going to go in as well?" I ask Viktor almost pleadingly.

To my horror, he shakes his head and motions at the door. I contemplate running, but that's impossible with Viktor here— unless I shoot him, and I don't want to do that.

I inhale deeply to dispel the shaking in my limbs and push the door open. It automatically clicks shut behind me, and I flinch, then I immediately scold myself.

What the fuck am I being so jumpy about? I'm not the one in the wrong here. He is.

And I'm not going to cower away from him.

It's just that…the wound is too fresh and too raw. I don't know if I can stop myself from being emotional when facing him.

And he's an apathetic psycho. If I'm the one being all over the place while he's calmly standing there, it'll look like I'm the irrational, crazy one, when it's the other way around.

"Going somewhere, Sasha?"

I freeze and stare at the dark corner where his voice came from. The dim lighting of the room makes him look like a devil slithering out of hell.

He has one hand in his pocket and the other wrapped around a glass of whiskey. There's a cut on his lower lip, exactly like the one on mine from when we warred last night.

Despite having his glasses on, his eyes pierce right through me, and it takes everything in me to stare back without feeling the need to bolt.

"I want to quit," I say in a surprisingly leveled voice.

A cruel smirk lifts his lips. "You can quit, but you can't leave."

"I'm getting out of here. I don't care if you agree or disagree."

"You're already packed and probably believe what you're saying, too." He steps toward me, and my legs shake, demanding I retreat, but it's too late when he stops in front of me and lifts my chin with two fingers. "I told you this last night, but I'll repeat it again, in case you were too drunk to remember. You can *never* leave me. That option isn't on the table, under the table, or even in the fucking room."

I let the duffel bag fall to the floor and slap his hand away. "Don't touch me."

He shoots for my neck this time, but I jump out of reach. My eyes must be blazing with volcanic anger.

"Sasha…" he warns.

"Don't Sasha me. You have a Kristina now, don't you? Go to her to fulfill your twisted fetishes."

"If you keep acting like this, I will."

My lips part.

"You don't like that, do you? The idea of me touching her has turned your face into that of a ghost. So stop being difficult and accept that she means nothing. Absolutely. Nothing."

I shake my head a few times. I can feel the emotions rushing through me and the fight slowly leaving my limbs. I don't want to feel this way, but I do.

"I can't watch you with her. Even if you say she means nothing, she'll be your wife, and I can't put myself through that. Don't make me, Kirill." I approach him and take his hand in my shaking one. "If I ever meant anything to you, spare me this torture and let me go."

His jaw tightens, and his hand feels stiff and heavy in mine. "No."

My nose tingles, and my eyes burn, but I release him with a jerk. "I'm leaving anyway."

I grab my duffel bag, but Kirill pushes it out of my hold and throws it against the wall. Then he grabs me by the hip. I freeze for a second, still unable to prevent my mind and body from reacting to him.

When I finally snap out of it, he's already released me, but not before he pulls my gun out of the hoister and slips it into the back of his pants.

He sighs deeply and looks at me as if I'm the villain in this story. "I was hoping you'd see reason so it wouldn't come to this, but you forced my hand, Sasha."

"What do you mean…?"

"You'll stay here until you come to your senses."

"Are you…locking me up?"

"I prefer not having to use this method, but you're being unreasonable and refuse to change your mind, so I have to resort to this."

"You can't do that, Kirill." I push against him, but he easily pushes me back, and I stumble and then nearly fall.

The man who looks back at me is more a monster than a man. A heartless person with no care whatsoever about what he's doing.

"You promised you'd never leave me, and I'll make sure you keep that promise." He strokes my chin, then the cut on my lip that burns. "No matter what, Solnyshko."

And then he leaves, and the door closes behind him, cementing the finality of the situation.

He really is putting me in confinement.

TWENTY-FOUR

Sasha

I'M GOING CRAZY.

I've been pacing the length of this room for the past two days, back and forth like a caged animal.

At first, I looked for an escape and tried the door, but it's made from blended material as if it was designed to withstand bombs or something. I can't even pick the lock, because it's thumbprint protected.

The windows at the top are a lost cause, too, considering they're made of tempered glass.

Since that asshole Kirill took away my gun, I'm completely defenseless and without a way out.

I glare at the bracelet around my wrist. The one I've been religiously wearing since he gave it to me on my birthday. I threw it down earlier, but soon after, I got to my knees to search for it.

Maybe there's something wrong with my head, because I don't seem ready to abandon this part of me yet.

The thought of Kirill's upcoming marriage always brings tears to my eyes, and while I don't expect myself to get over it this quickly, I also hate this.

I hate strong emotions.

The helplessness.

The emptiness.

And right now, I hate *him*.

The least he can do after he stabbed me in the heart is to let me be. But no. Of course the damn monster has other plans.

What? I don't know.

I feel like he's teaching me some sort of a lesson right now. Is he mentally torturing me? Maybe he's testing my limits and how far it'll take me to snap.

No one's come around, and there's no signal on my phone. A fridge that's stocked with food sits in the corner beside a microwave, but that's about it.

Under different circumstances, this place would be good for a small retreat. Not only does it look like a hotel suite, but there's also a Jacuzzi tub and a huge cinema-like TV in the living area.

Needless to say, I haven't used either.

And I have barely slept.

My mind has been pushed around and strained so many times over the past few days that I'm surprised it hasn't given up on me yet.

The worst part is that Kirill hasn't come around for over two days. Fifty-two hours, to be more specific. But who's counting?

I'm slowly losing it, though. I've never gone this much time without action or something to do. And the worst part is that I can't leave this prison until His Majesty Kirill decides I can.

I've been doing push-ups and using the few machines in the corner of the room, but those activities are barely keeping me focused.

After pacing for thirty minutes, I hop in the shower for the third time today and take an ice-cold one. Once I'm finished, I leave my bandages off and put on joggers and a T-shirt.

It feels weird to walk around with my breasts free, but they could use some air. It's super uncomfortable when they bounce, though.

I stare in the mirror and wince at my bloodshot eyes. So yes, maybe I cried myself to sleep last night and kept replaying the image of Kirill's stupid engagement.

When will I ever be free of these emotions?

My hair is getting longer again, reaching my nape. I swear it grows so much in so little time just to mock me for not being able to keep it.

I pull at it and then release a frustrated sigh.

Surely Maksim and Yuri are looking for me, right? Unless Kirill told them something that made them believe I don't need help.

A creak comes from the front door, and I stumble out of the closet and run to the living room. I come to a slow halt when I find Kirill standing by the door, looking more dashing than a model.

It's been only a few days since I last saw him, but it feels like forever. He's the same person, but for some reason, he's also not.

The jacket stretches around his bulging biceps, and the few undone buttons of his shirt reveal a hint of the tattoos on his chest.

He strides inside, his icy eyes filling with undeniable lust as he takes in the length of me. It doesn't matter what I wear, Kirill always seems to be able to see beneath every layer of fabric.

It's as if I'm always standing naked in front of him.

I clear my throat in a helpless attempt to chase away the lump stuck there. "Are you going to let me go?"

His attention finally slides back to my face, but that's not necessarily a good thing. Tension lurks beneath his narrowing eyes as if they're hiding something. "That depends on whether or not you've come to your senses. You've had plenty of time to think about it, no?"

"What does that mean?"

"Are you going to abandon that nonsense about leaving?"

"No! You can't make me stay here against my will, Kirill."

He adjusts his glasses with his middle finger, looking as cold as a statue. "News flash, I'm already doing that, and if you keep defying me, I'll take this further."

"Further...how?"

Is there something worse than keeping me as a prisoner and confiscating my freedom?

"You'll never leave this place until you stop being stubborn for no reason."

"No reason?" The emotions flow back into my words again, and I jut a finger at his chest. "How is being cast aside because Your Majesty is having an arranged marriage called no reason?"

He engulfs my forefinger, and the rest of my hand in his, then spreads my palm on his chest. More accurately, on the steady rhythm of his beating heart. My own heartbeat picks up and refuses to be brought back down.

His expression sharpens, and a tinge of strange emotion ignites in his light eyes for a fraction of a second. "That's where you're wrong. I never cast you aside. You're doing that yourself."

"Well, excuse me if I don't want to be the other woman."

"The only other woman in this equation is Kristina."

"But she's the one who'll be your wife!" My vision blurs, and I wipe my eyes with the back of my hand.

Why do I get riled up this easily? Why can't I be as detached as he is while he's ripping my chest open?

Just *why?*

"Is that what you want to be? My wife?"

My lips part, and his words do a strange thing to my bleeding heart. The gaping wound slowly closes as if it's been touched by a magic wand, and that's fucked up, because I know for a fact that he's just throwing me a bone right now.

I always knew Kirill excelled at mental torture. I just didn't realize I'd be on the receiving end one day.

This is just too cruel.

"Don't say things you don't mean." I sniffle.

"When have I ever lied to you?" He steps closer, killing the distance between us, and wraps his hand around my waist even as I push at his chest. "Answer the question, Sasha, do you want to be my wife?"

My fight wanes, partly due to his words and partly because I'm breathing his cedar and woods scent with each inhale. I didn't realize how much I missed it and him until right now.

My fingers curl into his jacket as I take his face in. He's so close that I see my reflection in his glasses—vulnerable and stupidly hopeful. But I still hold on to him, to the damn optimism and the smokescreen of happiness.

This is all I have left, and believing in the half-full part is better than wallowing in misery.

"If I say yes, will you make it happen?" I whisper.

A smile lifts his lips. It's not cruel or condescending. It's not sadistic or cunning. It's...triumphant. Happy, even.

This is the first time I've ever seen this expression on Kirill's face, and I don't know why that makes me want to smile back.

His free hand strokes my cheek, and I instinctively lean into his touch, then it lowers to my neck, and he wraps his fingers around it as he whispers in my ear, "Fucking mine."

He releases me as quickly as he grabbed me. "I'll be back."

I stare, dumbfounded, as the door closes behind him.

Once he's out of sight, I run toward it and bang on the stupid metal. "You can't keep locking me up, Kirill! Let me go!!"

No reply comes. I continue hitting the door for a few more minutes until my fists and legs ache. Then I hit my head against it.

What the hell was I thinking?

The fact that I even suggested being his wife is an anomaly

in and of itself, but to also be rejected so subtly makes me want
to scream.

Kirill is definitely a master of manipulation, because I can already feel the mental toll of this situation.

Damn it.

Damn it.

What if he keeps me here forever, and then I have to live
through being his mistress?

Oh, God.

I won't be able to survive that.

I straighten. No. I'm getting out of here no matter what.

The next time he returns, I'll attack him and run away. If he
doesn't want that, then he shouldn't have imprisoned me.

The question is, however, what if he doesn't come back anytime soon?

⁓

Just when I think I'll start hitting my head against the door again,
it opens.

Exactly two days later.

I jump up from the sofa and grab my chosen object of attack—a heavy vase—and run to the door. My feet come to a halt
when Kirill walks in with an older man while rolling a suitcase.

The vase remains suspended in midair. Obviously, I lost the
element of surprise, but that's only because I've been taken completely aback.

Kirill is dressed in a dashing tuxedo, his hair is styled to perfection, and his eyes shine with a rare gleam behind the spotless
glasses.

My arm loses strength, and I let it and the vase fall to my side.
"What's…going on?"

"Wait here," Kirill tells the man who's dressed in a smart
suit, has a small belly, and is wearing strong aftershave that I can

smell from here. He's also carrying a briefcase like some sort of accountant.

After he nods, Kirill walks to my side and grabs me by the arm. I don't have time to protest as he drags me and the suitcase to the adjoining bedroom and closes the door.

I twist my arm free and jump away from him, my mind racing with countless options. I can still hit him now and run. That man outside didn't look strong enough, so I can probably handle him—

"You should have everything you need here." He pushes the suitcase in my direction. "Make it quick."

Curiosity gnaws at me, but I don't touch it. "What's in there?"

"A wedding dress. Lingerie. Some makeup in case you need it." He reaches into his jacket and then retrieves a black velvet box.

My heart nearly stops when he opens it, revealing two rings. One is a simple band for a man and the other is a gorgeous gold solitaire with a huge green rock on top.

The vase falls and hits the mattress as Kirill walks in my direction.

I think I'm going to hyperventilate.

No, I *am* hyperventilating.

Is this a dream?

Because if it is, then it's too cruel.

"These took longer than I preferred." He pulls out the ring, and tears gather in my eyes.

Oh, God.

On the inside of the green ring, '*Kirill's*' is engraved. As for the band, it says, '*Sasha's*,' both done in cursive. "K-Kirill...what...?"

"You asked me if I could make it happen." He takes my hand in his and kisses the back of it. "I'm making it happen."

"But what about Kristina? Igor? The alliance? Your position—"

"Shh." He places a finger on my mouth. "Don't worry your head about any of that. Just get changed...unless you want to get married looking like this?"

I shake my head frantically. "I'll get changed… Just give me a moment."

A rare grin curves his lips. "Does that mean you agree to marry me, Solnyshko?"

"I didn't know I had a choice." Besides, he just proved that he chose me over Kristina, so why can't I choose him?

"You don't, so I'm glad we're on the same page."

I smile, and he brushes his lips against mine, then possessively bites the lower one before he leaves and closes the door.

He's really an asshole.

And I'm marrying this asshole.

Oh my God. I'm actually *marrying* Kirill.

Maybe I should think about this more or say no until I can process the consequences. If I marry Kirill, I can't be his guard anymore, and I have to be a woman. If this gets out, then both of us will be in trouble and…

I shake my head and open the suitcase.

You know what? I don't care. I've always made decisions for other people's sake. This is the only chance I've gotten to have something for myself.

Even my heart, which was battered to near death not too long ago, has stitched itself back together again and is already chanting Kirill's name.

He chose me.

After I begged him to pick me over Kristina, he did, and he's proving it with actions instead of words.

Happy tears cling to my eyelids when I bring out the carefully wrapped wedding dress. The material is soft satin and lace. There's also the most beautiful lingerie set I've ever seen—cream trimmed with pearly beads.

After I put them on, I'm struck by two things. One, they're the perfect size. Jeez. Even I don't know what size I am in women's clothes, but apparently, Kirill does.

Two, I feel so beautiful. So feminine at last.

I might be a tomboy, but I've always dreamed about wearing a wedding dress and dolling up.

There's a whole makeup case with items that I don't even know what to do with. I go for the simple things because I don't really know how to use the others. I put on some mascara and blush, and I finish with soft pink lipstick.

Those are the only things I trust myself with or else I'll paint my face like a clown.

There's also a jewelry set that matches the green ring he showed me earlier—a dazzling necklace, bracelet, and earrings.

He even thought to bring earrings that don't need piercings since mine have long since closed.

After I put them on, I stand up and stare at the mirror.

I almost don't recognize myself. I look so different from my male persona.

The dress hugs my waist and falls to the floor in an extravagance of lace, satin, and pearls sewn to the fabric.

It looks so elegant and stunning.

Even my face has a soft, more feminine feel than usual. My hair, though…I grab the huge flower bouquet, pull out some rose stems, and quickly form a small crown. Then I put on the veil and place it on top.

I smile at my reflection. I'm finally me.

After years of hiding behind another persona, today, I get to be myself.

A knock sounds on the door and Kirill's booming voice follows, "Are you done yet?"

"Yeah! Be right there." I stumble when I try to walk in the shoes. They're not high heels, but they're women's shoes.

I can't believe I forgot how to walk in women's shoes.

The horror.

After I spray some perfume he brought, something soft and flowery, I inhale deeply and exit the bedroom. The man from earlier is sitting at the dining table with some papers in front of him, but that's not what makes me stop.

It's the man who's waiting at the front of the room, who freezes upon seeing me.

Astonishment and awe fill Kirill's expression, and his icy eyes turn to liquid blue as his eyes follows my every step.

Once I'm across from him, I clear my throat. "How do I look?"

He doesn't answer.

I shift. "I know it's weird. I might have caused myself a bit of whiplash, too, and—"

"You're the most beautiful fucking thing I've ever seen."

My breath gets stuck at the base of my throat, and I have to hold back tears. Kirill grabs my hand. "Let's get this over with so I can unwrap you."

I suppress a laugh as he leads me to the man at the table, and we sit opposite him.

I can't stop looking at my fingers threaded into Kirill's. Is it weird that we're getting married, but this is the first time he's held my hand this way?

"Make it quick," he tells the man.

"I can just ask for consent, and then you both sign the certificate," he replies with a Russian accent.

"Let's do that."

"We need two witnesses."

Kirill taps something in his phone and a few seconds later, the door opens. I swallow thickly as Viktor strides inside then stops short upon seeing me.

My face must be different shades of red. Why did it have to be Viktor of all people? Yes, Kirill trusts him the most, but how am I supposed to react when he's looking at me as if I'm a ghost?

"What's the meaning of this?" Viktor asks, staring between us.

"I'm marrying, Sasha." Kirill announces ever so casually. "Be a witness."

"What the fuck—"

"Sit the fuck down and be a witness, Viktor." Kirill orders with no patience whatsoever.

He narrows his eyes on me then settles beside the man who's been watching the scene with careful quietness.

"Lipovsky, you little fuck," Viktor continues grilling me with his gaze. "You're a woman?"

"She obviously is, and watch your fucking tone when you speak to my wife."

Butterflies erupt at the bottom of my stomach and spread throughout my body.

Kirill called me his wife.

His. *Wife.*

"I still don't understand what's going on," Viktor continues. "I need an explanation."

"Later. For now, shut it and be a witness." Kirill turns to the man. "Proceed"

"We need another witness."

"You can be one. Now, go."

The older man nods. "Do you, Kirill Morozov, take Aleksandra Lipovsky—"

"Ivanova," I whisper and stare at Kirill. "My name is Aleksandra Ivanova."

If we're going to get married, he needs to know my real name. We're going to share our lives now, and that means trusting each other.

Kirill's eyes don't shine with recognition at hearing the last name, and that right there is proof that he had nothing to do with my family's death.

Instead, he squeezes my hand in his. "You heard her. It's Aleksandra Ivanova."

"We will need an ID for that..."

"I'll get it to you later. Continue."

The man clears his throat. "Do you, Kirill Morozov, take

Aleksandra Ivanova as your lawfully wedded wife, to love and to cherish, in sickness and in health, till death do you part?"

Kirill's attention never leaves mine as he says with blinding assertiveness, "I do."

I'm about to cry again. Damn it.

The man looks at me. "Do you, Aleksandra Ivanova, take Kirill Morozov as your lawfully wedded husband, to love and to cherish, in sickness and in health, till death do you part?"

I hold back the tears as I finally choose myself. "I do."

Kirill's eyes blaze in a deep, deep blue that nearly sweeps me under from the intensity. He lifts my hand and slips the band on my ring finger, then offers me his hand.

My movements are shaky as I do the same.

We then sign our names where the pastor or civil servant tells us to.

"I now pronounce you husband and wife. You may now kiss the bride…"

The man hasn't even finished his words, but Kirill has already tugged me toward him by the nape and slams his mouth to mine.

He kisses me like he's my husband.

And I'm his wife.

I'm Kirill's wife.

I kiss him as passionately as he kisses me, matching his intensity with mine.

This time, I let the happy tears loose.

TWENTY-FIVE

Kirill

I HAVE A WIFE.

And her name is Aleksandra Ivanova.

My perception of marriage was skewed from a young age due to Roman and Yulia's toxic and excruciatingly incompatible pairing.

They taught me to loathe the idea of tying oneself to another person for life, which is why I've always viewed marriage as a possible business opportunity. Nothing more and nothing less.

However, those feelings have changed dramatically since I witnessed Sasha's state following the news of my engagement to Kristina.

She was crying nonstop. I know because I have cameras here and I'm the only one with access. What made matters worse was how she was often looking for ways to escape me.

I didn't expect much when I asked if she wanted to be my

wife, but her reaction woke a foreign part of me. A poignant sense of possessiveness grabbed hold of me and still refuses to let go.

The room plunges into silence after Viktor escorts the civil servant out. Part because I can't get enough of studying the woman standing in front of me, looking like the best present I've ever received.

Her cheeks are covered with a pink hue, and her lips are swollen from how savagely I kissed them just now.

It's been a long time since she dressed as a woman, but she's not in just any clothes now. She's wearing a wedding dress to be my wife.

My. Fucking. Wife.

I bring out my phone. "Let's take a picture."

The man took a few of us before he left, but that's still not enough. I want to keep this image of her forever.

Sasha nods and stands beside me. I pull her by the waist, and she yelps as I raise the phone and snap a few pictures of us. Then I kiss her and take more. She smiles against my mouth, and I can almost taste her happy tears from earlier.

"You look so fucking beautiful," I whisper against her lips, and she shudders.

Her eyes meet mine. "You look gorgeous yourself."

"Gorgeous, huh?"

"You know you are." She hesitantly plants a hand on my shoulder. "May I have this dance?"

"There's no music."

"That's easy to fix." She grabs my phone and taps a few things, and soon after, cool classical music fills the room.

"I don't really dance," I say as she places the phone back in my pocket.

Her expression falls, but she interlinks her fingers with mine. "I can teach you. Just place your hand around my waist and follow my lead—"

Her words are cut off when I slam her against my front and

then twirl her around. When she lands back against me, her eyes shine with contagious joy. "I thought you didn't know how to dance?"

"I said I don't dance, not that I don't know how." I sway her in my arms a few times, then spin and catch her.

She's flat out laughing now, and her happiness makes me wish we could stay this way for eternity. It's rare to see her laugh, even when she's in a good mood. My understanding is that she's self-conscious about being too open.

Those concerns seem to disappear now as she throws her head back and laughs. She's an excellent dancer by every definition of the word. Not only is she disciplined, but she also has an easy elegance to her moves like a former rich young lady would have.

Halfway through, she wraps her arms around my waist and hides her face in my chest. My hand flexes on her back, feeling her tremble slightly as we sway to the music.

Sometimes, when she's being a fucking badass as my bodyguard, I forget that she can also be a vulnerable woman who needs hugs as a form of comfort.

She has this little personality trait where she loves and cares with all her heart.

And this woman is now mine. Fully. Thoroughly.

She'll never, *ever* be able to escape me.

"Are you falling asleep?" I whisper, my lips kissing the top of her hair over the veil and in the middle of the crown of roses that she improvised.

She nuzzles her nose in my chest as she shakes her head.

"Good, because I have that unwrapping thing to do, remember?"

Her head lifts in time for me to pick her up and carry her in my arms. Sasha yelps as she grabs onto me, her eyes turning a molten hazel.

I love how she wants me as much as I want her. It's almost as if she can't get enough of me, either.

Almost.

While I want to keep her in this dress for eternity, I also need to fuck her like I need air.

My cock has been jerking and demanding to be served ever since she said, 'I do.' I'm surprised she didn't feel the heavy weight rubbing against her stomach just now.

I gently place her on the bed and hastily remove my jacket and bow tie. I start to unbutton my dress shirt, then get bored and rip it down the middle, sending the buttons flying.

Sasha leans back on her hands, watching my every movement with keen interest as if this is her custom-made strip show.

Her greedy pretty eyes follow the lines of my tattoos to where they disappear beneath my pants. So I take my time removing my weapons holster and unbuckling my pants. My movements slow down whenever her breathing picks up or when she sinks her teeth into the corner of her bottom lip.

I wrap the belt around my hand and pull down my pants and boxer briefs.

Her chest rises and falls in an unsteady rhythm as she openly watches my cock. The fucker fully comes to life at her attention, the veins popping with the need to plow inside her.

"Look at your eyes devouring my cock." I wrap my belt around her neck and pull her forward. "How about you choke on it instead?"

Sasha kneels on the bed facing me and wraps her hands around my erection, looking at me with those glittery eyes. "That's wrong. It's *my* cock now."

And then she opens her mouth wide and swallows most of my length inside.

Fucking fuck.

I'm so close to coming at the feel of her hot wet mouth, but mostly, it's due to what she said before taking me. It's that sense of ownership that nearly matches mine.

Sasha keeps eye contact as she laps her tongue around my

cock, deep throats it until her face reddens, then bobs her head up and down, creating more friction with her tongue.

She's as intense as when I grab her head and face-fuck her.

Usually, I'd do that, but tonight, I let her do what she wishes. I let her show me just how much she wants me. How much she wants to please me.

My only hold on her is the belt that's straining against her throat.

"You're taking me like a very good girl, Solnyshko." I stroke her cheek and then pat her head over the veil and the crown of roses.

She hastens her rhythm at the praise, her hands pumping me up and down as she sucks my dick like it's a Popsicle.

"That's it. Worship my cock, so it's hard and ready to fuck your tight cunt."

She trembles, but she maintains her hard-core pace.

I fucking love seeing her from this angle. The ring on her finger shines under the dim light as she jacks me off and plays with my balls. Her eyes are filled with lust and intoxicating admiration.

Respect, even.

And she's wearing a wedding dress.

But as much as I want to keep watching her in this position, if she keeps going at this pace, I'll come down her throat. And that's not the plan tonight.

I tug my belt that's around her neck and pull her off. Her lips leave my cock with a pop, a trail of saliva and precum forming a line between us.

"I'm not done," she protests in a low voice.

"I know, but I prefer to consummate our marriage with my cum in your cunt."

Her chest heaves, and I release the belt to retrieve a knife from my holster and grab the edge of her dress.

Sasha swats my hand away. "No way in hell will you be cutting my wedding dress."

"How else will I get to the good part?"

"Oh, I don't know. Have you thought of unzipping it like a normal human being?"

"That fucking mouth." I let the knife fall to the mattress and pull her by the belt that's hanging on her shoulders.

My fingers tease the curve of her nape, and I bite the sensitive spot near her pulse as I slowly pull the zipper down. "Like this?"

"Mmm…" She shivers, goosebumps erupting all over her skin.

I take my time in lowering her dress to beneath her pearl-studded bra that's clasped at the front. My head drops between her heaving breasts, and I use my teeth to undo the clasps.

Her hands grab onto my head and condensation forms on my glasses so I throw them aside as I reveal one gorgeous tit at a time.

Her dark pink nipples are hard, and I tease one with my finger. "They look achy. Are they?"

She nods once, a whimper slipping from her lips. I love how she's so responsive to my touch that a mere nipple teasing can turn her into a mess of my own making.

I bite the other nipple and then suck on it. Her back arches, pushing them further into my face, her fingers digging into my shoulders for support.

"Oh, God."

"Not God." I run my tongue over her nipple and then kiss her lips. "*Me.* Tell me you're mine."

Her hands cradle my cheeks. "I'm already wearing your ring."

"Say you're mine."

"I'm yours, Luchik. Always." Then she seals her lips to mine, kissing me with a desperation I've never witnessed from her before.

It's like she's making sure I'm here and won't be going anywhere.

I bunch her dress up and shred the tights at her pussy. She gasps against my mouth, and I bite her lower lip as I push her panties to the side and thrust two fingers inside her.

"You're so fucking wet. You want my cock, Solnyshko?"

Her reply is a moan close to my lips.

"Do you feel yourself drenching my fingers? You're such a dirty little whore, wife."

Her nipples rub against my chest due to her erratic breathing, and she clenches around my fingers. "Say that again."

"My dirty little whore?" I ask, pretending to be oblivious as I tease her clit with my thumb.

"No, the other word."

"Wife." I thrust harder. "You're my fucking wife, Sasha, and you'll come for your husband, won't you?"

"Yes...yes..." Her lips hover over mine in an 'O' as her pussy tightens around my fingers.

Her head rolls back, but I pull on the belt. "Eyes on me. I want to see how you come for me."

Her hooded bright eyes remain on mine while she rides my fingers for her orgasm. I nibble on her neck, release her, and slide down her body, biting her tits, stomach, and any inch of skin I get a hold of.

Once I'm between her legs, I open them wider, tearing the tights further.

The dress remains stuck in the middle, spreading out on either side of her. This time, I grab the knife, turn it on its side beneath her panties, and cut right through the middle.

She jerks and when I pull out the knife, it shines with her arousal. I lick it, and her cheeks redden even as her lips part.

Sasha might not show it much, but she's as demented as me. She's the other half of my unbound lust and possessiveness.

We're two sides of the same coin.

I roll her around so that she's kneeling on the bed, her ass in the air, and I position myself behind her. "I'm going to claim you, wife, and you'll scream for your husband."

I dig my fingers into her hip and thrust inside her all at once. Her body jerks, but her cunt swallows me whole, milking my cock.

"Fuck. You feel like my wife." *Thrust.* "My woman." *Thrust.* "Fucking mine."

She nods frantically and tries to look over her shoulder at me, the veil forming a halo around her head. Her tits jiggle from the powerful rhythm of my thrusts. Her back lowers further. Every part of her welcomes me home.

No, *she* is my fucking home now.

The only home I've ever known.

As her whimpers fill the air, I slip the knife's handle against her back opening.

She goes still, her eyes widening as she angles her head back. "Kirill...what...?"

"Shhh. Don't move." I ram into her cunt with a steady rhythm. "Do you trust me?"

"I do," she says without any hesitation.

That's my fucking woman.

"I need you to stay still for me." I spit on her other opening, then thrust the handle in, the sharp edge facing up.

She tenses, her breathing turning shallow.

So I go deeper into her cunt, hitting her sensitive spot over and over until she relaxes again. I add another inch, but this time she's too focused on the pleasure to pay attention.

I release her hip, part her ass cheeks further and push the knife deep enough that I only have a small space to move it.

She watches me and moans as I pick up my rhythm until I feel the knife handle rubbing against my cock through the thin layer.

Then I ram the knife, shallower at first, and then more, until I match my cock's rhythm. Sasha arches her back, her moans and whimpers creating a symphony of pleasure.

"Every hole you have is mine to own, isn't it, Solnyshko?"

"Yes...yes..."

"This is my cunt." I pull out almost completely, then drive back in until my balls slap against her skin. "My ass." I thrust the knife harder and faster. "My fucking body."

She doesn't reply, because her head is thrown back. I can feel her milking my cock. Her arousal messes up the sheets, her, and even my inner thighs.

"Look at me."

She does, and her hands grab my arms as she trembles. Her face becomes a map of pleasure—tears cling to her eyes, and her lips are pink and swollen.

This woman is my wife.

My fucking *wife*.

"Tell me you love me." I go deeper, harder, and out of control.

I have to pull out the knife and throw it aside before I accidentally hurt her. I already cut myself and I smear the blood all over her ass, then slap it.

"I love you," she whispers.

I hit her sensitive spot again and spank her ass—again. "Now, scream it."

"I love you!"

Those words are my undoing.

I groan as I empty myself deep inside her cunt, then I pull out and spray my cum on her ass and back hole. Blood and cum mix, creating my favorite view. But that's not enough, so I thrust anything that's escaped back inside her pussy again and again until she's writhing and pushing back against my cock.

After she rides the wave, I turn her around and take her in. Everything about her glows. Her sweat-covered skin, her hard, pink nipples, and her slightly parted lips.

I fucked this woman three hundred fifty-two times, and I still can't get enough of her.

And yes, I'm still counting.

Sasha sits up, her legs on either side of me, and wraps her hands around my neck, a happy, satisfied smile on her lips.

"You're officially mine now, wife."

Her eyes close briefly as she nuzzles her nose against mine and murmurs in a soft voice, "I love you, husband."

Something in my chest squeezes so hard, I think I'm having a seizure. I really should get this shit checked.

But now, I need to fuck Sasha again, just so there's no mistaking that she's all mine. Body, heart, and fucking soul.

Because once this small honeymoon phase is over, I'm not sure she'll still be as compliant.

TWENTY-SIX

Sasha

I'M A LOST CAUSE.

I might have been staring at Kirill's sleeping face for the past hour or so, vehemently refusing to look away from him.

It's such a rare occurrence to see him sleep, but after I suggested helping him last night, he laid his head on my chest and closed his eyes.

So I stroked his hair and sang to him, and we somehow both fell asleep. It was the best sleep I've had in ages. No nightmares, no blood, and no reminder of who I'm supposed to be.

In fact, it was full of peaceful colors and Kirill's fatally beautiful face. I woke up with a smile on my lips and his erection pressed against my thigh.

Our clothes and my surprisingly intact wedding dress are lying all over the floor, and we smell like each other after the bath we had together before bed.

Kirill held me against him, then washed and massaged every

inch of my body. To say last night was the best night of my life would be an understatement.

Not only did we get married, but he also made me feel like I'm the only woman he sees. The only woman he wants to be his wife.

Yes, maybe the marriage part happened too quickly, but it feels so right.

His arm is thrown over my middle and his face is buried between my breasts. He didn't change his position during the entire night. I've noticed that about him before. He's a very still person. It's like he's conscious of his movements, even during sleep.

Kirill is the coldest, most enigmatic man I know, but right now? He feels like the closest thing I've had to a home after my family's death.

I run my fingers through his hair and pause as the rock shines under the dim light.

We're married.

This impossible man is now my husband. Not Kristina's.

Mine.

I kiss the top of his head, my lips lingering there for a second too long. Will I ever get used to this feeling?

Kirill might look like he's too possessive of me, but I'm worse. I can't handle seeing him with another woman, and if he'd really gone through with that marriage, the possibility of me turning toxic and somehow ruining that wedding was high.

I'm not one of those women who'd retreat with dignity. I'd curse him and her for eternity, from the grave, even.

Thankfully, none of that will happen now.

But I'm not sure how we move forward from here either. Or how he managed to break off the engagement without upsetting Igor or disrespecting the Pakhan himself.

What about his ambitions to get to the top, the problems with Juan and—

"Mmm." He nuzzles his face against my breasts, turning my nipples hard. "I think I found my favorite way to wake up."

And I think I'm in love with his sleepy, husky voice.

Kirill lifts his face from my chest, his light eyes droopy with sleep, and then something I've never seen before happens.

He smiles. It's not a smirk or a grin. It's a genuine wide smile that nearly stops my heart. "Morning, wife."

"M-morning," I whisper, stuttering like an idiot. "Husband."

It's really not good for my sanity when he does these unexpected things.

"That's right, your husband. You're Mrs. Morozova now." He pauses. "The only downside to that is that you share the same title as my mother."

"I can live with that."

"Ivanova, huh?" He lies back beside me and stares at me. "What's the story there?"

I gulp. "That last name doesn't ring any bells for you?"

"Not particularly. Should it?"

A breath leaves my lips. I knew he had nothing to do with my family's death. "I guess not."

"Are you going to tell me why you're hiding your identity?"

I bite my lower lip. There's no reason why I shouldn't tell him. After all, he already knows my last name, so he can trace back my story.

Besides, we're married now, and that comes with mutual trust. So I roll to my side and face him. "Remember when I told you my family was influential, but then we went bankrupt?"

He nods, "I suppose that's either not the whole story or a cover-up."

"Yeah. We were indeed influential, but we didn't really go bankrupt. We were attacked in our vacation house by soldiers from the army." My lips tremble as the events of that day play out in front of me. "We were all gathering for lunch on Christmas day when they barged in, in broad daylight, and opened fire on everyone, not sparing women, children, or even infants. I was pushed down under a table by my cousins, who paid with their life for the sacrifice."

Tears stream down my cheeks, and Kirill strokes his thumb under my eyes, wiping them away.

"I lost my parents and ten other members of my family. My brother, too. We never found his body, but it's been years, and I haven't managed to locate him. I was...sixteen at the time. I'm over twenty-two now, and I'm starting to think he died somewhere else."

"Who's we?"

"What?"

"You said *we* never found his body. Were there other survivors?"

Damn. Of course Kirill would pay such close attention to detail. "My uncle, grandmother, and young cousin were the only survivors, but we had to live in hiding because those who attacked us wouldn't be done until they eradicated us all."

"Is that why you were pretending to be a man?"

I nod. "Our hideout was discovered when I was around eighteen, and I was recognized immediately, probably because I look so much like my mother. So after they knew I could be the only survivor, these people had my image everywhere on their internal servers, and my life was in danger, so I faked my death, dressed up as a man, and joined the army."

"To search for the people behind the hit."

"How...did you know that?"

"It makes sense since you said the people who attacked you were soldiers."

"It was like intentional cleansing." I lean my cheek against his hand as he continues wiping away my tears. "I still don't understand why. We were rich, but we weren't involved in anything shady. Or at least, I didn't think so."

"You don't anymore?"

"I was too young at the time, so I didn't pick up on our family's business. I thought all the security we had whenever we went out was part of our rich status, but now, I'm sure there was more to it. My uncle is hiding things from me, because even though the hit came from within the army, they were only soldiers under orders. The actual mastermind could be...your father."

He pauses stroking my cheek for a beat. "Roman?"

"I...saw him in our main house a few days before the attack and then again before that last mission with the Special Forces."

"Hmm. So that's why you followed me to New York and were strangely upset when he died."

"Yeah..." I trail off, then blurt, "But that was only in the beginning. I wanted to search for information but didn't really find anything, and I liked being with you so...I swear I wasn't spying on you."

"There's nothing to spy on. I have no idea what the fuck Roman was doing with your family, and he left no records behind, which is admittedly strange since he left records about everything."

"Oh." My shoulders hunch. So it's another dead end.

"If Roman was involved, however, it probably was due to a bad move from the head of your family. My father's strongest point was mind games and pure sabotage. That's the only way he managed to get to the top and force someone like Yulia to marry him." He caresses my cheek gently, lovingly even. "I'll look into it from my position."

"You...will?"

"You're my wife. Your problems are now mine."

I didn't think I'd ever fall deeper in love, but I just keep falling for this man all over again.

Of course he has nothing to do with what happened. He didn't even know his father was associated with my family.

I grab his hand and then kiss the top of it. "Thank you."

"There's no gratitude between us."

Slowly, I sit up and look down at him, then bite my lower lip. "What do we do now? Should I go back to being your guard in front of the others or...what exactly?"

Kirill sits up beside me. "Do you want to be a man for the rest of your life?"

"No, but I also don't want to endanger your position."

"In that case, I have the perfect solution for this situation. You'll tell everyone you're leaving, and then you'll relocate to a cottage I own in the mountains. After I'm done with business here, I'll bring you back as my wife. It should take me about six months."

"Six months?"

"Don't worry." He grins. "I'll come by several times a week."

The mere idea of being separated from him this soon squeezes my heart. "But why would you need six whole months?"

"I just do." He kisses the top of my forehead. "Can you do that time for me?"

"I prefer to stay by your side as a bodyguard than leave as your wife."

"I want that, too, but I also want you to feel as happy as you were yesterday in that dress. I want you to feel comfortable in your own skin, Sasha. Besides, we have to give everyone time to get used to you being gone before I introduce you as...Aleksander's twin sister, maybe?"

I can't help the smile that stretches my lips. "You really thought this through, didn't you?"

"I always do."

"Are you going to visit me all the time?"

"Of course." He bites my lower lip. "Are you up for dressing as a man one last time?"

I nod.

While leaving everyone will be hard, the thought that I will return in a few months puts some much-needed balm on the wound.

Kirill will not only help me search for the truth about my parents, but he'll also fulfill my dream about living as a woman.

No more masks, disguising, or trapping myself inside.

I'll finally be...free.

My lips capture Kirill's and I kiss him with all the love and gratitude I feel toward him.

He might be a monster, but he's *my* monster.

And I refuse to have it any other way.

⌒

Saying goodbye is the most bittersweet process I've ever gone through.

Karina cried her eyes out and begged me to stay, then when I said I couldn't, she announced that we were no longer on speaking terms and ran back to her room.

Viktor pulled me to the side and said that he should've known I was a woman all along, but then he told me to not die out there until he gets to the bottom of this, which was the giant's way of asking me to stay, I guess. He continued to watch me with narrowed eyes after he gave Kirill the keys to the cottage that I'll be staying at.

Maksim was genuinely upset and couldn't understand why I wanted to leave in the first place. For him, none of this made any sense whatsoever, no matter how much I tried to explain that this life isn't for me anymore.

He and Karina were the angriest about this decision and gave me the cold shoulder.

Yuri appeared more disappointed than angry. I think I caught him glaring at Kirill, but I don't know if it was real or if I was imagining things.

Everyone else offered me best wishes, even if their expressions were turned downward. Some men even argued that leaving them under Viktor's ruthless reign was such a low blow.

Anna hugged me goodbye and gave me a bag full of food containers as a parting gift.

I had to hold back the tears as I climbed into the car Kirill lent me to drive. These people have become my family, and the fact that I have to leave them, even temporarily, drills a hole in my heart.

Kirill stands by the window and speaks low so that only I can hear him. "It'll take you about five hours to reach the cottage. Call me when you get there."

I nod and whisper, "When are you coming by?"

"A week from now."

"A whole week?" I don't attempt to hide the disappointment in my tone.

"I have a few important meetings this week that I can't get out of."

"Fine, I guess."

"Did you know that you look adorable when you pout?"

I smile and resist touching him when everyone is watching, including Karina from behind the curtain in her room.

Leaning close, I say, "I'm going to miss you."

"Fuck," he murmurs. "Now, I want to come along."

Yes, please.

"Go." He taps the top of the car. "Be yourself."

I grin, wave at everyone, and then I drive away from the mansion.

Goodbye, Aleksander Lipovsky. From now on, I'm Aleksandra Morozova.

TWENTY-SEVEN

Sasha

BY THE TIME THE WEEK ENDS, I'M BORED OUT OF MY mind.

During the first few days, I kept an open mind and explored the surrounding forest, hiked to the top of the mountain, and screamed from the bottom of my heart.

I was so happy to wear girl clothes and sports bras instead of chest bandages. Though I still wore my men's sweatpants and hoodies. What? They're comfier.

Then I did my daily workouts in the garden surrounding the small cottage.

Despite having wood stacked inside the house, I cut some more logs and threw them in the fireplace.

The cottage is located in the middle of nowhere, with only a mountain and a huge forest surrounding it.

On the inside, it looks like a fairy tale. The dark wood of the walls and the flooring gives the architecture an elegant feel.

There's a cozy sofa opposite the fireplace, over which hangs a TV. There isn't much service here, but there's a flash drive that's stacked with hundreds of movies and TV shows. I tried watching some, but I don't have the patience to stay still for hours. I'd rather be moving around.

Which is why I'm getting positively bored out of my mind.

I need to stay calm, though, because I have another six months of this.

Jeez. How am I supposed to survive that?

But anyway, that's for later. I stare at my phone for the hundredth time today, just to re-read the exchange I had with Kirill earlier.

Kirill: I'm coming tonight.

Sasha: Really? To the cottage?

Kirill: I meant in your cunt, but yeah, that, too.

Sasha: I can't with you.

Kirill: That's my charm. Do you need anything?

Sasha: Just you is fine.

Kirill: Fuck, Solnyshko. You need to stop saying shit that makes me hard while I'm surrounded by people.

Sasha: I'll make it up to you tonight. Promise.

To say I'm starved would be an understatement. I miss him like crazy. It doesn't help that he was busy with work these past few days, and we barely spoke over the phone or through texts. So I spent the whole week obsessing over our wedding pictures that he sent over.

I hate being away from him. Even during that period when he wasn't talking to me, I was by his side every day, so this distance is making me anxious.

I keep wondering if he'll be okay. What if someone attacks or attempts to assassinate him and the others don't act fast enough?

It's hard to chase away those thoughts despite knowing Viktor, Yuri, Maksim, and the others are there for him.

Guess that makes me a control freak, because sometimes I believe no one other than me will be able to keep him safe.

Which is both wrong and unfair to the others. Especially Viktor.

But anyway, Kirill is coming tonight, and I might have gone a bit overboard with the preparations.

There are still many containers of food, both the ones Anna gave me and what was in the fridge. However, I tried to cook a fancy dish I found on the internet.

Needless to say, I burned it.

So now, I'm moving to plan B, which is reheating my food. In hindsight, I should've just done that from the beginning.

I guess I wanted to cook for him—or try to. Obviously, I suck at this.

Planning missions and shooting targets? No problem at all. Everyday things such as cooking? Tragic failure.

I managed to at least set the table decently. I have his favorite drink—whiskey—on the table, and mine, too.

While I'm a stereotypical Russian who loves their vodka, Kirill is more sophisticated and only has Macallan. Neat.

He does drink vodka when it's offered to him, especially by the elders in the brotherhood, but it's not his drink of choice.

He's flexible that way, which makes him charming from the outside looking in.

Kirill is the type who's fine with bending his choices and preferences if it helps in getting close to the right people. That's why the smartest ones in the organization, namely Rai, Vladimir, and Adrian, are the most wary of him.

Rai often calls him a cunning fox, and she's not wrong. He's not too hard to be snapped or too mellow to be pushed around. He's just...an enigma.

And I love everything about him—including his manipulative

side. I like to believe that he wouldn't hurt the people he cares about the most, such as Karina and his men.

Konstantin, even.

Kirill acts like his brother is the most annoying existence on earth, but he refuses to take serious action against him. Yes, he sabotages him here and there, but it's not permanent damage, and I think he only does it to spite Yulia instead of Konstantin.

I'm also a bit too smitten, so I could be biased.

My opinion still stands, though.

After I make sure the table is all set, I shower and slip on a pair of dark green lingerie I got on a small shopping trip I made the other day.

I was struggling with women's underwear, but the lady in the store was super helpful without being judgmental about how a grown-ass woman didn't know her exact sizes.

It was weird enough that I went out as a woman (still dressed in joggers and a hoodie, though), and I automatically found myself in the men's section before I recalled that I'm not pretending anymore.

I thought about dying my hair back to blonde, but that's too much of a change for now.

I put on the matching nightgown the girl suggested, then look in the mirror. Oh, wow. I actually look good in this. The transparent nightgown molds against my curves, and the color brings out the green in my eyes—and my ring.

Since I didn't try them on in the store, I wasn't expecting much. Needless to say, I was too embarrassed to be buying this stuff when I never have in my life.

Then I sit in front of the mirror and try to experiment with makeup by following YouTube tutorials.

I wish I'd brought the case Kirill got for me, but he said since I was going back anyway, I should leave the wedding dress behind.

Two hours later, I scrap everything and go with simple mascara and lip gloss.

Looks like it's going to take me a long time to be a woman again, but hey, small steps. Right?

A knock sounds downstairs, and I flinch, but it's entirely due to excitement. It's still late afternoon, so I thought I had more time to tidy up the cottage, but maybe Kirill missed me so much that he came early.

At least, that's what I choose to believe as I slip into a robe and wrap the belt around me. I practically fly down the stairs and throw the door open with a huge grin on my face.

I'm about to jump him in a hug, but I freeze.

It's not Kirill who's standing in front of the door.

Not even close.

Yuri looks at me without a change of expression, his hands balled into fists on either side of him and his face hard.

Oh, shit.

Shit.

"Uh, I…" I trail off, not knowing what to say.

Sorry, I've been lying to you all this time?

Hey, so here it is. I'm actually a woman?

"Surprise," I say lamely.

"Far from it." He pushes past me into the cottage and slams the door shut.

This is the first time I've seen this part of Yuri. He's usually calm, collected, and the complete opposite of Maksim's turbulent energy. He's the anchor everyone turns to when they need reassurance. He's definitely been mine, especially when I was having an identity crisis after Kirill was shot in Russia.

Now, however, he looks ready to destroy a mountain and all living beings on it. If I hadn't known him for years, I'd be sure he's an imposter.

"You…you're not surprised I'm a woman."

When he says nothing and continues fixating me with that hard edge, I shiver. "You…knew? Since when?"

"Since the day you walked into that special ops unit."

"Wow, okay. Why...why didn't you tell me?"

"I was supposed to keep a low profile, but that's all in the past now." He walks around the place, checking power sockets, beneath the sofa and chairs, in the lamps—everywhere.

He's looking for cameras or listening devices, I presume.

"There aren't any," I say because I checked.

Yuri, however, doesn't stop his thorough scouring. I tighten the belt around my waist as I watch him. It's like I'm looking at an entirely different person. His movements are as sharp as his expression.

Once he's satisfied there aren't any, he comes down the stairs and glares at me.

"Why are you looking at me like that, Yuri? You're giving me the creeps."

"Good. You need more than that to come back to your fucking senses." He tightens his fists. "Go get your things. We're leaving."

"Why would I go anywhere with you?" I pause. "Did Kirill send you?"

"Fuck that motherfucker."

I flinch.

Okay. This is a lot more serious than I thought. Yuri has always respected Kirill. He doesn't consider it his life's mission to protect him like Viktor and me, but he's one of Kirill's most trusted men.

"What happened?"

"We need to go before he gets rid of you after you so stupidly told him everything."

"What...what are you talking about?"

"He's sending people over to get rid of you, idiot."

I shake my head. "You must be joking."

"Do I look like I'm joking?"

"That can't be true because...because...Kirill and I are married!"

"You really believe that shit?" He hits me upside the head, and I freeze. Fuck.

This brings back old, rusty memories. "I thought you'd be better than this, or I wouldn't have let you in."

"What..." I look at him as if he's an alien. "We really got married..." I lift my finger. "Look. I have a ring."

"Oh yeah?" He taps a few things into his phone and then thrusts it in my face.

It's a picture of the grand church where all the brotherhood weddings happen. There are familiar faces in the crowd—Damien, Adrian, Lia, the Pakhan, Igor, Mikhail, and a pissed-off Rai.

At the altar, Kirill stands with Kristina's hands in his.

And Kristina is wearing a wedding dress.

"This was from earlier today," Yuri comments. "He's being named the Pakhan by Sergei as we speak because of this marriage. He made sure everyone but Rai and Vladimir would vote for him."

"No..." I breathe out, my heart beating so loud, I can't hear anything else. "He can't marry her when he's already married to me. It's fake."

"Your stupid marriage is what's fucking fake, Sasha! Look at him! Do you see your ring on his finger? Did he give you that grand ceremony where the whole world knows you're his wife?"

A sob catches in my throat, and tears splash on the phone's screen. The more I look at them, the harder it is to breathe.

Oh, God.

I think I'm going to throw up.

Yuri snatches the phone from my hands and points upstairs. "At least change clothes. We need to get the fuck out of here before he eliminates the last person who knows about what he's done."

"That's not true, right?" I take his hand in mine. "He...didn't marry her, right?"

"Why do you think he sent you to the middle of nowhere? You obediently followed like a lovesick fool." He sinks his fingers in my shoulders. "Snap the fuck out of it, Sasha. That man never loved you. He used you like you were supposed to use him for information, but you ended up telling him everything you weren't supposed to."

"No..."

"I started to believe he has nothing to do with this shit, too, but he's Kirill Morozov. The motherfucker of all motherfuckers of manipulation. He almost got me, too. He surely got you."

"What—" My mind is such a mess of emotions and thoughts that I don't know what to think or say.

"He knows, Sasha. He knows everything about our fucking family. Uncle Albert was right. He plotted the whole thing for Roman, but unlike Uncle, I have hard evidence."

My shoulders tense, but the tears won't stop. "How do you know about Uncle Albert...who...who are you?"

He hits me upside the head again, and it's like I've been struck by lightning. "Stop being a crybaby, Malyshka."

Oh, no.

Oh, God.

"A-Anton...?" The word falls from my lips like a forbidden whisper.

Aside from Mama, he's the only one who's ever called me Malyshka, even after I grew up. And he's definitely the only one who hits me upside the head whenever I'm being an idiot.

"Finally," he whispers.

"But...but...you look and sound nothing like Anton...you... how?"

"Long story. Let's get out of here first."

"But—"

"We don't have time. After you so stupidly told Kirill our last name, he and Viktor were able to link everything together. He already sent men to Babushka, Uncle Albert, and Mike."

"No..."

He retrieves his phone and shows me a text exchange between him and Uncle Albert. There's a surveillance video that shows men attacking one of the usual warehouses Uncle hides in.

Yuri...no, Anton pauses the video on one of the attackers and taps the familiar eyes visible through the balaclavas. "Who does that look like to you?"

"Maks."

His lips lift in a snarl, anger and disappointment radiating from him in waves. "Fucking bingo."

"Are...Uncle, Babushka, and Mike okay?"

"Babushka is injured." He grabs me by the elbow. "We need to leave before he finishes the job with you."

My steps are lethargic as everything starts to fall into place. Did...Kirill pretend to marry me only so he could get information from me?

I was supposed to be the one who used him, but did he use me?

My stomach churns, and I trip and then fall.

Yuri catches me—no, fucking Anton—my brother. He's here. He's been beside me for years, and I didn't even recognize him.

"You need to keep it together," he says in his hard voice. "This is not the Sasha our parents brought up. Get your shit together."

"What if...what if he didn't mean to and—"

My words are cut off when the sound of ticking reaches us. The last thing I hear is "Lie down!" as my brother jumps on me. And then...

Boom!

TO BE CONTINUED...

The story continues in the final book of the trilogy, *Heart of My Monster.*

You can check out the books of the characters that appeared in this book.

Adrian Volkov: *Deception Trilogy.*

Rai Sokolov: *Throne Duet.*

WHAT'S NEXT?

Thank you so much for reading *Lies of My Monster*!
If you liked it, please leave a review.
Your support means the world to me.

If you're thirsty for more discussions with other readers of the
series, you can join the Facebook group,
Rina Kent's Spoilers Room.

Next up is the last book of the Monster trilogy,
Heart of My Monster.

ALSO BY RINA KENT

For more books by the author and a reading order, please visit:
www.rinakent.com/books

ABOUT THE AUTHOR

Rina Kent is a *USA Today*, international, and #1 Amazon bestselling author of everything enemies to lovers romance.

She's known to write unapologetic anti-heroes and villains because she often fell in love with men no one roots for. Her books are sprinkled with a touch of darkness, a pinch of angst, and an unhealthy dose of intensity.

She spends her private days in London laughing like an evil mastermind about adding mayhem to her expanding universe. When she's not writing, Rina travels, hikes, and spoils cats in a pure Cat Lady fashion.

Find Rina Below:

Website: www.rinakent.com

Newsletter: www.subscribepage.com/rinakent

BookBub: www.bookbub.com/profile/rina-kent

Amazon: www.amazon.com/Rina-Kent/e/B07MM54G22

Goodreads: www.goodreads.com/author/show/18697906.Rina_Kent

Instagram: www.instagram.com/author_rina

Facebook: www.facebook.com/rinaakent

Reader Group: www.facebook.com/groups/rinakent.club

Pinterest: www.pinterest.co.uk/AuthorRina/boards

Tiktok: www.tiktok.com/@rina.kent

Twitter: twitter.com/AuthorRina